GRIM TIDINGS

An Aisling Grimlock Mystery Book One

AMANDA M. LEE

WinchesterShaw Publications

Copyright © 2015 by Amanda M. Lee

All rights reserved.

No part of this book may be reproduced in any form or by any electronic or mechanical means, including information storage and retrieval systems, without written permission from the author, except for the use of brief quotations in a book review.

❦ Created with Vellum

ONE

"Bow down before the harvester of your doom!"

I rolled my eyes, glancing over at my brother, Aidan, as he stood before the cowering spirit in the corner with a devilish grin on his face. "Really? That's how you do it?"

Aidan's dimples deepened as he sent me a wink, while ignoring the middle-aged man and his pitiful whining as he kept trying to convince himself that he was dreaming.

"It's just a nightmare," the man tried to soothe himself.

"Do you have another idea?" Aidan asked.

"Have you tried talking to him?"

"That never works," Aidan replied. "They never want to believe they're dead. And, if they do, it's usually because they're depressed and they offed themselves because they were looking forward to the hereafter."

I ignored Aidan's blasé attitude and glanced down at the list in my hand. "Stan Parker, 54, accountant for Thompson and Hopkins."

"See, he's evil," Aidan said. "He's an accountant for a big law firm. You can't get slimier than that."

"It's an environmental law firm," I replied.

Aidan merely shrugged in response. He was clearly enjoying himself, if his flushed skin and gleaming eyes were any indication. I had a feeling it was because he had been put in charge of my "training," something I wasn't convinced I needed.

"It says here he's a Catholic," I said, reading further into Stan Parker's file. "I think I know how to handle this." I took a step toward Stan, squatting down so I was at eye level with him. "Mr. Parker, my name is Aisling Grimlock, and I'm here because there's been an … incident."

"Incident?" Aidan arched a dark eyebrow.

I ignored him. "Unfortunately, there was nothing that could be done and you've … um … passed on."

Stan Parker glanced up at me, finally focusing on something other than his own feet – and the uneven tile pattern in his bedroom – and fixed me with a bleak stare. "Are you an angel?"

"You've obviously never seen her in the morning before she's had three cups of coffee," Aidan scoffed.

I waved him off. "I'm not an angel," I said. "I'm a reaper."

Stan Parker looked confused. "Like a grim reaper?"

"Exactly," I replied, sending him my most encouraging smile as I brushed my long black hair – shot through with enough white streaks to give my father a coronary when he saw them – out of my face. "I'm here to help you get to your final destination."

"I don't know what that means," Parker replied, his voice dull and his eyes lifeless -- OK, no pun intended. "You make it sound like you're a travel agent."

Aidan snorted. "Yes, we're here to take you on a fabulous vacation to Greece."

"I am kind of like a travel agent," I said, shooting Aidan a withering glare. "I've got all your arrangements right here." I tapped the file in my hand for emphasis.

"That's a file on me?"

"It is," I replied. "It's all about your life."

"It's kind of thin."

"It sure is," Aidan agreed.

I kept my violet eyes trained on Stan's face. "It's not your whole life," I said, "just the highlights."

"And lowlights," Aidan added.

He was starting to grate, which I suppose is a brother's job. Since Aidan and I were closer than normal siblings – that whole twin thing had bonded us a little too closely – our new working relationship was starting to strain the easygoing thing we'd had going for the twenty-five years since our birth.

"What lowlights?" Stan asked, his lower lip trembling.

"I don't think they're important," I lied.

"I really like the one about you sleeping with your best friend's wife," Aidan said. "Then, when he confided his problems with the marriage, you pretended that he was imagining things until he started seeing a shrink." He'd moved away from Stan and was busy studying his bedroom, opening drawers and poking through the contents, something that was making Stan decidedly nervous.

"What are you doing? What is he doing?"

"Ignore him," I said. "We should really get going, though. Aidan, bring the scepter over here."

"The scepter?" Stan's eyes widened. "Is that like a magic stick to beat me with?"

"Why would you ask that?" Aidan seemed genuinely curious, until his bright purple eyes narrowed under the weight of sudden knowledge. "Is that what you're into?"

"No! Who told you that? That's not on the list, is it?" Stan tried to peer over my hand to see what had been written into his file.

"No," I replied, although now I was curious about what was buried in his file. I had read only the highlights. "Mr. Parker."

"Call me Stan. We should be on a first-name basis, after all."

"Stan," I said, forcing myself to keep my voice pleasant. "We really need to get going. We're kind of on a tight schedule today."

"Doing what?"

"Collecting souls," I explained, standing back up to my full five feet, six inches. My knees were beginning to ache from crouching.

"And this is your job?"

"It is now," I said. "Unfortunately."

Aidan grinned at me. "It's not as easy as you thought, is it? It's a lot harder than you gave us credit for."

"I never said it was an easy job," I argued. "I just didn't think it was as action-packed as you made it out to be." I glanced back down at Stan. "And I was clearly right."

"They're usually not this ... whiny."

"I am not whiny," Stan said. "I'm going through a shock. I just found out I'm dead, and it wasn't even a good death."

"What's a good death?" I asked.

"You know, running into a burning building and saving children from a fiery death," Stan said. "Or pushing an old lady out of the path of a speeding bus. Or riding a supermodel until your heart just gives out."

I glanced at Stan's paunchy stomach and thinning hair and couldn't help

3

but think that all three of those scenarios were very likely outside of his wheelhouse. "You can't control your death – unless you want to kill yourself," I explained. "And, if you do that, you don't go to one of the better final resting places."

Stan looked momentarily hopeful. "Am I going to Heaven?"

"Yes," I said, glancing at his file again for confirmation. I frowned, though, when I saw where he was really going.

"That doesn't look like I'm going to Heaven," Stan said, his voice rising an octave. "That looks like I'm going to the other place."

Aidan leaned back on Stan's bed -- blocking my view of Stan's body, which was thankfully buried beneath his plaid bedspread covers -- and waited for me to handle the situation.

"Define the other place," I said, taking a step so that I could again make eye contact with Stan.

"Define the other place? Define the other place? I don't want to go to Hell!"

"Well, good news," I replied, using my best faux tour director voice. "You're not going to Hell."

"I'm not?" Relief washed over Stan's shaking body.

"Nope," I shook my head emphatically. "You're going to Purgatory. It's an entirely different place."

Stan looked shocked. "Purgatory? Isn't that like limbo? Is that better than Hell? It certainly doesn't sound as good as Heaven."

He wasn't wrong. "The good news is, your file says you'll only be there for fifty years."

"Fifty years!"

"Your file says you have a few things to work out," I offered, hoping that my explanation didn't sound as lame to Stan as it did to me.

"What does that mean exactly?" Stan pushed himself to his ethereal feet and placed his hands on his hips. I think I was getting a glimpse of his courtroom persona, which was one of the reasons he was going to Purgatory.

"Well ... ," I hedged.

"I want to know exactly what that file says about me," Stan ordered.

"I'm not sure I'm supposed to tell you that."

Aidan groaned from his spot on the bed. "Oh, just tell him. Otherwise we're going to be here forever, and I'm ready for lunch."

I didn't know how he could think about lunch with a dead body – and the traumatized spirit that belonged to that body – in the room. "Well, under your transgressions list you have quite a few entries."

"Such as?"

"Well, it says here you put fifteen witnesses on the stand even though you knew they were going to perjure themselves," I replied.

Stan looked incensed. "I did no such thing!"

"Then there's that whole sleeping with your best friend's wife."

"I went to confession for that!"

"Each time?" Aidan asked. "You have to go each time."

Stan worried his lower lip with his teeth. "That wasn't made clear to me. That's not fair. I thought going once was a blanket confession that would absolve me of all of my sins."

"Did you do the required penance?" Aidan pressed.

"Of course I did." Stan was scandalized.

"That's not what the file says. The file says you were supposed to say fifty Hail Marys, but that you didn't say any of them."

"The priest still absolved me of my sins," Stan argued. "You can't possibly be telling me that fifty Hail Marys are standing between me and Heaven. I'll do them right now, if that's the case."

"It doesn't work that way," I said.

"It also doesn't count if you don't do the penance," Aidan shot back. "While you're still alive, that is. Aisling, seriously, enough with this crap. Let's just absorb him and go."

"I want to speak to your superior," Stan said. "You can't be the last word on where my fate lies."

"We're not even the first word," I answered. "We're just grunts. The list comes from higher up and we just follow it. We're really just the last word."

"Higher up where?" Stan didn't look convinced.

That was too long of a conversation for this particular moment. "Just higher up."

"Well, I still want to speak to your superior." Stan was adamant.

"We can arrange that," Aidan said, getting to his feet. "You have to come with us, though, and then we'll have to make an appointment for you."

"And how soon can I get this appointment?" Stan asked, new hope flitting across his face.

"I think the current wait time is seventy-five years," Aidan said. I had no idea whether he was telling the truth.

"Well, that's not fair," Stan complained. "I demand an immediate appeal."

I glanced at Aidan, waiting for his response. His world-class charm obviously wasn't working today.

"We can arrange that."

"And how soon will my argument be heard?"

"I think the current time frame is eighty-five years," Aidan replied. He was clearly bored with the direction of the conversation, his mind already focused on the hamburger in his future.

Stan's mouth dropped open in horror. "So, you're saying my only options are to go with you, climbing into some weird scepter of death and spending fifty years in Purgatory making up for my crimes or wait seventy-five years to plead my case?"

"Pretty much," Aidan said, nonplussed, "although, you don't climb into the scepter."

"That's something, I guess," Stan said, shuffling uncomfortably.

"The scepter just absorbs your soul," Aidan added.

Terror flitted across Stan's bland features. "Absorbs?"

"It's not as gross as it sounds," I offered.

"Oh, okay," Stan said. "Um, just give me a second to get ready. It's going to be fine. I'll wake up in a few minutes and everything will be fine."

"Of course." Clearly my approach was getting us nowhere.

Stan started pacing his apartment, stopping at each photo frame to give it a long gaze. I thought it was kind of sweet. He wanted to get a last look at his loved ones. Maybe he wasn't such a bad guy after all?

Stan was completing his circuit, moving back toward the open bedroom door when he suddenly disappeared into the living room. I glanced at Aidan worriedly. "What do you think he's doing?"

"He's probably running," Aidan replied, his disinterest evident.

"Shouldn't we stop him?"

"He's your charge," Aidan reminded me. "I'm just here to supervise."

"This sucks," I grumbled, moving into the living room to make sure Stan didn't try to run. I shouldn't have worried. He was standing at the door of his apartment, trying to turn the door handle so he could escape into the hallway. He clearly didn't realize that he could simply walk through the door because he was stymied by the fact that his hand just kept moving through the handle harmlessly. That was a small favor.

I opened my mouth in an attempt to talk him down once more, but Aidan shook his head to dissuade me. He was right – and I knew it. I sighed, pulling the sterling silver scepter – shaped like a snake with ruby red eyes (don't ask) – out of my jacket pocket and pointed it at Stan.

The scepter lit up, emitting a bright flash of light, and I could see Stan's spirit start to break up as it filtered into the scepter. The last look he managed to muster was one of abject terror before he completely disappeared.

"Well, that went well," I said finally.

"That's not what Dad is going to say," Aidan replied.

He was right. I scowled as I imagined the diatribe I was sure to be on the receiving end of later tonight. It sucks when your Dad is also your boss.

"You want lunch?" Aidan asked. He didn't look too worried about the ass-chewing we were sure to get in a few hours.

"Make sure it's some place we can get drinks, too."

"We're Irish," Aidan laughed. "That's a given."

I followed him out of Stan Parker's apartment without a backward glance. This was turning into a terrible first day of work.

TWO

"So, let me get this straight, you had five souls to gather today and two of them ran while another two demanded appointments to plead their cases? That doesn't sound like an auspicious first day."

Cormack Grimlock is an imposing sight. He's six feet, two inches of solid muscle, black hair and a constant five-o-clock shadow. Even in his fifties, he's still a breathtaking (and frightening) man. He's my father, and I love him, but I feel the weight of his disappointment like an anvil around my neck when he feels like cutting it loose. And tonight he obviously feels like cutting it loose.

"It's not as bad as it sounds," I said, throwing myself onto one of the leather couches that decorate his library. It's really only a library in the strictest sense of the word. To a normal person – one who didn't grow up in the dark shadow of the reaper world – it was something more akin to a library research room. The walls are covered with dark bookshelves encumbered with thousands of dusty tomes, which my father insists we might need some day. The far end of the room is dwarfed by my dad's mahogany desk, which he sat behind.

"And how would you describe your first day on the job?"

I glanced over to the adjacent couch where my brother Aidan was sitting and studying his fingernails and tried to send him a mental SOS. He either wasn't getting it or he was ignoring it – I had a feeling it was the latter. "Well, we did manage to gather all five souls."

Cormack sighed, letting loose one of those patented parental grunts that can only be achieved when you have more children than you have patience. Since I was one of five children, my father had long since ceded complete control, although he still likes to pretend sometimes. "I guess we can count that as a win."

"See," I smiled. "There is a bright spot."

"Don't push it."

Aidan snickered, leaning back on the couch and fixing me with an amused grin. "I told you."

"I don't know why you're so smug," my father said. "You were in charge. You should have had a better handle on things."

"You said to let her do it and just step in when things got out of hand," Aidan argued. "I was following your directions."

My father's back stiffened. "Apparently you and I have very different definitions of what constitutes a situation getting out of hand."

"Well, that sounds like your problem, not mine."

I was surprised by Aidan's tone. Every member of my family is plagued by foot-in-mouth disease. We don't usually put that particular trait on display with our father, when we can help it, though. It doesn't end well. Ever.

"What did you just say to me?" I feared that if my dad's face got any redder he might burst a blood vessel.

"I said you're right," Aidan sighed. "I'm sorry."

"That's what I thought you said."

When I was sure my dad wasn't looking, I shot a triumphant smile in Aidan's direction. He flipped me off, discreetly, but my father and his eagle eyes didn't miss the gesture.

"I saw that."

"Shouldn't we get the soul transfer over with?" Aidan asked, trying to change the subject.

"Fine," my dad replied. "Perhaps I should oversee the soul transfer, just to be on the safe side."

"Knock yourself out," Aidan grumbled.

My dad motioned for me to join him, holding out his hand so I could place the scepter in his palm. I watched as he took the silver staff – which was about ten inches long – and placed the bottom end into the purple urn in the corner of the room behind his desk. The process was a mild curiosity – until I joined the family business I wasn't allowed to see this part of the operation. The urn lit up, flashing once, twice, ultimately five times, and then going dark. My dad retrieved the scepter and handed it back to me.

"At least one job was done without incident today," he grumbled.

"The easy part," Aidan scoffed.

My dad opened his mouth to let loose with a choice verbal smackdown but was interrupted when the door to the office opened and the rest of my family filed in. My older brothers, Redmond, Cillian and Braden, were in the middle of a deep conversation.

"She was after me," Redmond said, sliding down onto the couch I had just vacated.

"You're crazy," Cillian said, his eyes flashing. "She wanted me."

"You've both gone blind," Braden interjected. "She kept touching my bicep. She wanted me."

"She kept touching all of our biceps," Redmond argued. "She tried to stick her tongue in my ear, though."

"She was coughing," Cillian replied. "That wasn't her tongue. It was spit."

Gross.

All of my brothers look exactly alike. No, really, they do. If not for the white streaks I had recently added to my hair, there would be no doubt that we all swam from the same gene pool. Every one of us had inky black hair and bright purple eyes, both traits passed on to us from our father. There wasn't a lot of deviation in our ages – apparently our parents were randy in their youth – so we were extremely close, and competitive.

Redmond is the oldest, and most stable at twenty-nine. Cillian is a year behind at twenty-eight, and he is a touch more volatile (and by a touch I mean he freaks out at the drop of a hat). Braden has middle-child syndrome at twenty-seven and, while the rest of us have straight hair, his is wavy like our mother's was before she passed away. Aidan and I are the babies at twenty-five and, if Redmond is to be believed, we were not exactly happy accidents. It's not as though my parents didn't love us as children, but we weren't explicitly in their family plan. They had intended to have three children – not five – so it's no surprise that my father's patience often wears thin with us faster than it does with my older brothers.

"What are you three arguing about?" My father's voice was gruff, but his eyes were twinkling. He liked hearing about my brothers' romantic conquests. Since my mother had died – almost a decade ago now – he had lived like a monk, except for their stories.

"Cillian tried to steal my date," Redmond explained. "She shot him down, though."

"She shot you down," Cillian argued.

"She obviously shot you all down because you all came back here alone," I interjected, shoving Redmond's foot from the coffee table so I could move past and settle into the open spot on the couch next to him.

Redmond slung his arm around my shoulder affectionately. "We actually came home early to see how Aisling's first day of work went."

My mouth dipped into a frown as I regarded him.

"That bad? It will get better, kid," he said, squeezing my shoulder in a show of solidarity.

"If she had finished her training when she was a teenager, she wouldn't be scrambling to catch up now," Dad said.

Redmond rolled his eyes. This was an old argument. When I was eighteen, I had gotten drunk at a holiday party and informed everyone that I had no intention of joining the family business as planned. We were raised knowing that we had to join the reaper fold, and my brothers had all fallen into line.

I had wanted something different, something that didn't revolve around death. So, instead, I dropped out of the reaper-training program and started classes at the local community college. After changing my major four times – nothing seemed to fit just right – I dropped out and took a job as a secretary at an insurance agency. Unfortunately for me, downsizing eliminated that position about six months ago.

With few options – and no degree to fall back on – I finally agreed to join the family business when my roommate gave me an ultimatum: Start paying rent or get out. He meant it in the nicest way possible. No, really, he did. He was just trying to give me some direction – one that didn't lead to a fast food chain -- at least that's what I keep telling myself.

So, here I am. I joined the family line, but there was no way I was going to move back into this mausoleum on the hill. It's kind of like a castle. I'm not exaggerating. When you tell people you live in a suburb of Detroit, they picture falling down houses and rampant gang bangers. We live on Grosse Pointe's Lakeshore Drive, though, in one of the richest areas of Michigan. Even for this area, though, our house is just a little bit too much. You know that show, *Downton Abbey*? They wish their house was this big. No joke.

All four of my brothers still live here, taking over one of the wings as their party pit (their words, not mine). I couldn't get out of here fast enough, though. To me, a home is supposed to be warm and inviting. The only thing this house invites is unrest.

"I don't want to argue about the training again," I said, my voice low.

"Let the training thing go," Cillian agreed. "It's over. It's done with. You've won. Move on."

"I've won what?" My dad looked incredulous. "Is this the lottery and no one told me?"

"You wanted her in the family fold since she announced that she wasn't going to do it," Braden said. "She's in the family fold. Give it a rest."

My brothers are nothing if not loyal. Sure, they're total pains, but they're loyal pains.

"I wanted her to go through the proper training and join the business when she was nineteen, like the rest of you," Dad replied. "I didn't want her to waste money and jump around from job to job before finally starting work with us because she had no other choice."

"I didn't jump from job to job," I grumbled.

"And she paid for her own college," Redmond reminded my dad. "Why don't you stop bringing it up?"

"Why don't you mind your own business," my dad shot back.

"Why don't we all calm down," Aidan suggested.

"You're the reason we're even having this discussion," Dad said, fixing his eyes on Aidan.

"How?" Aidan's voice was high and unnatural.

"You helped her pay for that community college," my dad charged on. "You didn't think I knew that, did you? But I knew."

"So what?" Aidan said, his voice angry and firm. "That was my choice, not your choice."

"And how did it work out? Was it money well spent?"

Aidan shifted his gaze over to me uneasily. "She wanted to see what was out there. I don't see what the big deal is."

"The big deal is she is one of us, despite whatever it is she's done to her hair – and I know you did that just to tick me off, young lady – and she should have been with us from the beginning. Do you know how many jokes I had to listen to at the reaper council because she chose to be a secretary instead of a reaper?"

"So you're angry because your friends are asses?" Redmond was rubbing his hands together, as though spoiling for a fight (which was often the case).

"I'm angry because, until now, she's been a tremendous disappointment."

The jab hit me where it was supposed to – right in the heart. His aim was always true, even if he regretted the words the minute they escaped from his mouth.

"She's not a disappointment," Braden growled, getting to his feet. "Don't call her that."

My father's face softened, instant contrition taking over. "I didn't mean that."

"Then why did you say it?" Aidan asked.

"Because ... I don't know why I said it. She just frustrates me. I didn't mean it, though."

"You frustrate us," Cillian interjected.

"How do I frustrate you?"

"By saying things like you just said. Why do you always have to harp on her?"

I listened to the argument continue around me with my ears but I tuned it out with heart and my head. *I can't let him get to me,* I reminded myself. He didn't mean what he said. No, he really didn't. Boys he gets. Adolescent boys. Teenage boys. Adult boys. He gets their feelings and emotions and he can deal with them.

High-strung girls with their drama and mean-girl attitude, though? That he doesn't get. He was fine with me when I was little, when I was digging in the dirt and wrestling with my brothers. When I wanted to be Batman he was perfectly fine. The minute I put on a skirt and discovered boys, though – in the same way (and at the same age) that Aidan discovered boys, by the way – he started to falter as a parent. That's when my mom swooped in and took over as the main parental figure for Aidan and me. Even though Aidan didn't know what he was at that point, my mom knew. My dad claims he didn't, but I find that hard to believe.

When my mom died while trying to collect a soul in a burning building – it happens more often than most reapers would like to admit – my dad had to take on our parenting again. He wasn't very good at it, by his own admission. Not that he didn't try. He did try – and those are the memories I cling to.

"Let's just drop it." I had said the words barely above a whisper, but every head swung in my direction and all arguing ceased.

"I'm on your side," Redmond said, gripping my shoulder tightly.

"I know, and I appreciate it. It's just not worth arguing about. I know I'm a disappointment. It doesn't hurt me anymore. Just let it go."

With those words, I got to my feet – fighting the shakiness that threatened to overwhelm me -- and exited the room. The one thing I need above all others right now is an escape from this house. I always need an escape from this house. Why I agreed to return is still a mystery to me.

It has to get better, right? Right?

THREE

While the rest of my family lives in luxury on Lakeshore Drive – maids and butlers included – I have opted for minimalism. Okay, maybe minimalism isn't the right word. Cozy. Yeah, that's the word that best describes the condo I share with my best friend in Royal Oak, a northern suburb of Detroit in the more affluent Oakland County.

Royal Oak isn't ritzy, but it's certainly not run down. It's comfortable – and the nightlife is to die for (probably not a great phrase for a reaper, I know). It's more hipster-meets-music snob, with great food on every corner thrown in for good measure. There's a festival every other weekend and something new to discover every month.

I love it here.

I unlocked the door to my condo – located within walking distance of Royal's Oak's bustling after-dark activities – and found my best friend, Jeremiah "Jerry" Collins, lounging on the couch watching *Golden Girls* in his boxer shorts.

Before you ask, yes, Jerry is gay. I've known since we met in kindergarten and he immediately vetoed my Converse and Levis, something he does to this day. I didn't know he was gay right away. I did ask my mom if he was a girl dressed up as a boy, though. She merely smiled, patted me on the head, and told me that someday I would appreciate his fashion sense. She was wrong on that one.

"Hey, Bug," he greeted me without looking up from the television. He had called me "Bug" since we were little, when my brothers were happily burning ants with a magnifying glass while I tried desperately to save them -- in vain, I might add. Nothing can dissuade my brothers from a task when they set their minds to it.

"Hey," I said, dropping my purse on the coffee table and sliding onto the couch next to him. "How was your day?"

"Oh, just so stupid," Jerry replied. "Mrs. Noonan came in again."

I wracked my brain for an identity hint. "Is she the one who wants the four-tiered wedding cake?" Jerry owned a chic little bakery – Get Baked – on Royal Oak's main drag. He's extremely creative and talented, and I'm not saying that just because he's my best friend.

"She's just unbelievable," Jerry continued. "She wants me to somehow include dolphins in it now."

"Dolphins? That doesn't seem very wedding-y. Is that a word? Wedding y? I don't think that's a word."

Jerry ignored my grammar constipation. "Dolphins have nothing to do with a wedding," he agreed. "She only asked for the dolphins after I told her that putting shirtless men on a gay wedding cake was tacky."

Yeah, because of who he is and how well known he is in the gay community, a lot of Jerry's business revolves around same-sex weddings in Michigan. That's a thing now because a recent court decision pretty much spanked Michigan's governor and told him that a gay marriage ban is repugnant – which he's still fighting. Jerry's business is booming, though.

"I thought you liked tacky?"

"For a bachelor party? Sure. For a wedding, though? Some things are sacred."

Sometimes I think Jerry is more of a girl than I am. When he thinks of wedding cakes he gets all twitterpated like in *Bambi*. When I think of wedding cakes, I don't get anything but hives.

"Well, what did you finally tell her?"

"That I knew what I was doing and to trust me."

"And how did she take that?"

"She told me I was bitchy."

I couldn't hide my smirk. Jerry idles at bitchy. That's what I love about him. "Then what happened?"

"Then I called her son and told him she was driving me crazy."

No, not bitchy at all.

"And he agreed with me and she backed off," Jerry added.

"And how did you end things?"

"She started crying and admitted that she's manic about the wedding because she wants to make sure her son realizes she's okay with it, him being gay and getting married and all."

"That's kind of sweet," I admitted.

"It is," Jerry agreed, slinging his arm over my shoulder and pulling me close so I could get more comfortable.

I thought about his response for a second and then smiled. "The cake is going to have dolphins, isn't it?"

"Small, tasteful ones," Jerry replied.

Tasteful dolphins on a wedding cake? I can't wait to see it. I turned my attention to the television, fighting to stifle a laugh as Rose launched into a story about St. Olaf. While *Golden Girls* may seem stereotypical for a gay man – and it is -- there are some stereotypes that have to be embraced. At least that's what Jerry always tells me. *Golden Girls* is one of our coveted nightly rituals. We also watch *Little House on the Prairie*. We're multi-faceted weird.

We watched the episode in silence for a few minutes, but then I felt Jerry stir beside me. "So, Bug, you haven't told me how your day went."

That was on purpose. "It was fine."

"Fine?"

"Fine."

"That doesn't sound very convincing. I would think a day of gathering human souls and helping them pass to the great beyond would be fulfilling."

Yeah, Jerry is in on the big family secret. I told him when I was eight. My dad had some sort of fit when he found out but he eventually got over it. Jerry is a part of our family, by right if not birth. My dad won't admit it, but even he is fond of Jerry and his antics.

"It was fine," I repeated, trying to convince Jerry -- and myself -- that I was telling the truth.

"Then why are you so stiff?"

"I'm not stiff."

Jerry ran his hands over my shoulders, kneading the knots out of my back. "You feel stiff."

"How do you know when a woman feels stiff?"

"Honey, there's nothing about anything stiff that I don't know about."

I wrinkled my nose. "Thanks for that visual."

"That's what I'm here for."

"I thought you were here to keep me entertained?"

"That's what I was doing."

"Oh, good to know. Sometimes it's hard to tell."

We lapsed into silence again. I was hoping that Jerry was going to forget about my first day at work. I should have known better.

"So, how was work?"

I blew out a frustrated sigh. There was no way out of this. So, I told him. I told him everything. I told him about Stan. I told him about Aidan. I told him about my dad and the big argument. When I was done, Jerry's body was taut with anger. "Your dad makes me mad."

"He loves you," I pointed out.

"He loves you, too, Bug," Jerry said, his voice low. "He just has trouble with you."

"Because I'm a girl?"

"No, not because you're a girl, although that probably doesn't help."

I glanced up at him in surprise. I was expecting the answer to be yes. "Then why does he have trouble with me?"

"Because you remind him of your mother."

That hit me hard so, of course, I denounced its truthfulness without even considering the possibility that he was right. "That's ridiculous."

Jerry ran a hand through his dark hair and fixed his somber brown eyes on me. "Bug, I love you dearly, but you are completely ignorant when it comes to your father."

"I grew up with him," I argued. "I think I know him a little better than you."

"In some ways, yes," Jerry agreed. "In others, though, it's like you've never met him."

I pondered the idea for a second, but forcefully pushed it out of my mind. "There's no way," I said. "I don't even look like my mother. I look like him."

"You all look alike," Jerry agreed. "Your mom was all blonde and sunny, and you guys are all dark and broody, but it's there."

"What's there?"

"The voice. The slope of your nose. The way your forehead furrows when you're thinking really hard – like now. That all comes from your mother."

I opened my mouth to argue, but Jerry silenced me with a look.

"Your dad is a good man, but he's also a man haunted by your mother's death," he continued. "And, when he looks at you, he thinks about what could have been. What should have been. He wonders what would have happened if your mother had waited to go into that building until the fire was completely out. What would have happened if she had been ten feet away when the roof collapsed. What would have happened if he had gone instead of her, as he was supposed to."

I felt my heart well up, even though I was fighting the sudden onslaught of emotion that was washing over me.

"Your dad feels guilt," Jerry plowed on. "Your dad thinks that he should have died instead of your mother. Does he handle things well? No. Does he treat you the way he should? No. But you should know he always regrets it when he lashes out at you. He just doesn't know how to say it."

I pressed my face into Jerry's side in an effort to hide the tears threatening to spill over. He patted my back.

"Just try to cut him some slack, Bug," he said.

"I do," I said, fighting back a sniffle.

"Try to get your brothers to cut him some slack, too," Jerry suggested.

"I'm not a miracle worker."

"Just try to get them to chill."

"They can't help themselves," I said. "They're loyal and I'm the only girl, so they're protective. Don't you remember when Dean Cooper dumped me on prom night and Tommy Wilkinson saw him making out with that girl under the bleachers and I came home crying?"

"I remember he looked like he'd been in a cage fight on graduation day," Jerry said. "It wasn't a girl, though. He was making out with Carson Franklin."

Holy crap. "No way."

"Yes, Carson told me the next day when we were at yoga."

"Why didn't you ever tell me?"

"Because I couldn't decide if it made things worse that he was making out with a guy," Jerry admitted.

I thought about it a second. "I don't know either," I said finally. "Now, I would have understood. Then? I probably would have freaked out more."

"That's what I thought."

"I think it would have made a difference to my brothers, though."

Jerry shrugged. "Ah, well, Dean was a douche. He had it coming for all those wedgies he doled out for the four years he thought he ran the school."

"Yeah, but now it just seems mean."

"Your brothers are mean."

"They're not mean," I protested.

"Not to you, no. They love you."

"They love you, too."

"They didn't always love me," Jerry reminded me. "They used to laugh when you put makeup on me and then tried to force me into a dress."

"They did that to Aidan, too."

Jerry frowned at the memory. "You know, come to think of it, your brothers were douches in high school too."

I wanted to argue, but he wasn't wrong. Instead, I rested my head on his shoulder and lost myself in some Dorothy-induced sarcasm until my eyelids were too heavy to stay open.

Tomorrow was another day. It could only get better. I was practically sure of it.

FOUR

"Wake up, Buttercup."

"Get off me, you freak." I tried to shift Aidan's weight from my midriff, but he was surprisingly solid – and determined when he set his mind to it. I was still rolled up and trapped beneath the blankets on my bed.

"It's almost eight. We're going to be late." Aidan always was a morning person. It's annoying. I didn't see how anyone could be so chipper after the day we had survived yesterday.

"You're a poet, and you didn't know it," I grumbled. I definitely need some coffee.

"No more rhymes now, I mean it." Aidan wasn't giving up – and a good movie quote never dies.

"Anybody want a peanut?" I pulled the blanket away and met Aidan's wide smile with a scowl to match. "Get off me."

"Are you going to get up?"

"Do I have a choice?"

Aidan's frivolity melted away as he met my sleepy gaze. "Are you okay?"

I knew what he was referring to, but I pretended otherwise. "You mean am I fine after being jolted awake by my annoying twin? Yes. Now get off me."

"That's not what I meant." Aidan looked determined.

"Yes it is," I countered.

"No it's not."
"Yes it is."
"No it's not."
"Yes ... ."

"Leave her alone," Jerry ordered. He was standing in the open bedroom doorway watching the two of us. Like me, he's not a morning person. It's another reason we get along so well. Aidan had obviously woken him up, too.

"I'm her brother," Aidan argued, his gaze flitting to Jerry's bare chest and chiseled abs. What is it with gay guys? They always have the best bodies. And, even though Aidan and Jerry had known each other since they were kids, there is a lot of faux flirting going on when they're in a room together. "It's my job to make sure she's all right."

"That's the best friend's job," Jerry countered, fixing Aidan with a small smile while making sure to flex his muscles as he posed in the door frame. "Your job is to annoy her and beat up her boyfriends."

"I've got that covered."

"I've noticed."

I rolled my eyes and pushed Aidan off of me, mustering enough strength to dislodge him while he was distracted by Jerry's abs. "You weigh a ton."

"I'm a prime piece of manly candy," Aidan informed me, winking at Jerry for emphasis. "There's no fat on this godly body."

"Don't make me throw up."

"Get in the shower."

"I need coffee," I argued.

"You can have it after you shower."

"Fine," I grumbled. "But this is going on my list."

"I can live with that."

"MR. JOHNSON, IT WOULD BE HELPFUL IF YOU COULD CALM DOWN."

Aidan and I were on our third and final job of the day and it wasn't going well, to say the least.

"Calm down? Calm down? How can you tell me to calm down?" Mitch Johnson was a wreck. He was forty-five years old and had worked out like a maniac his entire life. He didn't smoke. He didn't eat fattening foods. He had only one martini a week – and usually at a work function. And, yet, he had died of a heart attack while cooking his lunch before he returned to the office. He was in denial, there was no getting around it.

"I know it's hard for you to understand." I tried a different tactic. "These things happen, though."

"Happen? I never drank. I never smoked cigarettes. I never ate anything with any fat content that could actually give my food taste. And now I'm dead? How does that even happen?"

"Genetics?" I really had no idea. I've never met a cupcake I don't like, even when Jerry insisted maple frosting was awesome.

"My father is still alive. So is my mother. My grandparents lived until they were well into their eighties. How is it genetics?"

"A heart defect?"

"I go to the doctor every six months. He would have found it if I had a problem. What else have you got?"

"Bad luck?"

"I don't accept that," Mitch said, his voice angry and full of hate. "You take it back and fix this, you bitch."

I think I was starting to understand the problem. "You have a lot of rage, don't you?"

"So?"

"That probably killed your heart." Hey, I'm not a doctor, but it sounded plausible to me.

"I don't like you," Mitch seethed.

"Well, I think you're a peach."

Mitch glared at me, refusing to divert his gaze from my eyes, even though Aidan was noisily searching through his refrigerator in the next room for something to eat.

"I'm not going."

"You have no choice."

"I don't believe that."

"Well, nonetheless, you don't have a choice." All of my grand plans to lead souls to the light with a smile and sympathy had gone out the window after less than twenty-four hours on the job. That didn't say much for my follow through.

"I want to talk to the other one."

"Who? Aidan?"

"I don't know his name," Mitch said. "I want to talk to the man. He's obviously the one in charge."

I gritted my teeth. Aidan was in charge during my probation, but I didn't have to like it. "Aidan."

"What?" Aidan walked into the room, an apple in his right hand and a

Coke in his left. "What's the problem?"

"He wants to talk to a man."

Aidan smirked but ambled over to Mitch anyway. "What can I do for you, sir?"

"I want to lodge a complaint." Mitch put his hands on his hips and plastered a reasonable look on his face as though that would somehow fake Aidan out. I didn't know how to tell him that my brother would have simply sucked his soul without engaging in any of this pesky conversation I had stupidly insisted upon. I really didn't think it would help at this point anyway.

Aidan rolled his eyes in my direction. "And what is your complaint?"

"There's obviously been a mistake," Mitch explained. "I'm a good man. I've lived a good and clean life. I wasn't meant to die."

"Bummer."

"I don't think you're understanding me," Mitch said.

"No," Aidan countered. "I don't think you're understanding me. I don't care that you think you shouldn't have died. Ninety percent of the souls we collect think they shouldn't have died. I had a ninety-year-old former mineworker lodging a complaint just last week.. You just need to stand there and let us do our job. Shutting up would just be a bonus."

Tact is an acquired taste, one Aidan has no intention of acquiring.

Mitch crossed his arms over his chest and tapped his foot impatiently. "I want to talk to your boss."

"My boss is my dad," Aidan replied. "He's going to be a lot meaner to you than we are. Trust me."

"So, this is a family business?"

"Unfortunately," I muttered.

"Well, then I want to talk to your father's boss."

That was an interesting thought.

"He doesn't have a boss," Aidan lied.

"Well, then, I'm not going." Mitch was grasping at straws. I didn't really blame him; hey, no one wants to die.

Even though he'd been through this a thousand times, Aidan looked surprised. "You're not going where?"

"Wherever it is you're taking me," Mitch answered.

Aidan glanced at me. "Where are we taking him?"

That was a good question. I flipped the sheet on the file, found the appropriate line, and then gulped as I glanced back up at Aidan. "To a place."

Aidan read my face. "You're going to Hell."

There was that tact again.

Mitch was flabbergasted. "Hell? Hell? How do I deserve to go to Hell? That's not even remotely possible. Check again."

I did as instructed. It hadn't changed, though, not that I thought that was a reasonable possibility. I felt helpless. "I don't know what I'm supposed to say here."

Aidan ignored me. "You're going to Hell. Get used to it. You obviously did something to go there. You must know what it is."

Mitch screwed up his face as he concentrated. "Nope, not a blasted thing. There's been a mistake. Come back when it's corrected. I'm busy this spring and summer, but I can probably schedule you for an appointment in the fall. I'll just wait here."

Aidan looked to me for help. I looked back down at the file, searching for the transgressions list, frowning when I found it. "It says here that you've date-raped three different women."

"I have not."

"Sandy Winston?"

"She wanted it."

I gripped the file tighter. "Penny Lynn?"

"She was a slut. It's not my fault she was so drunk she couldn't remember begging for it."

I pursed my lips in aggravation. "Joanna Franz?"

Mitch's face contorted with rage. "She put her hand on my leg. She initiated the sex."

Well, that was my breaking point. "You're a dick."

"And you're another woman who can't admit what she wants." Mitch sidled up to me, trying to get a look down the vee in my shirt. I think he was trying to be charming, even though he was failing at a fantastic rate.

"Hey!" Aidan was pissed off now, too. "Don't look at my sister like that."

"Why don't you leave the room," Mitch suggested. "I'm sure your sister and I can come up with an agreement that benefits us both."

"If you had a body, this is where I would beat you to death," Aidan threatened.

I couldn't wipe away the feeling of a million small insect wings flitting across my body. "You're gross."

"You're hot. Are those things real?" Mitch asked.

"That did it!" Aidan exploded, moving toward me and pulling the scepter from my coat pocket. "I'm not listening to another second of this."

Fear colored Mitch's face. "What is that?"

"Your doom," Aidan shot back.

"That sounds a little dramatic," Mitch replied, although his voice had lost some bravado.

"I'm a dramatic kind of guy."

"Aidan," I started. "Maybe we should just … ."

Mitch seemed to realize he was out of options. Instead of accepting his fate, though, he did what came naturally to a woman-abusing coward: He ran.

Before we realized what was happening, Mitch bolted through the closed door of his apartment and was gone, leaving Aidan and I staring at some really ugly particle board, a flat-screen television and an otherwise empty room.

"Sonofabitch!"

FIVE

"I'm not going to say this is your fault."

"That's probably wise."

"It's your fault, though."

I cast a scathing look in Aidan's direction. "I thought you weren't going to say this was my fault?"

"I changed my mind."

Thirty minutes later and we were still searching for Mitch Johnson – something frowned upon in the reaper community. When a soul escapes, they prolong the inevitable. It may sound great – in theory, at least – to run and prolong your afterlife in the only world you've ever known. The problem is, though, that when it happens your soul slowly starts to lose cohesiveness with the real world and all that is left is an empty shell that goes through the motions. That's where ghosts come from. No, seriously. Sometimes a soul is just lost – and that's when we've failed at our jobs.

"Dad is going to be pissed."

Aidan's sympathetic eyes met mine. "This happens all the time. He can't blame you for this. I'll tell him that."

"Like that matters."

"I'll make it matter."

I reached over and squeezed Aidan's hand; the comfort was for him as well as myself. "So, how long do we look?"

Aidan seemed unsure. "I don't know. We might get lucky. If that jerk thinks he's shaken us he might circle back and return to his home. He might still be hoping this is a nightmare and he'll wake up and he can go back to his date-raping ways."

That didn't sound so bad – not the date-rape stuff, but the returning to his apartment stuff. "And if we're not lucky?"

"Then we're going to be in trouble when we get back to the house." Aidan looked grim.

"What do you think he will do?" I didn't say who the "he" was, but Aidan knew who I meant.

"Yell."

"And then?"

Aidan shrugged. "And then? And then nothing. He's a blowhard. He can yell. He can stomp. He can scream. He can pout. This is a danger of what we do. No one has a perfect recovery rate."

"He does."

"So he says," Aidan scoffed. "I don't believe it."

"Why would he lie?"

"He's a man," Aidan replied. "He likes to inflate his numbers. It's a man thing."

I smiled, despite myself, at Aidan's jovial smirk. I didn't believe him, though. He was just trying to put on a brave face for my benefit. "So, what? We should hide behind the trash cans or something?"

Aidan didn't look thrilled with my suggestion. "Let's circle around the block again. I'm not quite ready to give up."

I wordlessly fell into step with Aidan, letting him choose the direction. We were in downtown Detroit – one of the sections on Woodward that had seen some revitalization in recent years rather than the continuing dilapidation that seemed to be claiming a larger foothold in the city.

Aidan, never one for uncomfortable silence, couldn't help from trying to fill the dead air. "Are you sorry you agreed to go into the family business?"

I considered the question. Was I? I still didn't know. "Ask me that question again in a week."

"You're doing fine," Aidan said. "You're a little earnest; you need to build up a colder exterior. That's normal for novices. Don't sweat it."

"I shouldn't be a novice, though, should I?"

Aidan furrowed his brow. "What do you mean?"

"I grew up in this life," I explained. "I've always known what this life entails. This stuff shouldn't surprise me."

"You don't seem surprised," Aidan hedged. "It's more like you're conflicted. That's not the same as being surprised."

"Conflicted?"

"Like you don't know whether you really want to be claiming these souls."

"I don't think that's what I'm feeling," I replied. "I know that these souls have to move on; otherwise they'll be tortured for eternity. I know it's an important job. It's just that … there's something off."

"Then what are you feeling? That this is an important job … and then what?"

"Honestly?"

Aidan nodded, spurring me on.

"I feel like I'm disappointing myself."

Aidan moved his lips to the side, biting the inside of his cheek. It was a familiar expression, one I'd seen for twenty-odd years. "Because you're doing what Dad wants us to do?"

Did that make me shallow? Did I care? "Yes."

Aidan's charming smile graced his handsome face. "I know the feeling."

This was news. "You do?"

"Do you think I wanted to join this business?"

"Why did you?"

"It seemed like the easiest avenue."

That didn't sound like my brother — any of my brothers, for that matter. "Really? That's why you did it?"

"We were bred for this, Aisling," Aidan replied. "It's not like a family law firm or a family restaurant. We're born with special abilities. They're minor, but they're still special. When I thought about doing something else, the idea of shirking my responsibilities was too much to bear. So I did what I was born to do."

"Do you regret it?"

Aidan considered the question. "No."

"Do you think I'll regret it?"

Aidan wrapped an arm around my shoulder and pressed a quick kiss to my temple. "That's my biggest worry right now."

That wasn't an answer. I didn't point it out, though. "Do you think Dad is really happy that I finally joined the fold?"

"No."

I cracked my neck, mostly because I was looking for something to do that didn't include ripping my own hair out, and tried to fight my aggravation. "Why not?"

"Because you got out."

His answer stunned me. "What?"

"Cormack Grimlock is many things, Aisling," Aidan explained. "He's a reaper. He's a leader. He's a bureaucrat."

Tell me something I don't know.

"He's also a father. He doesn't want you to die like Mom did." Aidan's words were simple, but his tone was heavy. "He's all for family pride, but he's more for family safety. If you were to die ... if something were to happen to you ... well, he barely survived mom's death."

Aidan's sentiment stunned me. I couldn't form words.

"He couldn't survive your death." Aidan's voice was barely a whisper. He tightened his arm around me and then forced the serious look from his face. "Let's cut through this alley, check the apartment again, and then call it a day, shall we? I need a drink."

It took me a second to find words – and the ones I discovered weren't going to help our situation – so I grasped for something to lighten the mood. "You're smarter than you look."

"That's not possible. I look like Socrates."

I snorted derisively and followed Aidan into the alley, my thoughts jumbled and my heart clenched in my chest. Sometimes I wonder whether I'm reading the situation wrong -- where my dad is concerned anyway. Most of the time, though, I think he's in the wrong. When someone like Aidan stands up for him, though, I wonder whether I'm not as perceptive as I think I am.

Aidan picked his way around a pile of garbage as we navigated between two apartment buildings. I had lost my bearings fifteen minutes ago. I had no idea where we were. I could only hope Aidan wasn't in the same boat.

"Gross, what is that smell?"

Aidan glanced at the rusty metal door to our right and sniffed. "Day-old Chinese?"

"That killed my appetite for broccoli and beef for a week."

"How about egg rolls?"

My gag reflex reared up and I clamped my hand over my nose to fight the stench. "Don't be cute."

"I was born cute."

"Says you."

"Says everyone."

I wasn't going to feed his delusions. "I say we call it a day. The rancid Chinese is making it a necessity."

"What do you think we're doing?"

"I don't ... oomph!"

With my attention focused on Aidan, I hadn't been watching where I was going. I found myself momentarily suspended in the air, the ground rushing toward me, before I crashed to the pavement and grunted in pain as the gritty cement ripped through the knee of my jeans.

It took me a second to recover once I hit the ground. It took me a few seconds to gather my senses, and when I finally got my bearings, I wished I hadn't. I was on the ground, favoring my left side, when my gaze fell on what I had tripped over.

It was a body – and not the one I had initially been sent to investigate.

"Is that ... ? Oh crap."

6
SIX

"We should go."

Aidan's hand was in my face and he was waving it around in an attempt to snap me back to reality. He wasn't entirely successful. "I just tripped over a dead body."

"Bummer. We should still go."

"We can't go," I protested, finally taking his hand and letting him pull me back to my feet. I dusted off my jeans, checking carefully to make sure there weren't any errant bodily fluids marring their blue surface. "We have to call the police."

Aidan raised his eyebrows and fixed me with his best "are you crazy" glare. "That's a really bad idea."

"We can't pretend we didn't find him," I argued. "He's obviously been … cripes, are those stab wounds or burn marks? That's really nasty."

"Yes." Aidan seethed through gritted teeth, trying to pull me from my spot and move me out of the alley. "We don't want to be part of this."

"I think it's too late."

Aidan and I froze, slowly turning in unison to see who had joined our nightmare.

The man standing right behind us looked interested in our conversation – and mildly suspicious. His brown hair was several inches long and brushed back from his angular face. His dark eyes, the color of molten chocolate, were sharp and curious, while his mouth puckered in an unreadable expression. He was dressed in simple blue jeans and a brown leather jacket that was as rich in color as his eyes. His hands, which looked like they were always busy, were placed firmly on his narrow hips as he waited for an explanation.

He was obviously a cop – or possibly a drug dealer. I looked him up and down again, zeroing in his shoes. Nope, he was definitely a cop. Sometimes you just know. Crap.

"Um, hi," I greeted him lamely. "We, um, we found a body."

The cop glanced to the ground behind us, taking in the entire scene, before shifting his gaze back to us. "I see that."

I didn't dare glance at Aidan, but I could feel his unease as he shifted next to me. "We didn't do it," he said. "I just thought you should know."

"That was going to be my next question, so I'm glad you cleared that up." The cop's tone was droll. "Anything else you want to tell me?"

Don't answer. Don't answer. Don't answer. "I think he was stabbed – or possibly burned," I offered. Crap. Why did I answer?

Aidan kicked me, but I had already realized the stupidity behind my statement on my own.

"What makes you think he was stabbed?"

I looked the cop over again. He didn't have any identifying marks that proved he was one of Detroit's finest, but I was still sure I had pegged him right. He was playing it awful cool, though. "Those holes in his chest were my first hint." Two could play that game.

"And who are you?"

"Aisling Grimlock," I replied, squaring my shoulders. I refused to let his dour nature freak me out.

"And your boyfriend?"

Aidan and I exchanged a look. "Gross," we said in unison.

The cop waited for further explanation, clearly not amused with our twin response.

"This is my brother, Aidan."

"Ah," the cop said, turning his full attention to the body on the ground. "I guess that would explain why you look alike."

"I'm much better looking than her," Aidan said.

I rolled my eyes. "Is that really important now?"

"It's always important."

"Yeah, I see the family connection now," the cop said, squatting next to the body and using a pen to poke around on the ground next to him. "He was definitely stabbed. You were right about that. I guess you got up close and personal with the victim?"

I ignored the question and watched him for a few more minutes, my impatience finally getting the better of me. "And who are you?"

The cop straightened back up. "My name is Griffin Taylor. I'm a detective with the Detroit Police Department."

"Yeah, we figured that out."

"You figured out I was a detective?" Taylor rubbed his hand over his square jaw. "How did you do that?"

"Well, given our location – and the fact that there's a dead body here – it was either cop or drug dealer, and a drug dealer wouldn't be caught dead in those shoes." Sometimes I babble when I'm nervous.

Taylor glanced down at his black New Balance sneakers. "What's wrong with my shoes?"

Oh, where to begin. "Nothing," I lied. "If you're going to the gym," I muttered under my breath.

He looked me up and down a second and then smiled. "Are you wearing zombie Converse?"

"Yes."

"And you're making fun of my shoes?"

"I've told her about the shoes," Aidan agreed. "She doesn't get it."

Taylor narrowed his eyes as he regarded Aidan. "You told her about the shoes?"

Aidan scowled, which only made me smirk harder. He couldn't hide the fact that he was gay even when he tried – which wasn't very often. "Can we go? This clearly doesn't involve us, and we have plans for the night."

Detective Taylor snorted. "What do you think?"

"I think we're going to be late for dinner," Aidan replied.

"Well ... I have a few questions."

Taylor was playing a game, I realized. He was waiting to see how we reacted, and I think we were giving him a real show. Most people would be freaking out after stumbling over a body. Since we saw at least three a day, though, it wasn't exactly traumatic for either of us.

"Questions about what?" Aidan's incredulous tone is pretty impressive when you consider the fact that a frowning cop is facing him down, practically daring him to make a fuss.

"Well, for starters, how about the body?"

"We didn't do that," Aidan said. "We just cut through the alley and my clumsy sister tripped over that guy's foot. We probably wouldn't even have noticed him if she would watch where she was going. I can't take her anywhere."

"Hey!"

"Well, you're clumsy," Aidan grumbled, but he looked apologetic.

"You tripped over the body?" Detective Taylor focused on me.

"Yeah," I admitted.

"Did you touch the body?"

"No. Gross."

"Did you get any evidence on you?" Taylor was circling me, looking me up and down.

"I better not have," I said. "That would totally bum me out."

"And we can't have that," Aidan said. "We are going to be in so much trouble when Dad finds out about this."

I hadn't thought of that. If he thought my first day on the job was a disaster, this was going to send him through the roof.

"What does your father have to do with this?" Taylor asked.

"He's our boss." I realized my mistake too late.

"Your boss?" Detective Taylor looked interested in my slip-up. "And what do you do?"

Crap.

"We're antiquities dealers," Aidan said hurriedly.

"Antiquities dealers? In Detroit?"

"There are a lot of older homes here and some of the belongings in them are worth money."

Taylor didn't look convinced. "In this neighborhood? You were working in this neighborhood?"

"We work all over the region," I said, stalling for time.

"And you had an appointment around here?"

"No," Aidan broke in. "We were going to have lunch down here after we finished up an estate job in Grosse Pointe Park."

"In an alley?"

"No, we were actually going to have lunch at Giuseppe's." My brother can lie with the best of them. Giuseppe's Italian Bistro is a gem in this neighborhood, and people are known to go miles out of their way for their baked lasagna.

"Giuseppe's is two blocks over."

"We were taking a shortcut."

"Why would you park over here?"

"The parking lot at Giuseppe's is really small and I didn't want to risk my car being dinged."

"What kind of car do you drive?"

"It's a vintage Corvette."

It was like watching a Wimbledon final. Detective Taylor still looked suspicious. "I think, just to be on the safe side, we should all go into the precinct and get all of this on record. You know, just to make sure things are on the up and up – not that I don't believe you or anything."

Double crap.

"Why?" Aidan was starting to get his hackles up. He hated all authority, but Taylor's attitude was chafing more than usual.

"Because you're the first on the scene of a murder. That's just standard operating procedure."

"You don't know it's a murder," Aidan pointed out. "He could have killed himself."

"He stabbed himself in the chest four times?"

Aidan shrugged. "You don't know; he could have been dedicated."

Now that I looked at the wounds more closely – which was the last thing I wanted to do – the stab marks looked more like really long claw marks. That was a disheartening thought.

Taylor's lips thinned into a cross between a sneer and a grin. "Well, I still think that some questions are in order."

"Well I think … ."

"Let it go, Aidan." I accepted the inevitable defeat. "We don't have a lot of choices here. Let's just get it over with."

"You should listen to your sister."

"Not if I can help it," Aidan grumbled.

Aidan and I took an involuntary step back as the alley suddenly flooded with emergency personnel. Detective Taylor kept his eyes on us while he issued a few orders and then motioned for us to follow him. Aidan and I fell into place behind him and trudged back out of the alley.

It was going to be a long night.

7

SEVEN

"So, let me get this straight … ."

Yeah, my father wasn't taking our update very well.

"You lost a soul – one that was going to Hell, by the way. Do you have an idea how much paperwork this is going to entail?"

"He rabbited," Aidan said, shoving a stuffed mushroom from the plate he had relieved the maid of a few minutes ago into his mouth. We had been detained at the police department for four hours , but Aidan was acting like he hadn't had a meal for four days. "We couldn't stop him."

Dad gave Aidan a withering look. "Then, while you were out looking for the soul, you stumbled over another dead body and instead of immediately leaving you stayed long enough for the police to discover you there."

"We weren't there that long," I argued. "I think he would have seen us there regardless."

My father ignored my interruption. "So you went to the police station and submitted yourselves to hours of interrogation – without legal representation, which is just stupid – and not only are you still considered suspects but this cop … ."

"Detective Griffin Taylor," I offered. I can't help it. I like the way his name sounds rolling off my tongue, a mixture of mystery and strength all rolled up in a handsome package. Too bad he's a cop.

"Detective Griffin Taylor," my father said through gritted teeth. "He also confiscated your personal scepter, if I'm not mistaken."

I shrank down in my spot on the couch. This wasn't good.

"We told him that it was a recent acquisition but he didn't believe us," Aidan said around a mouthful of mushroom.

For their part, Redmond, Cillian and Braden were all sitting on the couch opposite Aidan and me and keeping their mouths shut, which went completely against their nature. They couldn't hide their occasional snickers – and humorous glances – as they listened to our tale, though.

"This is not funny!" My father exploded when Cillian poked Redmond for emphasis at one point.

"It's kind of funny," Redmond said, not even trying to hide his wide grin.

"How is this funny?"

"I really like the part where Aisling tripped over the dead body," Braden said. "That's so her."

"Thanks."

"You're welcome."

"My favorite part was when she identified the cop because he was wearing New Balance tennis shoes," Redmond offered. "I can just see this guy's face when she told him that."

"You don't even know what he looks like," I scoffed.

"He's hot," Aidan said, taking a break from his mushroom gluttony long enough to swig from a bottle of imported beer. "He's all muscles and brown hair. He's got these really intense eyes. I bet he looks good naked."

My other three brothers rolled their eyes. They had long ago become accustomed to Aidan's boy-crazy nature – but that didn't mean they liked to hear about it.

"Is he gay?" Cillian asked.

"No," Aidan shook his head. "He was much more interested in Aisling, despite the fact that she was wearing zombie Converse. I think those tight jeans were a little bit of a distraction from the shoes."

"My jeans aren't tight," I shot back.

"Honey, if you bend over in those things the wrong way you're going to split a seam."

"Stop talking about that," Dad ordered.

"I agree," Redmond chimed in. "I don't want to picture that. Only a freak would want to picture that."

"I'm not a freak."

"You're close enough," Cillian said. "Pick another subject."

"Anyway, I don't think that Detective Taylor is going to keep the scepter,"

Aidan said. "Just send a lawyer down with the proper paperwork and he'll hand it over."

It seemed simple to Aidan, but my father didn't seem to agree. "The proper paperwork? Where do you suggest we get that?"

Redmond is always the pragmatic one. "This can't be the first time this has happened. We've got all those fake templates in the system. Print one out and I'll go get it."

"That doesn't fix our other problem," my father pointed out.

"And what problem would that be?" Cillian asked, snatching his hand away from the mushroom plate when Aidan smacked it in an effort to protect his bounty.

"The part where Aidan and Aisling are murder suspects," Dad reminded them. "That's going to make doing their job a little difficult if they're under constant surveillance."

"We're not under surveillance," I argued. "We're just persons of interest."

"That's better?"

"Than being named as actual suspects? I should think so."

"Sometimes I wonder if you're my children," Dad grumbled.

Redmond sighed and pushed himself off the couch. He hauled himself over to the desk my father was pouting behind and pushed his chair out of the way. "Stop freaking out," he ordered. "We'll have this fixed in no time."

Since my father showed no signs of relinquishing his chair, Redmond dropped to his knees and began navigating through the computer system. With only the sounds of Redmond's fingers on the keyboard and Aidan's mushroom chewing breaking up the dismal ambiance, the room got uncomfortable pretty quickly.

"What's for dinner?" I finally broke the silence.

"Prime rib," Braden rubbed his hands together in anticipation. "Garlic mashed potatoes and corn, too."

I guess I could stay for prime rib, even though my fight-or-flight response was tilting in flight's direction.

"So what was the dead guy's name?" Cillian asked.

"Mitch Johnson."

"No, not that guy," Cillian shook his head. "The guy you found in the alley."

"Oh, um, I think his name was Brian Harper." I wasn't sure why Cillian was asking, but he seemed lost in thought. "Why do you ask?"

Cillian screwed up his face in a "well duh" expression. "Really? Don't you think that we should have had prior knowledge of Brian Harper passing?

You know, since we're the designated reapers for the surrounding five counties."

Oh, wow, I hadn't even thought of that. "He wasn't on any of your lists today?"

Everyone shook their heads.

"Is that possible? To not have a soul on the list?" I turned to my dad expectantly.

"It's not supposed to be," he said. "I can't remember the last time a mistake like that occurred. With computers now, it should never happen."

"Could another reaper be on our turf?" Cillian asked.

Turf? Really? What is this, *West Side Story*?

"Not without the council notifying us," Dad replied.

"Could someone be freelancing?"

Freelancing is frowned upon – but not unheard of – in our line of work. There are a handful of well-known reapers who have disavowed affiliation with the council but who still take individual jobs for certain interested parties as long as there is some form of monetary remuneration. This usually happens when someone is coveted by two religious groups – with the winning freelancer getting payment on delivery. It's a competitive field.

It's more likely for a freelancer to be engaged, though, when Hell has a bead on someone and thinks they might run. Timothy McVeigh, for example, had three freelancers hired to make sure he couldn't escape and his soul capture turned ugly. The same with Osama bin Laden. Brian Harper, though? That didn't sound like a typical freelancing assignment.

"What do we know about this Brian Harper?" Braden asked.

Aidan took a break from shoveling food into his face to pull his iPad from the coffee table. He was engrossed in his work for a few minutes, so the rest of us just watched and waited. I had no idea what he was doing, but he was the most technologically savvy member of our little clan so we let him do his thing.

The room had gone so silent that everyone jumped when the printer on the desk came to life and started spitting out pages.

"Sorry," Redmond said. "I need to get this paperwork in order so I can get Aisling's scepter back."

Everyone turned back to Aidan and waited. It was as though we were in a horror movie and the killer was about to make an appearance -- or something less obnoxious. I'm not great at making comparisons when hunger and stress collide.

"Uh-oh."

"Uh-oh what?" The suspense was killing me. Okay, that's an exaggeration. The suspense is starting to wear on me, though. I tend to drift toward the dramatic sometimes.

"Brian Harper is on the list."

"Whose?" Dad asked, his face instantly reddening.

"Redmond's."

"He is not." Redmond jumped to the middle of the room with his list in hand to prove that he hadn't been shirking his duties before I could blink.

"He's not on your list today," Aidan clarified.

"I don't understand," Redmond faltered.

"He's on your list for next week."

"How is that possible … oh." Realization bloomed in the corner of my mind usually reserved for serious books and cliffhanger Friday on *General Hospital*. "Someone killed him early to steal his soul."

"You're smarter than you look," Aidan said, patting my hand affectionately. His words were full of mirth but his eyes were full of dread. I was new at this, but even I knew this couldn't be good.

"So, who would do that?" Displaying ignorance in front of my father wasn't my first choice, but someone had to ask the question.

"We shouldn't jump to any conclusions," Redmond said, exchanging a wary glance with Dad.

"What conclusions are we jumping to?"

"Nothing," my dad said, rising from his desk chair. "Nothing."

"What aren't you guys telling me?"

"I want to check something," Dad said. "You all go into the dining room and start your dinner. I'll be there in a few minutes."

"But … ."

Aidan grabbed my arm, shaking his head as he dragged me out of the room. "Just let him do his thing," he whispered. "You're going to make things worse if you press him right now."

I didn't see how things could get much worse. I turned to Redmond for support but he was obviously on Aidan's side. "He's right, kid. Just let it go for now."

I still didn't understand, but I did what I was told. They would tell me what was going on as soon as it was confirmed. I was almost sure of it.

8
EIGHT

Someone was performing construction at an ungodly hour. That's what that pounding in my head had to be, because I hadn't imbibed enough alcohol last night to blame it on a hangover. I'm Irish; it takes a fifth – or a keg – to make me regret a bender.

After a few minutes, I realized that drifting back to dreamland was out of the question so I grudgingly climbed out of bed and made my way to the condo's cozy kitchen. I smelled fresh muffins and coffee before I rounded the corner, which meant Jerry was already up.

"I can't believe you're up at the crack of dawn," I mumbled. "Do you have an appointment or something?"

"It's after ten."

I froze when I heard the voice. It didn't belong to Jerry, but I did recognize it. "Detective Taylor?"

I rubbed the sleep from my eyes to find Jerry's handsome face at the counter before I turned my attention to Griffin Taylor, who was sitting at our small kitchen table eating a muffin and drinking from a coffee mug.

This had to be a dream.

"Good morning, Bug. Did you sleep well?"

I glanced down at my plaid, cotton boxer shorts and knit tank top – I don't sleep in a bra so my nipples were just kind of sitting there for everyone to see – and I felt awkwardly naked in front of Detective Taylor. Jerry is gay;

he doesn't look at my girl parts. And, if he does, he doesn't really care about them. Detective Taylor, though, couldn't look away.

"What are you doing here?"

Detective Taylor dragged his gaze from my chest and focused on my face. I caught a glimpse of my reflection in the glass cabinet doors and cringed. I need to remember to start putting my hair in a braid before I go to sleep to cut down on the bedhead. It was too late now.

"I have a few more questions."

"You didn't get your answers after four hours yesterday? There's nothing new to add."

"Four hours of what?" Jerry looked intrigued.

"Not what you're thinking."

Detective Taylor smiled at our banter. "What is he thinking?"

"Nothing."

"I was thinking you spent four hours doing the horizontal tango."

"Jerry!"

Detective Taylor coughed around a mouthful of coffee. "The horizontal tango?"

"You know, sex." Jerry is blunt, which I usually love about him. Now, though? I'm wishing for a sinkhole to open up in our kitchen.

"We didn't have sex," I hissed.

"How am I supposed to know?" Jerry asked. "You didn't come home until after I was already in bed. I have trouble believing you spent that much time with your family without blood being shed."

"We had some things to talk about," I grumbled.

"Like being taken in for questioning?" Detective Taylor asked.

"Are you a police officer?" Jerry looked intrigued.

"You just let him in without knowing he was a cop? He could have been a strangler or something."

Jerry shrugged. "He said he had to talk to you. I thought maybe he was looking for a morning quickie. He's too hot to be a strangler."

Detective Taylor chuckled as he popped another bit of muffin into his mouth. "Obviously you two aren't an item."

"She's not my type," Jerry said, sliding into the open chair next to our guest.

"No kidding. I don't have enough chest hair."

"Sarcasm isn't becoming, Bug," Jerry said, keeping his gaze on Detective Taylor's face. "And you know I don't like chest hair. He's never going to sleep with you if you keep acting like this. Now sit down and have a muffin."

"I don't want a muffin." And I most certainly don't want to have sex with Detective Taylor. What? I don't.

"Then have some coffee and make our guest feel welcome."

I was starting to rethink my lifelong friendship with Jerry. The coffee did smell good, though. And, as much as I wanted to retreat to my bedroom to change into something that didn't make me look like a teenage girl at a sleepover, I refused to cede my own home turf. Crap. Now I'm using the word "turf."

I grudgingly sat down in the chair next to Jerry and poured a cup of coffee – wishing just for a second that I could throw it in my eyes to wake myself up faster – and reluctantly sipped from it. "So, Detective Taylor, what can I do for you?"

"Why don't you call me Griffin."

"That doesn't seem very professional."

"Call him Griffin," Jerry said. "It's a nice name. Detective Taylor makes me think of Mayberry."

"Andy Taylor wasn't a detective," I countered.

"Don't be difficult."

I rolled my eyes, a move that wasn't lost on Griffin. "Fine. Griffin, what can I do for you?"

"I have a few more questions about the body you found yesterday."

"You found a body?" Jerry's eyes were wide as he hung on Griffin's every word.

"Aidan and I found one in an alley," I said. "Actually, I tripped over it."

"Of course," Jerry laughed.

"Griffin here thought that Aidan and I should spend the rest of the afternoon answering inane questions because we had the bad fortune of walking down an alley."

Griffin leaned back in his chair, studying me with unreadable cop eyes. "You don't think that coming upon the two of you talking about fleeing from a murder scene is a good reason to take you in for questioning?"

"You were going to leave the scene?" Jerry tsked. "That's not very smart."

"No, it's not," Griffin agreed.

I sipped from my coffee again before adding to the conversation. I didn't get a chance, though.

"I bet it was Aidan's idea to leave – you were with Aidan, right?"

"Yes."

"How many brothers do you have?" Griffin asked, as though he was making random conversation when I knew he was trying to catch me in a lie.

"Four."

"Older? Younger?"

"All older."

"Isn't Aidan your twin?"

I knew it. He was trying to trip me up. He had run a background check on me. "Yes," I nodded. "He is still six minutes older than me, though. So, while he's barely older, he is still older."

"He treats her like he's five years older, though," Jerry offered.

"I think that's a brother thing," Griffin replied, gracing Jerry with a friendly smile. "I have two younger sisters and I feel the same way about both of them."

"Aidan is still better than Redmond," Jerry explained. "Redmond acts like her father. It's a little disconcerting."

"He doesn't need an explanation of my family tree," I snapped.

Jerry looked momentarily taken aback. "You seem tense, Bug."

"Why do you call her Bug?" Griffin looked genuinely curious.

"Oh, that's a great story," Jerry said.

"No, it's not."

Jerry ignored me. "When we were in kindergarten, my mom let me ride home on the bus to their house for the first time. I was really excited. You should see Grimlock Manor; it's like a castle."

"Grimlock Manor?"

"That's where her family lives."

"They still all live there together? Everyone? Everyone except Aisling?"

"Yes," Jerry nodded. "It's tragically codependent, but what can you do?"

Griffin winked when he saw my perpetual scowl. "It's interesting," he said. "Continue your story, though."

"Oh, right." Jerry was clearly warming to his topic. If this were his life story he was rehashing, he would be equally effusive. It's just his nature. "Anyway, so we get off the bus and I'm all in awe of the house. It has actual turrets – I'm not exaggerating – and I had all these dreams of being a princess held prisoner in a turret and being rescued by a big, strong prince."

I couldn't hide my smile. Griffin seemed entertained, too.

"All of a sudden I hear her screaming. So, when I look over, she's fighting with four other boys – some of them a lot bigger than us – and she's pulling hair and kicking and swearing up a storm."

"You swore in kindergarten?" Griffin asked.

"My dad taught me."

"He also taught her how to beat a DVD player with a golf club when it won't work. That's why she's not allowed to fix any household items," Jerry continued. "So, when we get over there we find that Redmond, Cillian, Braden and Aidan are all burning ants with a magnifying glass."

Griffin nodded knowingly. "I did the same thing when I was a kid."

Jerry frowned at Griffin's admission, suddenly suspicious of our guest. "Anyway, Aisling started trying to round up the ants to save them and I thought she was a bug superhero, so I started calling her Bug."

"That's a cute story."

"It's a long story," I corrected him.

"That doesn't mean it's not cute."

This conversation was quickly veering into the uncomfortable. "So, what did you want to ask me?"

"I wanted to know if you saw anyone in the alley before you and your brother discovered Mr. Harper."

"I told you we didn't. There was no one there. It was just us."

"And you're sure? You weren't distracted by anything?"

Only deep conversations about my father's intentions and my constant feelings of inadequacy. "We were just talking."

"About what?"

"Lunch."

"At Giuseppe's?"

"Right."

"Giuseppe's? You went to Giuseppe's without me?" Jerry whined.

"We never made it."

"Karma," Jerry shot back knowingly.

"Whatever."

Griffin ignored our sparring. "We canvassed the area after the body was discovered," he continued. "We found two witnesses."

"Then why are you here?"

"What?"

"Well, your witnesses couldn't have possibly implicated Aidan and me, so why are you here?"

"Because what the witnesses described sounds like something out of a horror movie," Griffin replied, his face grim.

Uh-oh. "What did they describe?"

"Honestly? They said they saw a tall man – like seven feet tall – in a black robe with a face like a demon."

"A demon?" Jerry looked amused. "Was this a rough part of town? Were these witnesses all drugged up?"

"They're not the best witnesses," Griffin acknowledged. "They both described the same thing, though."

"So there are demons running around Detroit?" Jerry didn't look convinced until his eyes met mine evenly before realization washed over him. "Oh."

"Oh, what?" Griffin asked.

"Nothing," Jerry said hurriedly, suddenly fascinated with his mug of coffee.

Now Griffin was the one who didn't look convinced. I couldn't worry about that right now, though. I had to find Redmond. I knew what my brothers were trying to hide from me. It wasn't a freelancer that took the soul early. It was a wraith.

Now I was pissed – and a little scared.

NINE

Rushing a police officer out of your home when pretending to do the opposite isn't easy.

Thankfully, Jerry seemed to realize that I knew more than I was letting on and decided to be helpful.

"Don't forget you have to help me at the bakery today," he said. Jerry participates in community theater and he gets off playing a part. His current role was supportive best friend, and he wasn't above lying to a cop to get him out of our condo.

"You own a bakery?" Griffin asked. He was still playing the comfortable breakfast angle.

"Get Baked," Jerry replied, his pride evident as his chest puffed out.

"That's a great place," Griffin said.

"You've been there?" I asked pointedly.

Griffin looked momentarily abashed. "Well, no, but I've been to a few brunches where cupcakes from Get Baked were served."

"Brunches?" Jerry narrowed his eyes. "I thought you were straight."

"I am straight." Griffin looked flummoxed. "You know, straight people have brunch, too."

"Not in my world. She doesn't have brunch." Jerry pointed at me for emphasis. Unfortunately, he was lying. I remembered a series of Sunday brunches I was forced to attend with Jerry's posse. I didn't tell Griffin, though.

I couldn't fight the smile that flirted with the corners of my mouth as Jerry sank into his performance. Griffin frowned when he saw my reaction.

"I'm not gay."

"I know." I held up my hands in mock surrender.

"It's good you're not gay," Jerry said.

"Why?"

"Because if you're gay you can't end this one's dry spell." Jerry gestured toward me haphazardly.

My smile flipped into a scowl while Griffin's frown turned upside down. "Dry spell?"

"He's being dramatic."

"Six months," Jerry shook his head. "Six months isn't just a dry spell, it's a drought."

"Don't you have to shower before work?"

Jerry considered the question for a second and then winked when he got my inference. "Oh, right, you want a few minutes alone with our guest." He got to his feet and dropped his coffee mug in the sink. "I'll just leave you two alone."

He obviously didn't get my inference.

"Did you want some time alone with me?" Griffin asked after Jerry left the room. He seemed amused at the prospect.

"Not really."

Griffin raised his eyebrows, clearly not believing my answer.

"Don't you have somewhere to be? Murders to solve and all of that?"

"I'm still waiting for you to comment on the possibility of a demon murdering Mr. Harper."

Great.

"I think that the pot on the streets these days must be a lot stronger than the pot I smoked when I was in high school." Wait? A cop can't arrest you eight years after the fact, can he?

"That's all you have to say about it?" Griffin's eyes were serious.

"What do you want me to say?"

"I want you to say, 'Oh, that's crazy,'" he replied.

"Oh, that's crazy."

"Something tells me something else is going on here."

"Is that cop intuition?"

"More like human observation."

"You must be a big hit at parties."

Griffin regarded me for a second and then slowly rose to his feet. "I should probably go."

He probably should. I can't race out of the apartment and accuse my brother of being a big, fat liar if he is still here grilling me.

"I'll be in touch if I need to talk to you again," he said.

"Of course."

Is it wrong that I'm secretly yearning for another interrogation?

TWO HOURS LATER I WAS IN TROY WATCHING A HINDU TRY TO MAKE peace with Shiva.

"Seriously?"

Redmond refused to meet my accusing glare. "What does it hurt?"

"Aidan said that you guys don't do this," I said. "He says that you just go in, scepter blazing, and collect the soul and get out. He said that trying to talk to the souls is a waste of time and that I need to toughen up."

Redmond ignored my sarcasm. "Oh, by the way," he reached into his pocket and handed me a familiar object. "I got this back for you this morning."

I grudgingly took the scepter from his hand and shoved it into my pocket. "Thanks."

"You're welcome."

"Did they give you any crap?"

"No," he shook his head. "They were surprisingly easy to deal with."

"And they didn't have any questions about the paperwork?"

"Nope."

Redmond's soul was busily making promises to Shiva – and he wasn't in hearing distance – so I took the opportunity to grab the bull by the horns.

"So, Detective Taylor stopped by my place this morning."

"Is that the guy who took you and Aidan in for questioning?"

"Yup."

"Why was he at your condo?"

"Because he wants to torture me."

Redmond regarded me skeptically. "Why did he really show up?"

"Because he wanted me to confirm that the two witnesses he found really saw a seven-foot-tall guy who looked like a demon in a robe."

Redmond's breath came out in a whoosh. I knew it!

"You knew it was a wraith, didn't you?"

Redmond averted his eyes from my gaze. "No."

"Don't lie."

"I had my suspicions," Redmond replied. "That's different."

"How?"

"Don't look at me like that."

"Like what?"

"Like I lied to you."

I rolled my eyes. "You did."

"I did not."

"You did, too."

"I did not."

"You did, too. Now what is he doing?"

Redmond glanced back up at his charge and sighed. "Dedicating his life to Shiva in exchange for eternal worship."

"He's already dead."

"He doesn't believe it."

"They never do."

"I hate doing Hindu retrievals," Redmond sighed. "They're never violent, but they're always so earnest."

"Is that why you agreed to let him say goodbye to the statue?"

"Don't be a pain."

"So, what do you think about this whole wraith thing?" I returned to the problem at hand.

Okay, here's the situation. We live in a world where the paranormal exist. Not vampires (sorry, sparkly Robert Pattinson fans). Not werewolves (sorry, randy Joe Manganiello fans). Not zombies (sorry, gritty Norman Reedus fans). Not mummies (sorry … hmm, there have never been any hot mummies in pop culture, have there?). But other things do exist. Reapers. Witches. Fairies. Wraiths.

Wraiths are our current concern, though. They're essentially fallen witches and warlocks. They can live for centuries if they absorb the souls of the recently deceased. As for the owners of those souls, once they're gone they're gone. No afterlife. No Heaven. No Hell. No Purgatory. Nothing. It goes against the very fiber of nature.

Wraiths are a big deal – and they're inherently evil. If we have a rogue one in the area, we have a fight on our hands.

"I think we need more information." Redmond's face was drawn and serious.

I love Redmond, but his insistence on following the rules and not flying off the handle is tedious.

"Where are we going to get this information?"

"I have an idea."

I searched his face for answers and, when I found them, my heart plummeted. "No."

"Yes."

"No."

"Yes."

Crap. He wanted to go see Madame Maxine. I knew I should have picked a different brother to approach.

"Wait here," Redmond ordered. "I have to tear this guy away from the statue. I'll be right back."

I can't wait.

10

TEN

"I think this is a bad idea."

Redmond didn't even waste a tired look in my direction. "Then wait out here."

We were on Woodward in Royal Oak, on the sidewalk in front of Tarot and Tea, a magic shop. This was Madame Maxine's shop – and I have never had a positive experience here.

"I'm not waiting out here," I argued. "People might think I'm a prostitute or something."

Redmond glanced down at my Converse and shook his head. "Not in those shoes."

He had a point.

"Well, I don't want to rely on you to tell me what she knows."

It was a low blow, but I figured he deserved it.

Redmond rolled his eyes. "Are you ever going to let this go?"

"It's been three hours."

"That's like an eternity when a woman is hounding you," Redmond replied. "This is why I'm not married."

Whatever.

I squared my shoulders and followed Redmond into the store, letting him take the lead. It wasn't that I saw him as a leader; it was more that I found it easier to hide behind his impressive shoulders. I'm a coward where Madame Maxine is concerned. I admit it.

Tarot and Tea is one of those kitschy shops that appeals to faux wiccans and pagans. The shelves are covered with spell books and voodoo curses, while the racks are encumbered with incense bags and small glass balls. It's basically a haven for confused teenage girls and desperate guys who think being a warlock gives them an edge.

What most people don't know, though, is that Tarot and Tea has a hidden agenda: The owner, Madame Maxine, really does have the gift. What gift? The sight. Sometimes, she can see the future.

Madame Maxine is a self-taught witch and part-time clairvoyant. She's a fifty-five-year-old ball of energy and master of the snarky comment. Under normal circumstances, I would love her. Since she keeps telling me I'm wasting my life, though, I have a big chip on my shoulder where she is concerned.

Jerry had forced me into the shop during the Woodward Dream Cruise when we were teenagers. One tarot card reading later, Madame Maxine informed me that I was going to make one hundred wrong decisions before I finally made a right one. I wasn't keeping count, but I really couldn't argue with her insight -- not that I would ever tell her that.

I had stayed out of the store for five years after that initial reading. Then, when I was twenty-one, Jerry had talked me into another drunken visit after the Ferndale Gay Pride Festival. Madame Maxine had informed me I still had a lot of wrong turns in my future, but that the right ones would eventually come. Rather than acknowledging she might be right, I called her a fraud and fled. I hadn't been back since.

I wasn't looking forward to this visit.

I purposely matched my movements to Redmond's so I could remain hidden from prying eyes at the back of the store. Unfortunately, Madame Maxine was at her small tarot table – with a clear view of the door -- when we entered.

Crap.

"Well, look who has come back for another reading."

Redmond glanced down at me curiously but he didn't comment. "Maxine," he said, moving over to the table with his arms stretched wide. "It's so good to see you."

"You, too, handsome." She sent him a saucy wink as she got to her feet and hugged him. "It's been too long."

"I'm not in this area often enough," Redmond admitted. "I come in whenever I can, though."

"Every six months is whenever you can?" Madame Maxine didn't look convinced.

Redmond's neck flushed with embarrassment. "I'll do better."

"I surely hope so," Madame Maxine pressed her lips to his cheek affectionately. "And who is this small girl hiding behind you?"

Redmond stepped to the side to give Madame Maxine a clear view. "This is my sister, Aisling."

"I remember her."

"You've met?" Redmond didn't exactly look surprised as much as he looked conflicted.

"A few times," Madame Maxine acknowledged at the exact same time I said "no."

Amusement flitted across Redmond's face. "How do you two know each other?"

"I've given her a reading or two," Madame Maxine replied. "I don't think she liked my insight."

I was suddenly fascinated by the Wild Berry incense display so I pretended that I didn't hear the conversation. Since Redmond and I were the only customers in the store, though, it was difficult. I could feel Redmond's eyes boring a hole in my back as I fingered the incense sticks, occasionally lifting one to my nose to test the scent. Maybe I should have stayed outside. Getting mistaken for a prostitute couldn't be as uncomfortable as this, could it?

"And what did those readings say?" Redmond was intrigued.

I screwed up my face in disgust as I readied myself for Madame Maxine's pronouncement.

"You know that I keep all my readings confidential," she said. "Don't try to be cute."

I let out a long, shaky breath and finally found the courage to meet Madame Maxine's blue eyes. I expected to find mirth and consternation, but all I discovered was warmth and sympathy.

Hmm. Maybe Madame Maxine wasn't as bad as I thought.

"Are you still making bad decisions, girl?"

Or maybe she was evil incarnate.

"We're not here about me," I replied.

"I figured."

"How?"

"You both have dark auras," Madame Maxine said, sinking back down in her chair. "That means you have serious issues on your mind. You're worried."

Redmond maneuvered himself to the open seat across from Madame Maxine, settling his large frame in the small chair with more grace than I would have thought possible. "We have a problem."

"Define problem."

"There's a wraith in the area."

Since Madame Maxine was aware of the supernatural population, I expected some sort of reaction. Fear. Panic. Mild interest. None of those emotions moved across her face, though.

Instead, Madame Maxine reached up and pulled the wooden pick out of her gray hair, letting it fall to her shoulders in a mass of silky waves. For an older woman, she really was breathtaking. That bohemian chic thing she had going for her was pretty impressive, and I'm not just saying that because her ankle-length purple skirt had me considering trading in my Converse for comfortable pumps – or at least sensible flats.

Redmond was the first to break the silence. "This isn't a surprise to you?"

"No," Madame Maxine admitted. "It's not."

"Why didn't you tell anyone?" I asked, my mind tangling with a series of insults.

"Who should I tell?"

"The Authority?" I suggested.

Yes, we have a paranormal council. The members don't have a lot of power, but they do have a wide range of information dissemination avenues. They could have at least made everyone aware of what was going on.

"I'm not part of that group," Madame Maxine reminded us. "I'm a solitary practitioner."

"That doesn't mean you're not responsible for what happens in this town," I said.

"How am I responsible?"

"If you know a wraith is here – a wraith that's killing people and sucking souls, mind you – you should report it to someone."

"Why?"

"Because it's wrong."

"It's wrong to you," Madame Maxine said, choosing her words carefully. "You're a reaper, I get that. You have a job to do and a mantra to embrace. That doesn't mean everyone believes in that mantra. People believe differently, young lady."

"So you think it's okay for a parasite to live off the eternal life of others?"

"I didn't say that."

"What are you saying?"

"Aisling," Redmond warned. "Don't."

"Don't what?"

"Don't do what you're doing?"

"You can't think she's right?" I was incredulous. Redmond is notorious for not rocking the boat, but he's not exactly known for just sitting there and watching it sink.

"I didn't say that," Redmond replied, his voice low and his purple eyes serious. "Why don't you let me do the talking?"

I crossed my arms over my chest obstinately. I hate it when he treats me like a child.

"Let the girl talk," Madame Maxine interjected. "She has an opinion and it's her right to express it."

Redmond seemed surprised by Madame Maxine's chiding. "I thought … ."

"Just be quiet, boy," Madame Maxine instructed. "This is between me and her."

Redmond opened his mouth to argue and then wisely snapped it shut. He sent me a sympathetic look before focusing on Madame Maxine and avoiding my heated glare.

"You didn't answer my question," I pressed.

"I forgot what the question was."

"Are you okay with an abomination sucking the afterlife from people and then tossing them away like garbage?"

Redmond cleared his throat in warning but I ignored him. Madame Maxine didn't even seem to realize he was in the room.

"No."

"No?"

"No."

"Then why didn't you tell someone that there was a wraith in the area?"

"Wraiths," Madame Maxine corrected me.

"Wraiths? Plural?"

"There are at least three," Madame Maxine acknowledged. "I would guess there are more, though."

I wanted to explode. I wanted to shake Madame Maxine until she admitted she was wrong – about more than just keeping quiet on this topic. Instead, I opted for a different tactic.

"How do you know?"

"It's just a feeling," Madame Maxine answered. "There's a dark energy descending on us."

"And that's something you just feel?"

"I can't explain it," Madame Maxine admitted. "It's just something I know."

"Why would they be here?"

"Why not?"

"It's Detroit." I'm not being derogatory. I love the city. Pretending it doesn't have issues would be a waste of time, though.

"So?"

"So, it's not exactly a bustling community anymore."

"That's why the wraiths are here."

I wasn't following. Redmond was a different story.

"Because of the abandoned houses?" His hands were steepled in front of his face as he considered the possibilities.

Madame Maxine nodded.

I still don't get it.

Redmond turned to me, his face voice racing with energy. "Think about it, Aisling. All those abandoned houses are perfect places for wraiths to hide. The streets are full of junkies and prostitutes – throw-away people. The whole area is rife for a takeover."

I didn't like the sound of that. "But how have we not noticed?"

Redmond's jaw tightened. "Because we weren't looking."

"Isn't that our job?"

"Sure," Redmond agreed. "If you don't see the signs, though, you don't know what you're looking for. They're easy to miss."

I turned back to Madame Maxine. "What do they want?"

"I'm not sure they're on their own," she said.

"What does that mean?"

"I can't be sure," she said. "I have this feeling in the pit of my stomach, though."

"And what does that feeling tell you?"

"That something bigger is here and it's drawing them together for a purpose."

Well, that couldn't be good.

"What do they want?" I asked, already dreading the answer.

"A reckoning."

ELEVEN

"What do you think?"

We had left Tarot and Tea and were now sitting in Redmond's car in the store's small parking lot.

"I think that this could be serious," Redmond replied after a beat.

"I'll get the ark, you get the animals."

Redmond wrinkled his nose and reached over and pinched me. "Don't be smart."

"Do you think Dad already knows?"

Redmond rubbed the bridge of his nose. "I think he has an idea."

"That there are multiple wraiths in the area? You think he knows and he's not telling us? That doesn't sound safe."

"I don't think that he knows there are multiple wraiths," Redmond clarified. "I think he knew last night that a wraith was responsible for the body you found but he wanted to be sure before he said anything."

"You knew that, too." I crossed my arms over my chest and fixed him with a petulant stare.

"I had a suspicion; I didn't know."

"Semantics," I grumbled.

"Let's not get all female here," Redmond said. "We need to think strategically and not go off on a mission before we even know what that mission is."

"Get all female? That's a little insulting."

"That doesn't mean it's not true," Redmond said. "You've always been a little dramatic – and this would is a prime example."

"I am not dramatic," I sniffed.

"Yeah, you're really easygoing."

"I don't appreciate the sarcasm."

"Then don't dish it out."

Since this debate was going nowhere, I decided to end it with a little bit of class. I stuck my tongue out and blessed Redmond with a loud raspberry. Despite the seriousness of the situation, Redmond couldn't help but laugh.

"And you wonder why you're single."

We lapsed into silence for a few minutes, the only noise the steady drum of Redmond's fingers on the steering wheel. I don't have a lot of patience on a good day, so on a bad day I'm practically apoplectic.

Finally, Redmond put his key in the ignition and turned the car engine over. "Call Braden."

"And tell him what?"

"Tell him to get the information he gathered on that guy … what was his name?"

"Brian Harper."

"Yeah, Brian Harper. Tell him to get the information and meet us at his place."

I was surprised, but at least it was forward momentum. "Where is his place?"

"Right upstairs from where you found him."

"We're going back to the alley?" That didn't sound like fun.

Redmond shook his head, his attention focused on pulling into the heavy traffic clogging Woodward. "No. We're going to the apartment above the alley."

That was better?

Almost forty-five minutes later, Braden, Redmond and I were standing in the apartment complex's parking lot and flipping through Brian Harper's file looking for clues.

"This guy was slime."

Braden tugged on a strand of my hair absentmindedly and nodded his head in agreement. "I can see why he was going to Hell."

"Yeah, this scam where he put contractor liens on people's homes after doing substandard work so he could take ownership of them and sell them at a profit is pretty disgusting," Redmond agreed.

"I'm more offended with the racism when selling the houses," I said. "Only whites need apply."

"That's low," Braden said. "That's not as bad as the adoption scam he was running, though."

"I didn't see anything about an adoption scam."

Braden ran his finger down the page – which was in Redmond's hand – stopping when he got to the line he was looking for. "It says he was taking $50,000 from each interested family but he only had one kid for every three families – even though he was taking money from every family."

"Where was he getting these kids?"

"That's a pretty good question. It doesn't say."

"With as many fingers in as many pies as this guy had, his operation had to be bigger than just him," Redmond said.

"Our files don't go that deep, though," Braden mused. "We only get the highlights for our specific charge. We don't get a list of his associates, even though that would be really helpful right now. That's just not how it works."

"I'm lost."

Redmond tousled my hair. "We know."

I jerked my head away and smoothed down the mess. "I mean that I don't understand what Brian Harper being an ass has to do with anything. Maybe it was just a crime of opportunity."

"I think that would be too much of a coincidence," Redmond said, shrugging his broad shoulders until we heard an audible crack. "I think there's something here – something specific about Brian Harper – that we need to know."

"What makes you think that?"

"It's just a feeling," Redmond admitted. "I think there's more going on here."

"Well, with multiple wraiths in the area, I think that's a gimme," I said. "I still don't understand how Brian Harper's illegal activities during his life figure into the scary happenings surrounding his death."

Braden's face broke out into a wide grin. "You have a way with words."

"I'm an intellectual."

Braden pointed down at my DC Skate Shoes. "Yeah, because most intellectuals wear shoes that could be found in a teenage boy's closet."

I screwed up my face in a pointed scowl. "Don't hate the shoes. They don't like it."

"You know," Redmond said, finishing with the file and flipping it shut. "When you pretend your shoes have feelings it makes me uncomfortable."

"It makes Dad crazy," Braden added.

"They do have feelings," I countered. "They're just like people. They like to be put on display, taken out to a nice dinner and they don't like to go out in the rain."

"Good to know."

Redmond turned to Braden. "So, are you thinking what I'm thinking?"

"That we need to get into that apartment and find out what other shady dealings Brian Harper was up to?"

"Pretty much."

Wait. What? "You're going to break into his apartment?"

"Keep your voice down," Braden ordered, shoving his hand over my mouth instinctively. "There might be a few homeless people on the corner who didn't hear you announce the fact that we're about to break the law."

I clawed Braden's hand away from my mouth. "You can't just break into his apartment."

"Why?" Redmond was nonplussed.

"Because it's illegal."

"Technically we're breaking into someone's house or apartment when we go to collect a soul," Braden pointed out. "So that is illegal, too. I don't hear you screeching like a banshee about that."

I hate it when he has a point.

"What if the cops have it sealed off?"

Braden and Redmond exchanged a look. They obviously hadn't thought of that. Point for me.

"I guess we'll find out when we get there," Braden said. "It's unit 405, so let's get it over with."

"I don't want to break in."

"You're not going to," Redmond said.

I wasn't? Wait, why not? "Why is that? Because I'm a girl?" I narrowed my eyes in warning, just in case they didn't think I was serious.

"Yes," Braden nodded.

Redmond punched his shoulder. "No. It's because we need someone to act as a lookout and you're going to be less suspicious hanging around in front of the apartment complex than we are."

Nice story. "I think it's because you don't think I can do it."

Braden sighed. "Are you going to turn this into a thing?"

"What? The fact that you guys don't think I can do certain things because I'm a girl?" My hands were on my hips and my voice was stern. Sometimes I get it when they call me dramatic. It works for me, though, so I'm sticking with it.

"Why does everything come down to this women's lib crap with you?" Braden asked.

"Women's lib? Get out of the sixties, Braden."

"Well, what would you call it?"

"Reverse sexism."

"Is that like reverse racism?'

"Are you trying to confuse me?"

"No, I think you're doing that to yourself," Redmond said, opening his car door and dropping the file on the front seat. "Can't you just act as lookout and yell at us about how sexist we are later? Like over dinner when we have enough drinks that your voice doesn't sound like nails on a chalkboard."

"Fine."

"Good."

Redmond and Braden rolled their eyes, sending a silent message to each other that twenty-five years had taught me how to interpret: She's crazy.

"So, what do I do if I see a cop entering the building? Caw like a crow?"

Redmond snickered. "Or you could just text us so we can get out of the apartment."

That was a better idea.

I followed Redmond and Braden to the main entrance of the building. It was an older hotel that had been converted to apartments by Detroit's Downtown Development Authority about ten years earlier as part of the city's ongoing revitalization project. I'm not going to lie; the project isn't going well. There's too much blight to keep up with. Still, the cement steps leading up to the building and the big lion sculptures on either side of the front door were kind of cool. If you had to live downtown, this wasn't a bad place to live.

"How long do you think you guys will be up there?"

Redmond shrugged. "I have no idea. Just hang out down here and watch the front door. We'll be done when we're done."

Once Redmond and Braden disappeared inside of the building, I busied myself by pacing the length of the front sidewalk. When I got to the end of the block, I turned around and paced back. Since boredom was creeping in, I started playing the sidewalk crack game – trying to make the trek without stepping on a crack. That entertained me for about five minutes. Then I moved to the bottom step of the stairs and did some calf-lengthening exercises. If I was stuck here, I might as well get part of my workout in.

I was so caught up in what I was doing, I didn't notice the figure move in behind me until the distinctive sound of a man clearing his throat broke my reverie.

"What are you doing here?"

I froze when I heard the voice. Crap. Caw. Caw.

TWELVE

"Detective Taylor."

"I told you to call me Griffin."

"Griffin. What are you doing here?" My voice was unnaturally shrill, but I was having trouble reining in the panic.

"I was just about to ask you the same question."

Of course he was.

Griffin's face was hard to read. Amusement was flitting through his dark eyes – even if it wasn't fully expressed, but a frown was playing with the corner of his mouth, which I didn't take as a good sign.

"What question?" I was going for cute, wrapping a strand of my black and white hair around my index finger and flashing him a flirtatious smile. I was so nervous I was afraid the smile looked more deranged than sexy.

"What are you doing here?" Griffin wasn't taking the bait.

"Just hanging out."

"Here?"

"Yeah, it's a cool building. I like architecture."

"You're just hanging out in front of a random building in downtown Detroit?"

"Yup." My hands found my pocket and fingered my cell phone desperately.

"The building where a murder victim – one you discovered – lived?"

"Huh? Did he live here? That's a coincidence. Creepy."

Griffin pushed his lips out, clearly not sure where he was going to take the conversation next. Unfortunately, he went someplace I wasn't expecting. "Weren't you working at your roommate's bakery today?"

Crap. This is why you shouldn't lie – or at least remember what lies you've told so you don't accidentally step all over them. "I helped him for an hour, you know, frosting emergency, and then I was done."

"Because you had to come here?"

"No, because I had to meet my brother on an assignment." What? That's not a lie. It's an omission. I did meet Redmond on an assignment.

"Where is your brother now?"

Uh-oh. "I lost track."

"And this would be the same brother you were with yesterday?"

"No, a different one."

"Which one?"

"Why does that matter?"

"Why don't you want to tell me?"

What is it with men trying to confuse me today? I took a deep breath to calm myself. I needed to alert Braden and Redmond that Griffin was here, but if I pulled out my phone and started texting he would be suspicious -- even more suspicious than he already was, if that was possible.

"I was with my oldest brother."

"Doing what?"

"We had a job to do. An estate sale."

"Find anything good?"

"No, it was really just a glorified garage sale."

"And that's bad?"

Griffin's rapid-fire questions were starting to grate. He was trying to catch me off guard – I was well aware – but I couldn't dissuade him without tipping him off. He already knew something was up. He didn't know what, though. I'm a master at throwing off suspicion. Just ask my father.

"We're only interested in high-end antiques," I explained. "You usually don't find anything like that at a garage sale, although it's not unheard of."

"I see."

Something told me he didn't.

"You still haven't told me why you're here." The sun glinted off Griffin's brown hair, giving it an ethereal quality that wasn't lost on my libido. Unfortunately.

"I was just looking at the building."

"So, you're saying that you hang out in front of random buildings in the middle of the week in downtown Detroit for fun?"

"Yup."

"Because you like looking at architecture?"

"Yup."

Griffin cocked his head to one side. "Do you want to know what I think?"

Not really. "So, they let you dress really casual when you're a detective, huh?"

I don't think Griffin was expecting that response. "Excuse me?"

"Well, I mean jeans, a leather jacket – it's spring, aren't you hot in that? – and then there's the whole New Balance thing."

Griffin glanced down at his feet. "I'm wearing Nikes today."

"That's a step up," I acknowledged. "With those jeans, though, you really should try boots."

"Like cowboy boots?"

I looked him up and down again, shaking my head. "You can't pull off cowboy boots. Just some nice black boots – brown if they're not tacky – and it would totally change your vibe."

Griffin broke into a wide smile – the first I had seen grace his handsome face. He was striking, and I felt my heartbeat increase. Crap. I cannot be crushing on the cop investigating me for murder. That's not allowed.

"You don't think like most people, do you?"

"I have no idea what that means," I sniffed.

"Maybe I'll explain it to you one day," Griffin said, his smile turning from jovial to flirtatious.

"Not today?"

"No, today I'm going to just say goodbye and wish you well."

"Really?"

"No," Griffin shook his head. "Today I'm going to go up to Brian Harper's apartment and arrest whichever one of your brothers is up there snooping around."

Crap. "None of my brothers are in that building."

"Hey, Aisling, we're hungry."

I froze when I heard Braden's voice. Griffin, who was still standing a step down from me, peered around my shoulder until his gaze fell on Braden. When he turned back to me, his eyes were shiny and intense.

"You want to change that statement?"

Ugh. "I have no idea who that is."

"Really?" Griffin's tone was dry and sarcastic. "That guy isn't related to you? That guy with the same black hair and kind of purplish eyes isn't related to you?"

Hmmm. There was no way he could see Braden's eyes from where he was standing. He was guessing. It was a good guess, but it was still a guess. What to do? What to do?

Braden was descending the steps, his arms swinging lazily but his gaze worried. "Is that guy bothering you? Dude, get away from my sister or I'll beat you to within an inch of your life."

Griffin met Braden's challenging glare evenly. "That would be an impressive feat."

"There are some hookers around the corner, I saw them when I pulled up," Braden continued. "My sister isn't on the menu so find somewhere else to eat."

"That is gross."

Braden ignored me. Once he was on even footing with Griffin, their broad shoulders equal to each other, his expression shifted from annoyance to curiosity. "Why are you still here?"

Griffin reached into his pocket, pulled out his badge, flashed it in Braden's face, and then waited for my brother to put his foot into his mouth. Again.

I risked a glance at Braden out of the corner of my eye. The badge had obviously shaken him, but he wasn't going to let Griffin know that. "You're a cop?"

"This is Detective Taylor," I said quickly. "Griffin Taylor."

"The guy who rousted you and Aidan yesterday?"

Rousted? "He questioned us."

"And now he's harassing you on the street?"

Of all my brothers, Braden is the one who inherited my father's hair-trigger temper. And hypochondria, but that's a whole other story. Okay, if I'm telling the truth, we all inherited my father's hair-trigger temper. It's a curse.

"We were just talking," I said, putting my hand on Braden's forearm to still him. I had no idea whether he would actually throw down with a cop, but I wasn't taking any chances.

Griffin was watching us carefully. "And which one of your brothers is this? You said you were with your oldest brother, so that would make you Redmond, right?"

"Have you been studying our family tree or something?" That was kind of creepy.

"I ran you and your brother through the system yesterday," Griffin replied, his tone clipped. "Your family tree is part of public record."

It's still creepy.

"Well," Braden said, grabbing my wrist and tugging me in the direction of the parking lot. "We should be going. We're going to be late for dinner."

Griffin held up his hand to stop us. "Wait a second."

"We're going to be late," Braden repeated.

"I'm sure you have a minute to answer a few questions."

"Not really."

"Why don't you at least try."

"No thanks."

This wasn't going well.

"What were you doing here?" Griffin asked again.

"What were we doing where?" Braden lies as poorly as I do.

"Here. At Brian Harper's apartment complex." Griffin's tone was cold.

"Who is Brian Harper?"

"He's the man your sister and brother discovered stabbed to death in an alley yesterday."

"Oh, I forgot about that," Braden replied. "It must just be a coincidence."

"Then what were you doing here?" Griffin pressed.

I sent Braden a silent message. Reapers aren't telepathic, but I always fantasized about being able to talk to my brothers without words, especially when I was pouting in my bedroom as a teenager.

"I heard there was an apartment open in this building and I wanted to see if it was something I was interested in."

Yeah, that wasn't the message I had been sending.

"Don't you live in a castle?"

"A castle?" Braden furrowed his brow.

"With turrets."

"You've been talking to Jerry," Braden said. "He's the one obsessed with turrets."

"Detective Taylor dropped by the condo this morning and Jerry regaled him with stories of our youth," I explained.

"Why doesn't that surprise me?"

"Because he's Jerry."

"It's a good thing he can bake," Braden agreed, his face taut.

"So, you're thinking of leaving the castle?" Griffin asked.

"I'm twenty-seven," Braden explained. "I think it's about time I move out on my own. I'm really looking forward to it."

I snorted.

"What?"

"You can't even do your own laundry."

"So that wasn't your bag of laundry I saw in the back of your car yesterday? I know Laverne still does your laundry."

Dammit. He's not wrong. Laverne, the head maid at Grimlock Manor, presses my jeans, though, and they always have such a nice crease. I'm not lazy. Okay, I'm a little lazy.

Griffin had just about had it. "Do you two want to tell me what you're really doing here?"

"We already told you."

"So, your story is he's looking for an apartment and you like architecture?"

"What? That's a thing."

Braden's eyes rolled so high I thought they were going to get lost in his hairline.

"What are you two still doing here? I told you to have her ride with you and I would meet you back at the house? We're risking the cops showing up."

Oh, good, here comes Redmond.

Braden and I stiffly split apart so Redmond, who was jogging down the steps, could see we weren't alone. He slowed his pace when he caught sight of Griffin.

"Who is this?"

"Detective Taylor."

"Oh, good. The day wouldn't be complete without a visit from the cops."

Griffin's eerie smile was going to haunt my dreams tonight.

13
THIRTEEN

"So he let you all go?"

Jerry was standing in the middle of our living room trying to pick out a shirt – shiny purple vs. shiny blue -- for the bar this evening. I wasn't really a fan of either. When I told him I wasn't interested in going out, and then explained why, he was flabbergasted. I didn't blame him.

"He didn't have much of a choice," I said. "He couldn't prove we had been in the apartment; my brothers are good at being covert. There was no sign of forced entry, and Braden and Redmond stuck to their stories."

"And you stuck to being an architecture buff?"

"I didn't have much of a choice."

Jerry laughed. "I don't think he believed you. He doesn't seem especially stupid."

"Of course he didn't believe us. Who would? That doesn't mean he's some sort of rocket scientist."

Jerry narrowed his eyes. "So, now he knows you guys are up to something. Do you think he believes you killed that guy?"

That was a good question. "I don't know. I think, if he thought I was a murderer, he would be a little less flirty."

"He's flirting with you? That's promising."

"Kind of. Sometimes. I'm not sure."

Jerry smirked. "He likes you."

He does not. "How do you know?"

"I can tell."

"You always say that. You're not psychic, no matter what you think."

"Let's not get snippy, Bug," Jerry chided me. "No one likes a snippy bitch."

"You do."

"I'm a unique man."

"So you've told me."

Jerry moved over and took a seat next to me on the couch, making sure not to wrinkle one of his satiny sartorial options, and patted me on the knee. "I know things have been rough for you the past few months."

"Do you mean losing my job? Or do you mean my roommate giving me an ultimatum so that I had to join the family business? Or, could you possibly be referring to the dead body I tripped over yesterday?"

Jerry's mask of concern didn't falter. "I'm talking about your 'poor me' attitude."

"I don't have a 'poor me' attitude," I griped.

"You could have fooled me."

I cracked my neck to tamp down my irritation. "Don't you have a bar date to gussy yourself up for?"

"It's not a date," Jerry corrected. "It's just a handful of us meeting at the new drag bar on Trumbull."

"You're going to a drag bar?" That seemed counterproductive.

"Yes. Why do you have that tone?"

"Well, you're gay," I started.

"Thanks for the news update."

I ignored him. "Which means you don't like women."

"Huh, I would have never figured that out on my own."

"So why would you go to a bar where men are dressing up like women to pick up a guy?" I was genuinely curious.

"Drag is not about picking up men," Jerry explained. "It's about exploring a lifestyle – complete with fruity drinks with little umbrellas in them and music that makes me want to shake my ass."

"Didn't you do that in college?"

Jerry squeezed my knee a little harder than necessary. "Get dressed, Bug."

"I am dressed."

Jerry's gaze wandered from my plain tee to my frayed jeans and shook his head emphatically. "You are not going out in that."

"I was out in this all day."

"You are not going out with me in that," Jerry clarified.

"That's good, because I'm not going out."

"Yes you are," Jerry said, getting to his feet and wandering toward his bedroom.

"No, I'm not," I grumbled under my breath once he disappeared from view.

Jerry stuck his head back out of his open bedroom door. "Yes you are."

"THIS WAS a terrible idea."

My outfit might have changed, but my attitude hadn't. After twenty minutes of waiting in line with six-foot-tall hairless men – some of them trying to drape feather boas around my neck – my attitude was probably worse.

Jerry kept a firm grip on my arm – I think he was afraid I was going to bolt – and led me toward a group of men sitting at a rectangular table near the far wall of Mount Vesuvius. No, I'm not making up the name.

"I don't know anyone here," I hissed.

"You know Aidan."

"Aidan isn't here."

"Sure he is," Jerry said. "He's the one dressed up in the paisley shirt."

I narrowed my eyes and followed Jerry's finger to the end of the point and frowned. "That shirt is offensive."

"Paisley is in again. Read a magazine, Bug."

I let Jerry lead me to the table, sliding into the open seat next to Aidan and fixing him with a hard glare. "I can't believe you're here. That sound you hear is Dad's head imploding."

Aidan ran a hand through his hair, smiling down at my purple peasant blouse and skin-tight black pants. "I take it Jerry dressed you. I didn't even know you owned a shirt that girly."

"I wish I could say the same thing about you."

Aidan shifted his head back and forth in a mocking manner. "Who peed in your cornflakes?"

"Detective Griffin Taylor," Jerry said, signaling a waiter for two drinks. I had no idea what he ordered, but I was crabby enough that any alcohol would do at this point.

Aidan's face clouded over. "What does he want?"

"He stopped by this morning," Jerry said. "He's really cute."

"That's what I thought at first, too," Aidan said. "Then he grilled me for four hours and that dirty, sexy thing he has going on started to fade pretty quickly. Why did he stop by?"

"To ask Aisling a few more questions about the body you two discovered."

A few heads at the table turned in our direction at the mention of the word "body." Great. We were drawing attention to ourselves – and not good attention.

"Why didn't he want to ask me more questions?" Aidan asked. "I was there, too."

"She has better legs," Jerry replied.

"He couldn't even see her legs," Aidan said.

"I don't think you have the right parts," Jerry tried again.

"We're twins, we have the same ... oh, I get it. He's warm for her form." Aidan pinched my side in a teasing manner.

"The 1980s called: They want their saying back."

Aidan smacked me on the back of the head lightly. "Cheer up. Detective McHottie likes you. Maybe he can end your dry spell."

I glared at Jerry, but he was suddenly focusing on something on the other side of the room. "Speaking of the 1980s ... ."

"What?" I craned my neck, hoping to get a glimpse of someone dressed up as David Bowie. What I found, though, made my dark mood go completely black. "What is she doing here?"

My tone tipped Aidan into curiosity, so he followed our gazes. His reaction was much more demur. "That bitch. I can't believe someone hasn't run her over with a car yet."

The guy on the other side of Aidan was intrigued by our hate. "Who is that?"

"Angelina Davenport," Aidan replied through gritted teeth.

"She's pretty, although, her hair is a little big."

"She's the devil," I replied.

"You're just saying that because she kept trying to sleep with your boyfriends in high school," Jerry said.

"Tried? She slept with three of them."

"Three?" Aidan looked interested. "I thought she only slept with Mark and Mike."

"She slept with Keith, too," Jerry said.

"Oh, I forgot about Keith," Aidan mused. "I always liked Keith. He was like a big teddy bear."

"That's because he was a closeted homosexual," I replied.

"That was probably it," Aidan agreed.

"She sounds like a real slut," the guy said. "I wonder what she's doing here."

"Well, she probably used her powers of evil and realized I was having a bad day and decided to make it worse," I said.

I kept my gaze focused on Angelina. She was in the middle of a group of guys and she was regaling them with a story that had them all chortling. For a second, I couldn't help but hope she would drown in the collective puddles of baby oil that were surely pooling at her feet.

She was tall and willowy – although there was still a possibility she would get fat and dumpy like her mother (I kept hoping) – and her long brown hair was far too puffy to get there without a gallon of hairspray and some hick beauty pageant inspiration.

"I hear she's selling real estate these days," Aidan said.

"In her vagina?"

"Meow." I jumped at the chorus of voices that let loose with the simultaneous catcall. Apparently all other conversation had ceased in our corner of the bar.

"Oh, don't look," Jerry said. "She's seen us. Everyone act like we're talking about something important. Just laugh at whatever I say."

I refused to take my eyes off Angelina as she strutted across the room in our direction. I had never backed down where she was concerned. I certainly had no intention of doing so now.

Angelina stopped her forward momentum about a foot from us, striking a pose straight out of *America's Next Top Model*, and fixed me with a fake smile. "Aisling Grimlock. It's so good to see you."

"And then I told him he had no idea what he was talking about because stripes can never be worn if they're horizontal," Jerry said.

Everyone at the table broke out in spontaneous applause.

Angelina wrinkled her nose. "I see you're still hanging around with Merry Jerry."

I frowned. Jerry hated that nickname.

"I see you're still hanging out with yourself – since you're the only person that can stand you," I shot back.

What? Fake pleasantries are a waste of time.

Angelina pursed her unnaturally plump lips. Someone is overdoing it on the fillers.

"And how is your brother?"

I stiffened. Angelina had dated Cillian for a year when she was twenty and he was twenty-three. He had finally wised up and dumped her – he found her in bed with some guy from an accounting firm – but not before I had to sit through a multitude of uncomfortable family dinners.

"I'm fine, thanks for asking," Aidan replied, his eyes dark.

"I wasn't talking about you," Angelina said. "I was talking about Cillian."

"He's fine," I said. "His taste in women has vastly improved over the past five years. He hasn't brought a wildebeest home in years."

Angelina was trying to keep her anger in check, so she ran her tongue over the front of her teeth as a calming mechanism. "I see you haven't changed any since high school."

"Nope. I still hate you."

Angelina ignored my pointed dig. "What are you doing these days? I heard you dropped out of community college and were working as a secretary."

"I gave that up," I replied. "Now I'm working as a prostitute. It seemed to be working for you."

Angelina tapped the toe of her shoe on the floor irritably. "Do you think that's funny?"

"Did it bug you?"

"Yes."

"Then it's funny."

Everyone at my table started to laugh, which only served as further kindling to the fire burning in Angelina's cheeks. "You're still a bitch."

"I like to go with my strengths," I agreed. "I think that's why you're still a slut."

Angelina's drink was all over my face before I even had a chance to register what was happening. Jerry squealed when part of it caught him on the shoulder. "Hey! This shirt is dry clean only."

"Well it should be garbage only," Angelina shot back. "You're gay; you're supposed to know how to dress."

That did it. I launched myself out of the chair and was on Angelina before Aidan could stop me. We rolled around on the sticky floor – I was hoping it was just day-old drinks, I wasn't giving it any more thought than that – grunting and swearing at each other.

"Get off me, you cow!" Angelina shrieked.

"You're wearing a girdle? I knew it!"

"It's not a girdle," Angelina gasped, trying to dislodge my hand from her hair. "They're Spanx."

"Is there a difference?"

"Girdles are for old ladies," Jerry offered helpfully. "Now rip that hair out of her head!"

I could hear the crowd chanting behind us when someone -- finally -- stepped in to try to pull me off of her. I had no idea who it was and, quite frankly, I was beyond caring at this point.

"Get your hands off my sister."

"Which one is your sister?"

"The one who is winning."

"Well, there's no fighting in here," the stranger said. "Either I put my hands on your sister or everyone gets kicked out."

I couldn't see Aidan's face, but the feeling of big hands wrapping around my waist told me the stranger wasn't giving up and Aidan had given in. "Hey, that's my boob!"

The body that had been trying to force me off of Angelina was suddenly gone. A glance out of the corner of my eye told me that Aidan was grappling with him a few feet away, while Jerry stood on a nearby chair shouting out helpful suggestions. "He's bigger than you; you're going to have to punch him in the naughty bits."

This had gotten out of hand really fast. I eased up on Angelina, suddenly feeling foolish. That's when I heard my blouse rip and Angelina's yell of triumph.

Slamming her head into the floor a few more times couldn't hurt.

14

FOURTEEN

"Are you proud of yourselves?"

Since we were in the lobby of a police station at nine in the morning on a weekday, I think we could all agree that the answer was a resounding "no." Things had gotten just a little out of hand the previous evening – yes, just a little – and we found ourselves in holding tank in the custody of Detroit's finest until bail could be set the following morning. Since they separated men and women, I had been shoved into the same drunk tank as Angelina.

With few options in front of us, Aidan had finally broken down and called Redmond. We all agreed to plead guilty at arraignment and received fines – and a stern warning not to set foot into Mount Vesuvius again. Angelina was apparently taking her case to trial, which was just like her.

"Thank you so much for bailing us out," Jerry said, throwing his arms around Redmond. "I'm too pretty for prison."

"We weren't in prison," Aidan complained. "We weren't even in cells. They just threw us in the drunk tank, which isn't nearly as fun when you're not drunk."

I rolled my eyes. "At least you weren't in the same area with Angelina."

Redmond's eyes darkened. "Angelina? Angelina Davenport? Is that how this happened?"

"She wears a girdle."

I expected Redmond to smile at the gossipy tidbit. I was disappointed.

"She threw a drink on me," Jerry said. "She totally ruined my shirt."

Redmond patted his back absentmindedly.

"She threw the drink at me," I corrected. "You just got a little bit of it. I got the full blast."

"And what did you do?"

"I tackled her and beat the crap out of her."

"No," Redmond shook his head, but a small smile was playing at the corner of his mouth. "What did you do to antagonize her?"

"Why do you assume I did something to antagonize her?"

"Because I know you."

"Maybe she antagonized me."

"I'm sure she did," Redmond agreed. "You could have been the bigger person, though."

"She asked about Cillian," Aidan interjected.

"And that sent Aisling into a rage?"

"She also made fun of her dropping out of community college – and Jerry's shirt."

"I've always hated that bitch," Redmond growled. "I hope you ripped her hair out."

"Just a few clumps."

"Well, next time." Redmond slung an arm around my neck, rubbing his face against my hair. "Wow, you smell."

"We were rolling around on the ground."

"I guess I don't want to know what's in your hair then." Redmond moved away from me slightly, grimacing.

I didn't want to know either.

The four of us looked up when the front door of the police station chimed and a familiar figure walked through. Crap.

"Morning." Griffin Taylor looked as though he had enjoyed a good night's sleep, and he didn't seem surprised to see us there. Something told me – since this wasn't his precinct – that someone had tipped him off about our legal problems.

"Morning," Jerry said, running a hand through his hair to tame the unruly mess.

Griffin walked over to us, focusing on everyone in turn, before finally settling on me. "You look a little rough."

"I have no idea what you're talking about."

Aidan snickered, while Redmond coughed into his hand.

"You should look in a mirror, Bug."

I ignored the three of them. "What are you doing here?"

"I heard that you were picked up last night," he replied. "I was curious, so I came down to see for myself."

"Are you made aware when everyone is arrested at a drag bar in Detroit?" What? It's a reasonable question.

"No. Your name – and Aidan's, for that matter – have been flagged in conjunction with my investigation."

Well, great.

"Why would their names be flagged?" Redmond asked.

Griffin glanced over in his direction. "You're Redmond, right?"

"We met yesterday," Redmond reminded him

"I remember. There are just a lot of you to keep straight."

"And you haven't even met Cillian yet," I said.

"I'm looking forward to it."

Something told me that was a lie.

I jumped when the back door that led into the inner sanctum of the police station buzzed, letting another familiar figure out. Angelina. Double crap.

Angelina's night hadn't been any better than mine. Her hair – which was already big – was standing on end and there were some noticeable follicle gaps thanks to my rigorous hair pulling the night before and she limped.

"What did you do to her?" Redmond looked happy.

"I don't even remember doing anything to her feet."

Griffin regarded Angelina with interest. "Is this the woman you got in a fight with?"

"Fight?" Angelina spit out. "She blindsided me and pulled my hair."

"Oh, you had it coming." I took a step toward her, thoughts of finishing what I started dancing through my head. Redmond's arm around my waist stopped that fantasy.

"You are a menace," Angelina spat out. "You've always been a menace."

"At least I'm not a slut."

"I am not a slut! It's not my fault that Mark and Mike liked me better in high school."

"And Keith," Jerry added.

I shot him a death glare.

"Keith was a lost cause," Redmond said.

"Who are Mike, Mark and Keith?" Griffin asked.

"They were my high school boyfriends," I replied, my eyes never leaving

Angelina's sallow face, even as Redmond's arm tightened to the point where I was having trouble breathing.

"They liked me better," Angelina said.

"That's because you used to pretend you were a 7-Eleven," Redmond replied.

"What does that mean?"

"It means you were open twenty-four hours a day," Griffin supplied.

"Who asked you?" Angelina turned on him.

"The city of Detroit," Griffin replied, flashing his badge.

"Oh, great, now what?" Angelina wailed. "Whatever they've said about me is a vicious lie."

"She wears a girdle," I announced.

"You already said that," Redmond reminded me.

"Yeah, but not when Griffin was here and not when I could see her face when I said it."

"I do not wear a girdle! At least my bra isn't hanging out like I'm some transvestite hooker on Eight Mile."

I glanced down, realizing that hints of my Victoria's Secret bra were poking out from my torn blouse. I realized that Redmond and Aidan were looking anywhere but at my bra, while Jerry and Griffin both seemed interested.

"Is that the bra we bought when we were shopping last week? It looks different on," Jerry said.

Redmond groaned. "Can we not talk about Aisling's bra?"

"Especially since she stuffs it," Angelina said.

"I don't stuff, girdle girl."

"I'm going to claw your eyes out!"

Griffin stepped between us, shaking his head as he did. "I think you should go."

Angelina looked incensed. "Why shouldn't she go?"

"Because I'm not done talking to her yet."

"And he likes her bra." Jerry looked smug.

Angelina shifted her gaze between the five of us and then slowly made her way toward the front door. "Tell Cillian I said hi."

I fought against Redmond's arms, seeing red. "Stay away from Cillian, you witch!"

Angelina scampered out of the building, just in case Redmond's arms weren't strong enough to contain my rage. Once she was out of sight, the fight in me fled. "Let me go."

"Do you promise not to chase her down and beat her ass again?" Redmond asked. "I don't have enough bail money on me to secure your release again."

"I promise."

Redmond cautiously loosened his grip.

"So, if I'm following, that girl used to sleep with your boyfriends and then slept with your brother and that's why you created a riot at a drag bar last night and got yourself arrested," Griffin said. "Am I missing anything?"

"She wears a girdle."

"And she wears a girdle," Griffin conceded, his brown eyes flashing with a hint of amusement.

"No, that's about it."

"So, basically, last night had nothing to do with my dead guy?"

"No." Why would he think that?

Redmond was equally suspicious. "Is that why you came down here?"

"I was just curious," Griffin replied. "Oh, and I wanted to ask you another question."

Uh-oh.

"I'm too tired to answer questions right now," I said. "I'm tired. Try again tomorrow or something."

"You have work today," Redmond reminded me.

"Oh, come on," I complained. "Can't you get me out of it?"

"Not unless you want me to tell Dad why."

That was a big, fat no. "Fine."

"Who did you want to ask a question?" Jerry asked, while I fought the urge to kick him.

"I just wanted to make Redmond aware that the crime scene techs who went to Brian Harper's apartment yesterday seemed to think that someone had been in the apartment recently," Griffin said, his gaze fixed on Redmond's face. "What do you think about that?"

"I think that, since the guy lived there, that would probably make sense." Redmond is cool under pressure. He always had been. When we were trying to think up lies to cover our misdeeds as kids he was always the one to deliver the lie. He doesn't break under intense scrutiny.

"Yes, but it seems someone was in the apartment after we completed our initial search," Griffin continued. "There was a digital seal on the door that had been tripped."

Uh-oh.

"Well, I hope you find out who it was," Redmond replied. "That's probably who killed your victim."

Or not.

"That's all you want to say?" Griffin asked, raising an eyebrow in challenge.

"That's all I have to offer."

"Well," Griffin said, resting his eyes on my face briefly. "I'll be in touch."

I can't wait.

15

FIFTEEN

"So, what did you get arrested for?"

As part of my penance, Redmond assigned Cillian to work with me after my night in the city jail.

"He didn't tell you?"

"He just said you, Aidan and Jerry were arrested after getting in a brawl at a drag bar," Cillian replied. "I figured someone got dramatic and Jerry got mouthy."

That was a good assumption on a normal night. "Um, well, I don't really remember who started what," I lied.

Cillian paused mid-stride. We were on the west side of Detroit, hanging around outside of a Middle Eastern restaurant that smelled fabulous, waiting for a hit-and-run accident to transpire.

"You're lying."

"No I'm not." I averted my gaze and focused on Cillian's shoes.

"You are so," Cillian charged. "I can tell when you're lying."

"How?"

"You won't make eye contact."

I forced my eyes to his, seeing the same purple reflected back. "Everything from last night is a blur." What? That's not a lie.

Cillian gripped my forearms, forcing me to remain still. "What started the fight?"

83

"Someone threw a drink on me – and it hit Jerry, too. There was a lot of squealing and then a fight." That was true.

Cillian didn't release me. "Who threw the drink?"

I bit my lower lip and looked to the left. "I don't know."

"See! You're lying. You better tell me or I'll call Redmond."

Crap. There was no way out of this.

"Angelina."

All of the air whooshed out of Cillian. His hands dropped from my forearms and slipped into the pockets of his jeans. "Oh."

"See, this is why I didn't want to tell you." For some reason, one I couldn't fathom, Cillian was still sensitive when the Angelina situation reared its ugly head.

"What did she say?" Cillian regained his equilibrium and tried to pretend Angelina -- or any mention of her -- didn't bother him.

"She asked how you were."

Cillian smirked. "So you attacked her?"

"She also made fun of me dropping out of college and of Jerry's shirt."

"She's always been a bitch," Cillian ceded. "That still doesn't seem bad enough for you to kick the crap out of her."

"I was already having a bad day," I replied.

"Because that cop is sniffing around? Aidan says he's hot and he's ... ."

"Warm for my form? Don't repeat that hateful phrase."

"I was going to say interested in you, but okay." Cillian couldn't hide his grin. "You're not interested in him?"

"He thinks I'm a murderer."

Cillian reached over and brushed a strand of my bi-colored hair out of my face, searching for an answer to an unasked question. "You do like him."

"I do not."

"You do, too."

"I do not."

"You're avoiding eye contact again."

I need to work on that. "Fine," I blew out a sigh. "I can't like him."

Cillian cocked his head to the side. "Why? Does he wear polyester? Because I know Jerry won't put up with that, but he might overlook it if you ask nicely."

"Because he's a cop," I said.

"So?"

"He's a cop who thinks I'm a murderer," I tried again.

"He doesn't think you're a murderer," Cillian countered. "If he thought you were a murderer, he wouldn't be flirting with you."

"Who said he's flirting with me?"

"Jerry told Aidan."

"Jerry has a big mouth," I grumbled.

"That's why we love him."

I couldn't argue with that. I decided to change the subject. "Did Redmond tell you whether they found anything in Brian Harper's apartment?"

"He didn't tell you?"

"I don't think that would be proper conversation for a police department, and I haven't seen him since we left yesterday."

"How did you get home?"

"Braden."

"Why didn't he tell you?" Cillian asked.

"I forgot to ask," I admitted. "Running into Griffin at the apartment complex threw me for a loop."

"Griffin?" Cillian was smiling again. It was an infuriating expression.

"Detective Taylor," I corrected, my cheeks starting to burn.

"You call him Griffin?"

"He told me to," I replied defensively, although I couldn't fathom why.

Cillian nodded knowingly. "I see."

"The apartment search," I prodded, kicking Cillian in the shin as I moved past him.

"Oh, yeah, they didn't find anything at the apartment except some kinky sex toys."

Eww. "That's a bummer."

"They did find something online last night, though."

"What?"

"It seems that our Mr. Harper had just acquired an interesting book," Cillian said, his voice lowering to a conspiratorial whisper.

"Like what? The Kama Sutra?"

Cillian swished his mouth to the side. "Um, no. And don't ever say anything like that to me again."

"Why?"

"It sends me to a scary visual place."

"What was the book?" I asked. My brothers liked to pretend that I still don't know what sex is.

"It was a grimoire."

"Seriously?" A grimoire is a book of spells. Witches usually utilize them, but other people have tried to use them for nefarious reasons throughout the centuries. They usually mean bad news – or bad witches, to be more precise. "What kind of grimoire?"

"I don't have the specifics," Cillian admitted. "I know it's eighteenth century, though. Redmond and Dad are looking up more about it. Dad seems to think that whatever this grimoire is, though, it's what got him killed."

"And Braden and Redmond didn't see it in the apartment?"

"I think that would have been a clue they couldn't have missed," Cillian replied.

He had a point. "Well, now what?"

"Now? Now we wait for this poor sap, what is his name again?"

I glanced down at the file in my hand. "Myron Goldman."

"Where is he going?"

"Sheol." Jewish Hell, for those wondering. A customer's final resting place hinges on their personal belief system. So, while a lot of Jewish people don't believe in Sheol, it is a reality for those who do believe.

"Oh, bummer, what did he do?"

"He's a thief."

"We've been having a lot of people go to Hell -- and the alternatives – lately. Have you noticed that?" Cillian is interested in religion, more than I find healthy sometimes.

"I've been doing this for three days."

"You've been living it for twenty-five years, though."

I rolled my eyes. "You sound like Dad."

"Take that back."

We both looked up at a screech of tires, my eyes landing on a small man moving across the street kitty-corner from our location. I had only glanced at the photo attached to the file – we really need to go digital at some point so we don' t have to deal with all this paperwork – but I would recognize that bald head anywhere.

"This is going to be gross, isn't it?"

Cillian's eyes were glued to Myron Goldman as he shuffled across the street. "If we're lucky."

Boys are strange creatures sometimes.

The owner of the screeching tires came barreling around the corner – dark sedan, white guy with blond hair behind the wheel, looks to be in his early twenties – and slammed into Myron.

It wasn't like the movies – not that I thought it would be. Myron didn't jump up and roll over the hood of the car. Instead, he kind of flew to the side and crashed into the gutter next to the street.

The sedan never slowed.

"Should we get the license plate?"

"That's not our job," Cillian reminded, moving into the middle of the street. "Let's do this quick. Someone could be here within minutes, and you don't need another run-in with the cops."

Wasn't that the truth?

I followed Cillian, reaching into my pocket for the scepter. I could see Myron's spirit detaching from his body already. At least he hadn't suffered.

I slammed into Cillian, who pulled up short, before I realized he had stopped in the middle of the street. I peered around his shoulder, freezing when another figure stepped out of the doorway of the building next to Myron's body.

Cillian and I watched as the figure moved over to Myron, pulled a scepter from a pocket, and absorbed the soul before it fully formed into something resembling a human. The figure then glanced up at the two of us, winked, and got to his feet.

Unfortunately, I recognized him.

"Duke Fontaine," Cillian exhaled.

Oh, good, he recognized him, too. I was going to need him when things got ugly in five, four, three, two, one … .

16

SIXTEEN

"Hey!"

"Hey yourself, cutie pie." Duke Fontaine didn't bother running. Apparently, the sight of Cillian and me racing across the street to confront him wasn't cause for quaking in his military boots.

When we were all on the same side of the street it became obvious why our two bodies didn't equal his one. At more than six feet tall, Cillian was dwarfed by the six feet and seven inches of pure muscle (and tacky camouflage pants) that made up Duke Fontaine. His right thigh was bigger than my torso, for crying out loud. He had mercenary – or prison barber – written all over him. For all I knew, the Chinese symbols tattooed onto his bald scalp signified just that.

I didn't let his stature deter me. I planted my hands on my hips and a stern expression (the one that had my brothers screaming PMS and hiding under their beds when we were teenagers) on my face. "That is my soul."

Fontaine shook his head from side to side. "That's not how it looks to me, sweetheart."

"Don't call me sweetheart. And that guy is on my list."

"He's on mine now, my little pretty." Fontaine was trying to be charming, but all that did was further infuriate me.

"Hand him over."

"Possession is nine-tenths of the law," Fontaine countered.

"My foot up your ass is going to be ten-tenths of law in a second," I warned. "Give me my soul."

Cillian remained silent, but his face blanched when I threatened physical violence. I was making the threats, but he would have to back them up.

"I like you, button," he said. "You're fiery." He looked Cillian over and dismissed him before turning back to me. "You're a Grimlock, aren't you? You all have a certain look about you. I like it better on you than them, though."

"I'm pissed off is what I am," I shot back. "Give me my soul."

Fontaine smiled, giving me a shot of teeth that were probably used to gnawing raw meat off of bones, and tilted his head in my direction. "What will you give me for this soul, sweetie pie?"

"A hearty handshake, douche bag."

"I'm going to want something more than that."

Fontaine reached over and rubbed his fingers through my hair. I jerked back, repulsion squirming through my belly. "Don't touch me."

"Don't touch her," Cillian growled, taking a step forward. He might not have Fontaine's size, but that wouldn't stop him if he felt the need to protect my honor. I was hoping it wouldn't come to that.

"Listen, you two are cute," Fontaine said. "He's almost as pretty as you are, sweet thing. I think I should be going, though. I try to avoid the cops whenever possible and they should be here any second."

"I can see that," I replied. "They probably give you wet dreams."

It took a second for my jab to land but, when it did, all pretense of flirting disappeared from Fontaine's face. "You're not so cute now."

"Wait a few seconds," I replied, tapping my foot. "I'm about to get downright ugly."

"I don't doubt it," Fontaine said. "I'm still not giving you this soul. This is worth five grand to me. There's nothing you're offering that's worth even a quarter of that. Although, if you want to take your top off I might consider adjusting my fee."

My mouth dropped open as every curse word I had ever uttered fought to escape at the same time. Nothing came out, though.

"If you want to just pull your shirt down and give me a little peek, I might consider it then, too."

This time, I didn't even get a chance to consider responding. Cillian's fist slammed into Fontaine's face before the words had finished coming out of his mouth. The punch wasn't strong enough to knock Fontaine down, but the hit was hard enough to catch him off guard and he stumbled to the side, slamming into the brick wall behind him.

Cillian was on him with a flurry of fists and angry language, not giving Fontaine a chance to recover. Fontaine did what came naturally, and raised both of his hands to cover his face. I knew it wouldn't take him long to recover, though, so I darted into the melee and slipped my hand into the pocket Fontaine had slipped his scepter in after collecting the soul.

I rooted around the pocket for a second – praying I wouldn't inadvertently grab onto any other rod in there – and then pulled the sterling silver staff out and took a step back.

"I've got it. Let's go."

Cillian was still working out his aggression and Fontaine was about done letting him. I grabbed Cillian's ear and twisted it without mercy, pulling him with me as I moved away from Fontaine.

Fontaine seemed surprised that Cillian was suddenly gone – no more than Cillian, though, when he realized what had pulled him off Fontaine. "That hurts!"

I waved Fontaine's scepter in front of his face. "Let's go."

Cillian looked impressed. "When did you get that?"

"When you were smacking him around."

"I was pretty badass, huh?"

"Deranged is more like it."

"When we tell this story to the others, you're going to say I'm badass."

"Fine."

"Hey!" Fontaine was back on his feet and his hand was in his pocket. I couldn't be sure, but I definitely felt I had tilted over into the ugly category where he was concerned. "That's mine!"

Cillian grabbed my arm, all traces of badassery gone. "Run!"

"YOU BEAT UP FONTAINE?"

Redmond looked both proud and doubtful.

"I don't know if beat up is the right phrase," I hedged.

Once we were in the car and safely on our way home, Cillian's bravado had slipped under the weight of worry that accompanies pissing off Duke Fontaine. Once he was sure Fontaine wasn't following us, though, he had turned downright boastful. I guess I couldn't blame him.

"I beat his ass," Cillian said, sipping from a bottle of beer. We were all congregated in Dad's office to regale the family with our tale.

Braden turned to me. "How big of an ass beating was it? Was there blood?"

"No."

"He wanted to bleed, though," Cillian said.

I patted his knee. "I could see that."

"I want to know what he is doing here," Dad said, his elbows resting on the top of his desk and his expression serious. "Last I heard he was sticking close to his home turf in Las Vegas. Someone had to call him for him to come back to Detroit."

"He said he was getting five thousand for the soul."

"From who?"

I shrugged and turned my palms up. "I didn't have time to grill him on it. I took the opportunity to steal the soul back and then we ran."

"You ran?" Aidan asked, his gaze fixed on Cillian.

"Well ... Aisling ran," Cillian said. "I took the opportunity to leave him there on the street with a little bit of dignity."

"You're the one who told me to run," I reminded him.

"Drink your beer."

Cillian's neck colored as our brothers chuckled.

"He still didn't hesitate to jump in and protect my honor when Fontaine asked to see my boobs."

The chuckling stopped.

"Fontaine said what?" Redmond was on his feet. "You left that part out of the story."

Cillian slid me a look. "The guy is a pig. It shouldn't come as a surprise."

"Still, to say that ... to even think that ... ."

Cripes. "They're just boobs, Redmond," I grumbled. "It's not the first time a guy has asked to see them."

"Who? When? Who?"

"I think the better question is who hasn't?" Aidan chortled. "Even gay guys want to see boobs. They're like unicorns in our world. They're cool to look at, but they're mythical and scary to consider touching."

Dad cleared his throat. "Let's get back to Fontaine."

"I agree," Braden said. "I don't want to hear Aidan compare boobs to unicorns. It's going to give me nightmares."

I rolled my eyes and sent Aidan a sarcastic thumbs-up. He pushed his lips out and sent me an air kiss in response.

"You guys are never going to get married if boobs scare you," I pointed out.

"I happen to like boobs," Braden replied. "As far as I'm concerned, though, you don't have any."

"Exactly," Redmond pointed at Braden appreciatively. "You're flat as a board and twelve years old where we're concerned."

"Ah, it's like middle school all over again, huh Aisling?" Aidan teased.

"Stop talking about boobs!" Dad slammed his hands down on his desk.

My brothers had the grace to look abashed. I didn't bother since Dad refused to look me in the eye. I was twelve to him, too. You should see them when I bring up tampons.

"Dad is right," Redmond said after a beat. "We have to find out what Fontaine is doing in the area."

A normal freelancer is cause for worry when you're in the reaping business. Duke Fontaine is a whole other story. He was coming on the scene just when Dad was retiring from day-to-day operations and moving into a management position in the organization. He had stolen two souls from Dad – something unheard of at the time, if you believe the stories – and my father had hated him since. They had come to blows and – ultimately – Fontaine had agreed to relocate his services. I never quite understood what had gone down, just that Dad considered it a win. Something had obviously changed on that front.

"Don't worry about Fontaine," Dad said. "I'll handle Fontaine."

"How are you going to handle him?"

All eyes in the room turned to Dad for an explanation. We were all equally curious.

"Don't you worry about that."

"Are you going to handle him the way you handled him before?" I pressed.

"Aisling, why don't you give me Fontaine's scepter," Dad changed the subject, holding out his hand expectantly. "I'll handle the soul transfer and then make sure Mr. Fontaine gets his property back."

That didn't sound like Dad, but I didn't argue. I handed the scepter over and then followed my brothers out of the office and toward the dining room. There was nothing a home-cooked meal couldn't fix. I just hoped the cook wasn't serving chicken breasts – or unicorn.

17

SEVENTEEN

Three days later Dad insisted everyone had to go to a "work function." Attendance was mandatory. I assumed it was one of those lame charity events that his boring co-workers and their wives attended each month so they could gossip, swill wine and donate money to help the "little people."

I was right.

And wrong.

"I'm glad you made me come."

I glanced over at Jerry, not bothering to hide my grin. This wasn't what I was expecting either. It was a charity event, it just happened to benefit the Detroit Police Department.

"You're happy because there are so many men here."

"Men in uniform," Jerry corrected. "I'm happy because there are so many men in uniform here."

"You know not all of them are gay, right?"

"Don't ruin my fantasy, Bug."

"Sorry."

I reached over and brushed a small piece of lint from Jerry's tuxedo, marveling at how well he cleaned up. Jerry caught me looking at him and smiled down at me. "You look nice tonight, Bug."

My smile faded as I glanced down at my dress. I'm not one for getting all gussied up and putting on heels. I had settled on a simple black dress with a dangerously high slit up the right thigh – just enough to make Dad wish he hadn't made attendance mandatory.

"How long do you think we have to stay?" I asked.

"We just got here. We haven't had dinner or danced yet."

"I'm not dancing."

"Yes you are. You made me come to this shindig."

"You wanted to come," I shot back.

Jerry brushed off my argument. "That's not the point. I'm here. This is your thing. You're going to dance."

"You're going to have to dance with all of us," Redmond interjected, joining us around a bistro table with hors d'oeuvres spread out on top of it.

"You didn't bring a date?"

"You don't bring a date to a sausage fest," Redmond explained. "That's how you lose a date."

"How do you figure?"

"Women love a man in a uniform," he said, "especially when those men carry guns and put their lives on the line to keep the general populace safe on a daily basis."

One glance at the hundreds of men – only a handful of which had women on their arms – told me he was probably right.

"How long do you think we have to stay?"

"Already looking for an exit, sis? I'm shocked. Usually you love dressing up for a party."

"Like you aren't looking for an exit?"

"I'm fine," Redmond argued. "I like making nice with local law enforcement. You never know when it might come in handy."

Realization washed over me. "That's why we're here. I couldn't figure it out."

"What?" Jerry hadn't caught up yet.

"The police are investigating us," I reminded him. "This is Dad's little way of reminding them of what a big donor he is."

"Plus," Redmond added, "by making sure you and Aidan are here, he's also saying that we have nothing to hide. Murderers don't go to police balls."

"So, he's lying," Jerry said.

"Pretty much," Aidan said, sidling up to the table next to Jerry. "We're just all law-abiding, normal citizens enjoying dinner, dancing and as many disapproving stares from Dad and his friends as possible."

"Aren't you the cheery one in your dashing tuxedo," Redmond teased.

"Why should I be?" Aidan asked, preening under the compliment.

"Because you're the reason we have to be here," Braden offered as he and Cillian joined our group.

"Aisling is the reason we have to be here," Aidan corrected.

"Aisling wasn't in charge," Cillian pointed out.

I sent Aidan a triumphant smile.

"It was your job to make sure she didn't do something stupid," Braden agreed.

My smile faltered and I shot Braden a pointed scowl.

Jerry wrapped an arm around my waist in a comforting manner. "Don't listen to them, Bug. I think you're doing great."

Jerry is always on my side. Even when I don't have a side, he's on it.

"You don't even know what she really does," Redmond challenged.

Jerry is an honorary member of the family, so Redmond's position in the hierarchy doesn't daunt him. "I know enough."

Redmond rolled his eyes. This wasn't the place for an argument – especially this argument.

"Well, this looks like a fun group."

I wasn't surprised that Griffin was at the ball. I wasn't even surprised that he sought us out. I was surprised – and a little relieved – that he appeared to be alone. What? He's hot. I can look, I just can't touch.

"Griffin," Jerry greeted him, a broad smile on his face. "You clean up nice."

One look at Griffin in his dress uniform and I couldn't help but agree. He'd even tamed his wild hair and shaved, although I was partial to the five o-clock shadow he usually sported.

"Yes, Griffin, you look divine," Braden mocked.

I kicked him under the table but inadvertently made contact with Redmond instead. "What was that for?"

"I don't know what you're talking about," I lied.

"You kicked me."

"I did not."

"It must have been someone else wearing really tall heels," Redmond complained, rubbing his leg and fixing me with an angry glare.

"Don't look at me," Jerry said. "I left all my heels at home tonight."

Braden and Cillian cleared their throats as Griffin's face colored. I shifted my face to the side to hide my smile. Jerry is a great party date, no matter the party.

"So, do you guys always come to the police ball?" Griffin asked.

"We're very involved in our community," Redmond said, choosing his words carefully.

"That's not what I asked."

"We attend a lot of benefits," I said. "This just happened to be on the list."

Griffin didn't look convinced. "Well, I have to say, you look nice – even if this is only one of the many events you have on your schedule tonight."

Jerry swished his hip into mine. I knew what he was trying to indicate, but I ignored him and looked down at the bistro table. "You look nice, too."

Redmond, Cillian, Aidan and Braden were all staring at me as though I had suddenly grown a second head when I finally raised my eyes. I felt my cheeks burning under their scrutiny. I glanced over at Griffin and he looked equally uncomfortable.

"Isn't that your friend?" Griffin asked suddenly, pointing across the dance floor.

Everyone at our table turned, but the individual Griffin referred to was no friend of the Grimlock family. Redmond swore under his breath while Cillian turned white.

"What is she doing here?" Jerry asked.

"Hoping for round two, I think," Aidan said. "Yank all her hair out this time, Aisling."

"You're going to fight at a police ball?" Griffin asked. "That doesn't sound like a smart idea."

"Yeah? Well Aisling isn't smart."

"Thanks, Braden."

"That's not what I meant."

"I know what you meant."

Angelina was busy talking to a group of men – all in their dress blues – next to another bistro table. She hadn't seen us yet. I was sure of that. If she had, she would have left little heel marks on every cop who got in her way as she made a beeline for Cillian.

"Well, I think we've done our due diligence," I said, visions of fifty cops pulling me off Angelina as I ripped her acrylic nails off her fingers flitting through my head. "We should go."

"Dad won't like that," Redmond said. "He won't care what the reason is."

Griffin was incredulous. "You guys are really going to leave because she's here?"

He clearly hadn't spent enough time with Angelina at the precinct earlier this week. "She's the devil."

"Oh, I got that," Griffin said. "I just don't understand why you guys are all running from her."

"We're not running," Cillian said, his voice low.

"Okay, running isn't the right word," Griffin said. "Fleeing might be a better word."

"No," Cillian said, his voice firm. "We're not going anywhere."

"Cillian, it's not a big thing," I said. "We don't have to stay here. We'll just make sure that Dad sees us and then we'll sneak out."

"I can be in the same room with her," Cillian replied. "It's not a big deal."

"You shouldn't have to be in the same room with her," Redmond interjected, putting his hand on Cillian's shoulder in a show of solidarity.

"No," I agreed. "She should crawl under a rock and die and we should never have to see her again."

"Don't wish for the death of another person, Bug," Jerry chided me. "It's gauche."

"It's Angelina, though," Aidan argued.

"Fine," Jerry ceded. "Don't wish for a painful death, though."

Slowly, everyone turned their attention back to the finger foods and assorted drinks and we lapsed into an uncomfortable silence.

"Maybe we should mingle," Redmond suggested.

"With whom?" Mingling is not part of my vocabulary.

"There are hundreds of hot men here, Bug," Jerry said. "Even you could get laid."

Redmond shot Jerry a dark look. "Don't be cute."

"I'm always cute," Jerry said.

"You're not right now."

My shoulders shook with silent laughter. I risked a glance at Griffin, who was still loitering at the edge of the table, and saw that his gaze was still fixed on the other side of the room. The petulant part of me wondered if he was as taken with Angelina and her long legs, just like every other man I had ever met.

"Your friend is coming over here."

Crap.

"We could run," Jerry offered.

"That wouldn't look obvious," I replied.

"It's too late anyway," Griffin said, lifting his beer to his lips and taking a drink. He looked amused – and curious. I think he was interested in seeing what would happen.

"Cillian, it's so good to see you."

My spine stiffened at the sound of Angelina's voice. I can't beat her up in front of a roomful of cops, but maybe I can cut her tongue out without anyone noticing.

"Angelina." Cillian's voice was hard and empty. I barely recognized it.

"How are you? How are all of you? Braden, it's good to see you, too."

"What about me?" I asked. "Isn't it good to see me?"

"I just saw you."

"Great. Let's do it again in five years," I suggested.

"I'm not talking to you," Angelina replied curtly. "I'm talking to Cillian."

"Well, he doesn't want to talk to you," I said.

"Yeah," Jerry agreed.

"I think he can talk for himself," Angelina said, reaching out and rubbing her hand along Cillian's forearm suggestively. "Isn't that right?"

Cillian met Angelina's flirty look with a dark one of his own. "I don't have anything to say to you, Angelina."

For the first time, uncertainty flashed across Angelina's heavily made up face. "If we could just be alone for a second … ."

"Over my dead body," I said, fighting to keep my voice low enough that we didn't start drawing unwanted attention.

There was a hand on my arm within seconds. I figured it was Jerry, but the firm grip caused me to send him a questioning look. That's when I found out it wasn't Jerry, after all, it was Griffin. "Actually, I think you and I are going to dance," he said.

"Since when?" Dancing with Griffin was tempting, but making Angelina cry had a lot more appeal at the moment.

"Right now." Griffin was firm as he dragged me out to the dance floor. There weren't a lot of couples out there, but it wasn't so empty that we stood out. It was a slow song and Griffin wrapped his arms around my waist and pulled my hips flush with his. I lifted my arms and hooked them around his neck, swaying to the music, but never taking my eyes off Angelina. I couldn't hear what was going on at the table, but it didn't look good. Angelina's face was screwed up into one of those ugly scowls that often precede bursting into tears.

"Why are you smiling?" Griffin asked, drawing my attention back to him.

"Because Angelina looks like she's going to cry." I saw no point in lying.

"You really don't like her, do you?"

"I hate her."

"Because she slept with your boyfriends?"

"No," I shook my head, trying not to focus on how warm Griffin's body felt next to mine. "That only warrants dislike."

"Then why?"

"Because she messed with my brother," I admitted, chewing on my bottom lip.

Griffin smiled. "You guys are close."

"They're my brothers."

"Not all brothers and sisters are as close as you guys, though," Griffin replied. "You guys seem especially close."

"We're all close in age," I said. "It doesn't seem weird to me because it's always been this way."

"They seem protective of you."

"They are."

"And you seem protective of them."

"When they need it," I said.

"I like it," Griffin said. "In my line of work, most of the families I deal with have done something horrible to each other. I'm not really worried about that with you guys."

"What are you worried about with us?"

"That you'll cover up crimes together." I guess he was going for honesty, too.

"That's a bummer for you," I said.

"It is," Griffin agreed, tilting his head to the side. "Still, I don't think you guys are covering up murder."

Alarms started clanging in my head. This couldn't be good. "What is it you think we're covering up?"

"I haven't decided yet," he said. "But I plan on finding out."

18

EIGHTEEN

Dinner was slow. Dancing afterward was mildly entertaining. I took a turn around the dance floor with each of my brothers – and Jerry – and then excused myself to go to the bathroom. That's where I found Angelina trying to fix her makeup after a crying jag. I thought about kicking her while she was down but figured that would just be petty. What? I'm mean, but I'm not heartless, especially when I win.

Instead, I hid in the stall until her sniffling diminished and I was sure she had exited the bathroom.

When I rejoined the party, I couldn't find my brothers or Jerry.

"Looking for someone?"

Griffin was at my side. I hadn't seen him since our dance earlier, not that I was looking or anything.

"Did you see where my brothers and Jerry went?"

Griffin scanned the room and shook his head. "They wouldn't have left you, would they?"

"No." At least I hoped not.

Griffin put down his beer and grabbed my hand. I thought about yanking it back, but I couldn't quite bring myself to do it. Instead, I let him lead me around the room as we searched for them. After twenty minutes, we gave up.

"I'll just call a cab," I said.

"You didn't drive here?"

"No," I replied. "Jerry drove."

"Why would he leave you?"

"He probably figured I dodged out and got a ride home," I said. "It's not a big deal. I can probably get a cab here within twenty minutes."

Griffin didn't look so sure. Detroit's cab companies aren't known for being reliable – or safe. "What about your dad? Didn't your brothers say he was here, too?"

I'd rather ride Angelina home. I didn't say that, though. "I'd rather not."

Griffin sighed. "Why don't I just take you home?"

There was a slight tingle in the tips of my fingers. A brief flash of Griffin rolling around in my bed with me – naked – rushed through my mind. "Um, no, I can call a cab."

Griffin looked exasperated, as though he had read my mind. "It's just a ride home," he said. "No sex has to be involved."

I gaped at his words. "What the hell?"

Griffin smiled. "I won't turn it down if you offer, though."

"YOU SHOULD TURN RIGHT ON MAIN STREET," I INSTRUCTED Griffin twenty minutes later.

The ride to Royal Oak had been uncomfortable – and it wasn't just because you could cut the sexual tension in the car with a knife and fill a sandwich with it.

"I know where you live," Griffin reminded me.

"I was just trying to help."

"No, you were being a backseat driver."

"You can't be a backseat driver when you're in the passenger seat."

Griffin glanced over at me, his expression unreadable. "Are you always this much of a pain?"

"You'll have to ask my brothers," I sniffed.

"I'm guessing they're going to say you are."

"They're idiots."

Griffin smirked but didn't say another word for the rest of our drive. Jerry's car was parked in front of the condo when we pulled into the driveway, and a fresh wave of rage washed over me when I saw it. "He ditched me. I can't believe it."

"He doesn't strike me as the kind of guy to ditch a woman, especially you," Griffin said. "Maybe he thought you left with one of your other brothers?"

"Why would I do that when we live together?"

"You'll have to ask him."

I was going to do just that. I opened the door and moved to slide out of the car, stopping long enough to remember the manners my mother had drilled into my head since I was a little girl. "Thank you for the ride."

Griffin switched off the ignition and opened his own door. "I'll walk you to the door."

"That's really not necessary."

"No, but it's what a man does when he dropping a woman off," Griffin said. "It's the polite thing to do."

This wasn't a date. Did he think this was a date? "We're not on a date."

"That doesn't matter."

It does to me. I climbed out of the car and slammed the door, fixing Griffin with a hard stare across the roof of his car. "I'm perfectly capable of walking twenty feet to my front door."

"I didn't say you weren't," he replied, swinging his door shut.

"So, you don't need to walk me."

"Why do you care if I walk you? Does it offend your feminine sensibilities?"

No, because I needed to get away from him before I ripped his shirt off. "Because I'm an adult and I don't need men smothering me with ... man stuff."

"What kind of man stuff are we talking about here?" Griffin asked, a smile moving across his lips.

Okay, maybe that came out wrong. "You know what I mean."

"No, I want to hear about all this man stuff you don't want to be smothered with," Griffin said. "I think I need a visual."

"Men," I huffed, moving toward the front door of the condo and giving my hips just a little bit of extra swing for emphasis. Unfortunately, Griffin wasn't deterred by my bad attitude.

He walked me the entire way up the front walk, not pausing until we were both at the front door. I turned to him, my heart pounding in my chest, and tried to read the emotions behind his dark eyes. "Well," I said finally. "You walked me to my front door."

"You're not safely inside yet, though, are you?"

"Really?"

"Really what?"

"Are you just doing this so I'll invite you in?"

"And what? Show you my man stuff?" Griffin's eyes were heavy-lidded and the meaning behind his double entendre wasn't lost on me.

"You're unbelievable," I grumbled, rummaging through my small clutch purse until I found my keys. I selected the right one, slipped it in the lock and turned the handle. If I was worried about what might happen when Griffin finally said his goodbyes, I shouldn't have been. The sight waiting for me on my couch was enough to give me nightmares for a week – and kill any romantic yearnings that I had where Griffin and his tight butt were concerned.

"Oh my God!"

Griffin must have misread the horror on my face, because he pushed me to the side and bolted through the door to face the terrifying scene that greeted me. His gun was in his hand (where had that been the whole night?) and all of the flirt he had been exuding only seconds before was gone.

I'm sure Griffin has seen some horrible things. I should have prepared him for what he was walking in to, because he'll never be able to wash that sight from his mind.

I know I won't be able to.

So, was Jerry forced at gunpoint to leave the party and then return to our home? It depends on what kind of gun you're envisioning. Actually, speaking of guns, I wonder if Griffin would loan me his so I can shoot myself in the head?

"Aisling! I ... what ... where did you go?"

I strode into the room, covering my eyes as I went. Since Jerry and Aidan were in varying stages of undress – and they'd been groping like teenagers on prom night on the couch when I opened the door -- they'd been so caught up in each other they hadn't noticed me enter the condo.

"I'm blind," I screeched.

I risked a side look at Griffin, but his face was hard to read. It was red – from the obvious embarrassment – but he looked as though he was fighting the urge to laugh as well. This was not funny.

"Let's not be dramatic," Aidan said, pushing away from Jerry to leave a small gap on the couch between the two of them.

"Not be dramatic? You're making out with my best friend on my couch."

"So? We're both adults."

"You're my brother."

"I think that whole sharing a womb at the same time tipped me off," Aidan drawled. "Just don't freak out."

"My brother is making out with my best friend on my couch," I said. "This is the time to freak out."

"You're spazzing, and it's not attractive," Aidan said. "Why don't you have a drink and calm down." Aidan patted the open seat on the couch next to him.

"That couch has to be burned," I said.

"Why? This is a nice couch."

Griffin cleared his throat. "Um, I'm going to leave you to … this."

I had almost forgotten he was still here. "Thanks for the ride, although I'm betting you're rethinking that whole 'walk a woman to her door' thing you insisted on."

"No problem," he said, shooting Jerry and Aidan a stern look. "You really shouldn't have left her in Detroit to find her own way home."

"We thought she left with you," Aidan said. "We never would have left her there."

"Why would I leave with him?" I was scandalized – and embarrassed.

"Because you're warm for his form," Jerry said simply.

"I told you to stop saying that," I hissed.

"What? That you're hot for me?" Griffin looked interested.

"No," I shook my head, ignoring his pointed look. "Warm for your form. It's a stupid saying and it bugs me. He and Aidan have been saying it for days."

"If you went home with him, Bug, things wouldn't bug you as much," Jerry said. "Bug being bugged. That's kind of funny."

I would murder him if a cop wasn't in the room.

Griffin chuckled, not trying to hide his wide smile. "Well, that's flattering. I think. I'll … be in touch."

I met his gaze, feeling a weird mixture of emotions – fear, longing, regret – wash over me. "I'll see you."

"You will," Griffin agreed, shutting the door behind him as he left.

Once it was just the three of us, I turned back to Jerry and Aidan. "Do you two want to explain yourselves?"

"I think he likes you," Jerry said.

"That's not what I'm talking about," I shot back.

"That's good for us," Aidan said. "If he's hot for you, that means he can't possibly think we're murderers."

"That doesn't mean he doesn't know that we're up to something," I countered.

"He doesn't know what, though," Jerry said. "He'll never be able to figure that out. I know and I still don't believe it."

"We're getting off point."

"What's the point again?" Aidan asked.

"That you two were about to get all ... groiny on my couch."

"Groiny? That's not a word."

I crossed my arms over my chest. "It should be."

"Just chill," Aidan said. "It's not a big thing. We had a few drinks and we were watching some television and one thing led to another ... it was an accident."

I glanced down at the Blu-Ray case on the table and knew he was lying. "You were watching *Pretty Woman* and thought that wouldn't lead to something?"

Pretty Woman is like catnip for Jerry.

"Nothing happened, Bug," Jerry said. "A few kisses, a little petting."

"Don't say petting!"

"Maybe you should get some sleep," Aidan suggested. "You're obviously exhausted from all the flirty looks you and Detective Taylor were giving each other all night."

That did it. "I can't even look at you!"

"Then go to bed."

I stalked toward my bedroom, pausing in the open door, one hand ready to slam it shut. "You better not be here in the morning and I better never hear about this ever again!"

"Good night, Bug."

"Sleep well, sis."

Men.

NINETEEN

"You're kidding!"

After a long night spent tossing and turning – dreams of a sweaty Griffin warring with the memory of Aidan and Jerry groping on the couch fighting for supremacy in my brain – I left the condo early, before Jerry was up.

I just couldn't look him in the eye.

I went to Grimlock Manor to see how much headway my brothers had made in their research on the grimoire. Cillian and I were locked in the library – him behind a computer, me lounging on a couch pretending I was leafing through research books -- and searching for any information.

I had promised not to tell anyone about Jerry and Aidan's dalliance. So, of course, I lasted fifteen minutes before I broke.

"No, I'm not kidding," I replied. "I'm scarred for life."

Cillian laughed, his eyes filled with the mirth I was worried would be missing for days after his run-in with Angelina. "That's horrifying. What did you do?"

"I pitched a fit," I said. "What should I have done?"

"I don't know," Cillian said, shrugging. "Turn off the lights?"

"What?"

Cillian bit the inside of his lip as he regarded me. "Aisling, this really can't come as a surprise to you."

"Of course it's a surprise," I said. "Aidan is my brother."

"And Jerry is like a brother," Cillian said. "He's not a real brother, though. He's just a good friend to us. He's only a brother to you."

"It's still gross."

"It's ... interesting, not gross. I expected more from you."

"It's not gross because they're gay," I clarified. "It's gross because we're all the same age and we all grew up together."

Cillian reached over and tousled my hair, stopping to examine a strand of it for a second. "I like the white highlights."

"Dad hates them."

"That's why you put them in, isn't it?"

"That's an ugly thing to say."

"Am I wrong?"

"Let's go back to talking about how gross Aidan and Jerry licking each other on my couch is."

"Licking? Don't go into detail." Cillian held up a hand in an attempt to keep the visual out of his mind.

"Who was licking?" Braden poked his head into the room. When he saw it was just Cillian and me, he joined me on the couch, shifting my legs to give himself enough room to sit.

"Aidan and Jerry were making out on the couch when Aisling got home last night," Cillian said, his violet eyes twinkling.

I expected Braden to freak out. Instead, a wide smile took over his handsome face. "It's about time."

What the hell? "How can you not be freaking out about this?"

"Because some of us have been waiting for it to happen for years," Braden said.

"What? You can't be serious. They have nothing in common – other than being gay – and you can't build a relationship on that."

"They have a lot in common and very little of it revolves around them being gay," Braden said. "You're just too close to the situation to see it."

"And you're not?"

"We're close to Aidan," Braden said.

"You're close to Jerry, too." I may be angry at Jerry, but I was still his biggest cheerleader. "He's a great guy."

"He's an awesome guy," Braden agreed. "He's a great catch for someone."

"Someone who isn't Aidan," I grumbled.

"Why not Aidan?" Braden asked. "Don't you think he's good enough for Jerry?"

"Of course he's good enough for Jerry," I shot back. "Aidan is a catch, too."

"Then why shouldn't they catch each other?" Cillian asked, searching my face for answers.

"Because ... because ... because I said so."

"Because you think that if Aidan and Jerry get together, you'll somehow lose your best friend," Braden said.

"I don't think that," I scoffed.

Braden captured my hand with his, bringing his other hand to it to make sure I didn't yank it away. "Jerry loves you. He's never going to just throw you over. Not even for Aidan."

"I never said he was."

"No," Braden agreed. "I think that's why you're fighting this, though."

"That's ridiculous!"

"Is it?"

Cillian had stopped his tapping on his laptop – which was resting on his lap as he sat on the floor in front of one of the wingback chairs across from us – and waited for me to answer. The problem was, I didn't have an answer. Was Braden right? Was I keeping Jerry from something special because I was jealous?

"I want Jerry to be happy," I said finally.

"I know you do."

"I want Aidan to be happy, too."

"I know."

"I don't think I can share a bedroom wall with Jerry while he is banging my brother."

"Ugh," Braden said, dropping my hand. "Did you have to take it there?"

It wasn't so funny when the shoe was on the other foot, was it? "It just freaks me out."

"Okay," Braden said. "I can see that. The question is, when it comes down to it, are you going to stand in their way?"

"They said it was just an accident," I argued.

"And you believed that?"

My mind flashed to the *Pretty Woman* case. "No," I admitted.

Braden patted my hand. "Just think about it, kid," he said. "It might be really great."

"How?"

"Because, if they get together and stay together, Jerry would be an actual member of our family," Cillian supplied.

"He's already a member of our family," I grumbled.

"Just think about it," Braden pressed.

I blew out a sigh. "Fine."

"Good girl," Cillian said, turning back to his computer screen.

"What are you two doing?" Braden asked.

"Researching the grimoire," I replied.

"Oh, did you find anything?" Braden looked interested.

"It's hard," Cillian admitted. "There are a lot of generic references to grimoires in the records. Finding a specific grimoire, though, is like finding a needle in a haystack."

"That's actually a misnomer," I offered.

"What's a misnomer?"

"Finding a needle in a haystack," I said. "If you want to be correct you should say that we're looking for a specific needle in a pile of other needles."

Braden rolled his eyes. "Do you always have to be such a pain?"

"That's what Griffin said to me last night," I muttered. "I am not a pain."

"Griffin?" Cillian's eyes lit up. "Do you mean Detective Taylor?"

"He had to drive me home after you all ditched me at the ball last night."

"We didn't ditch you," Cillian said. "We thought you left with Jerry and Aidan."

"And they said they thought I was with Griffin, like that would happen."

Braden and Cillian exchanged a look – and it wasn't lost on me. I pretended I didn't see it, but neither one of them appeared ready to let it go.

"Do you like Griffin?" Braden asked, reaching in to tickle me for emphasis.

I shifted away from him, irritation bubbling up. "He's a cop."

"That's not a 'no,'" Cillian said.

"Why can't you like a cop?" Braden asked.

"Because he's investigating Aidan and me for murder."

"Besides that."

"Oh, yeah, because that's such a little thing," I scoffed.

"It's not like he believes you're a murderer," Cillian said. "You can tell he's interested in you."

"How can you tell that?"

"Because he watched you the entire night," Braden supplied.

"Oh, please, how do you know that?"

"Because we were watching him."

"You were watching him? You spent all night watching him?" That was creepy.

"If you didn't notice, there was a decided lack of women there last night," Braden said. "It was either watch him or watch Dad. He was more interesting."

"And he was watching me all night?" I tried to hide my interest.

"Would that make you happy?" Cillian teased.

"No."

"I think you like him, too," Braden said.

"I think you two are delusional."

"Fine," Braden blew out a sigh. "Keep denying it. We know, though. It was written all over your face."

"Whatever," I said, dismissing the topic of Griffin from today's conversation agenda. "What are we going to do about the grimoire?"

"I set up a trap and trace," Cillian replied.

"For those of us who aren't computer geeks, what does that mean?"

"It means I've gone to all the regular online dealers and typed in the specifics of the grimoire we're looking for," Cillian said.

"And what will that get us?"

"Maybe nothing," Cillian said. "If someone tries to sell it, though, we'll be able to find out who."

It wasn't much, but it was something. "And you know how to do that?"

"I'm smarter than I look."

"That's good," I said. "Because you're never going to catch a woman with the way you look. It's good you're smart, so you have something to fall back on."

Cillian slipped the computer onto the floor and launched himself on top of me. I've wrestled with my brothers for as long as I can remember, so I have a few moves, but he caught me off guard and I was utterly helpless in seconds. Once he managed to pin me beneath his weight he had me at his mercy.

"Who is the best-looking and smartest brother you have?"

"Braden," I laughed, despite myself.

Cillian tickled me harder. "Who is the best-looking and smartest brother you have?"

"Redmond."

"Try again."

"Aidan?"

"You have thirty seconds," Cillian warned.

"You," I ceded.

"And who is your favorite brother?"

"You." Cillian let off just enough for me to catch him off guard and shift my hips, tumbling him onto the floor next to me. "You're all schmucks, though."

20
TWENTY

"Did everyone enjoy the ball last night?"

Family dinners in my house are tough. My brothers make it fun but, depending on his mood, my father can make them hell. Not actual Hell, just hell on Earth. He was in a good mood tonight, though, so things were fairly light and entertaining.

"I think Aidan had a good time," I said pointedly, shooting him a mischievous look from across the table.

"Oh, yeah? What did you do?"

My family is close. We remain close by leaving Dad out of the gossip loop.

"I hung out with Aisling," Aidan replied through gritted teeth.

"And Jerry," I added.

Aidan pursed his lips. He was angry. I didn't blame him. I was being catty – and I knew it.

"And Griffin," Aidan said. He had obviously decided to play dirty, too.

"Who is Griffin?" Dad asked.

"Detective Taylor," Redmond supplied, his eyes shifting between Aidan and me. It was a good bet that Cillian and Braden had filled him in on the gossip.

"The detective who took you in for questioning? He was there?"

"It was a police ball," I said, fixating on my dinner plate. "I think it was probably expected of him."

"Did he talk to you?"

"Not only did he talk to her, but he danced with Aisling, too," Aidan said.

"And he drove me home when you all ditched me," I said, glaring at Aidan.

"You all ditched her?" Dad didn't look happy.

"We thought she left with Aidan and Jerry," Redmond said. "We never would have left her."

Dad turned to Aidan expectantly.

"I thought she left with Griffin," he said. "They were looking at each other like two dogs in heat all night."

"That's enough," Dad warned. "Don't say things like that about your sister."

"Sorry," Aidan mumbled, looking down at his dinner.

Dad turned to me. "Are you interested in this cop?"

"No," I said, my voice lifting an octave.

Braden snorted.

"Is she interested in him?" Dad turned to Braden.

Now Braden and Cillian were fascinated with the food on their plates.

"We're not really privy to the inner workings of Aisling's mind," Redmond supplied. He always was the diplomat in our family. "Although, if I had to guess, there's some interest there. On both their parts."

He's also an ass when he wants to be.

Dad kept his gaze trained on me. "Is this true?"

"No."

Dad narrowed his eyes. He's not privy to our gossip, but he knows when we're lying. I squirmed under his pointed attention. "Getting involved with a cop wouldn't be good for us."

"I know that."

"Make sure that you do."

"I do. I'm not interested in him. They're just being jerks." My heart pinged in my chest when I told the lie. Crap.

Dad must have considered the topic closed, because he shifted his attention to Aidan. "What are you and Aisling fighting about?"

"Wait a second," Redmond interrupted. "Why can't she date the cop?"

Dad turned back to Redmond, reluctance stifling his movement. "You know why."

"No, I don't."

"We can't tell a cop what we do for a living," Dad said. "The relationship would never work."

Redmond wasn't convinced. "We've told other people, people we've grown close with. You told Mom."

"That's different."

"How?" Redmond pressed.

"I married your mother."

"What if Aisling marries Griffin?" Aidan asked, suddenly on my side again. "I don't see why she can't eventually tell him if it gets that far. We're putting the cart ahead of the horse."

Wait, am I the horse in this analogy?

"Do you think a cop is going to understand what we do?" Dad looked nonplussed.

"I think it depends on the cop," Aidan said. "We don't know enough about Griffin to say either way."

"So, she shouldn't get involved with him," Dad replied. "It's pretty simple."

"I think we shouldn't be talking about this," I said, my voice low.

"I think we should let Aisling decide on her own," Cillian said. "They've only known each other a few days. We don't even know if he could put up with her attitude. I don't think we should be worrying about forever when we don't even know if a month is an option."

"Or, we could just nip it in the bud here," Dad countered. "That seems like the smart thing to me."

"Or, we could pretend Aisling is a grownup," Redmond said.

"Do you even like this cop?" I thought he was asking me, but his attention was focused on Redmond.

"I don't know him well enough to like him or not," Redmond hedged.

"You don't like him." Dad sat back in his chair so he could take us all in. "If Redmond doesn't like him, he's obviously not good for Aisling."

"So I can't date a guy unless you all like him?" I tried to keep the bitterness out of my voice. "When did that become the rule?"

"It's always been the rule," Dad said.

"It wasn't the rule when Cillian dated Angelina." It was a low blow, and I regretted it the minute I said it.

Cillian cleared his throat. "I don't think that's making your case. We all know how that turned out."

"And Griffin isn't Angelina," Aidan said. "So far, all we know about him is that he's a cop."

"And he's suspicious of you and your sister," Dad added.

"For now," Braden said. "When this is over, things might be different."

"Well, why don't we cross that bridge when we get there," Dad said, his tone gruff. "By the way, someone needs to go on a night run tonight."

The drastic swerve in topics was vertigo inducing.

"I'll do it," Braden said. "Let's go back to Detective Taylor."

Dad slammed his fork down on the table. "We're done talking about Detective Taylor. He's not going to be a problem because Aisling isn't going to let him be a problem, right?"

My throat was dry, but I answered. "Right."

"Good," Dad said. "Aisling can collect the soul tonight."

"Alone?" Redmond looked angry.

"It's a comatose patient in the hospital," Dad said. "He's been there for ten years. Nothing can go wrong. You'll have to go cloaked, but it should be easy."

I nodded, my mind busy with other thoughts. "Fine."

"I'll go with her," Aidan offered.

I sent him a mental apology wrapped in a small smile but shook my head. "No, I can do it by myself."

Dad puffed out his chest, exuding pride. "See."

"This family is a trip," Braden grumbled, turning his attention back to his food. "And not a good one. We're like the family trip to Ohio instead of the family trip to Disney World."

I followed Braden's example and focused on my dinner, shoveling a spoonful of peas into my mouth. I couldn't help but agree with him.

COLLECTING SOULS IN A HOSPITAL IS MUNDANE AND TEDIOUS. THE truth is, a high percentage of people pass away in hospitals. And, since we have to collect souls soon after they pass so they can't wander away, we often find ourselves in busy emergency rooms and intensive care units – which means we have to make ourselves invisible for the trip.

We don't have a cloak, like Harry Potter, but we do have a ring. The ring, which looks like a gaudy family heirloom, masks us so humans can't see us. It doesn't hide our voices, though, and it doesn't stop people from accidentally bumping into us either. It also doesn't hide us from other supernaturals. The odds of me running into one of those on this job, though, were pretty slim.

The other problem with hospital gigs is that they take some time to pass. The list we're supplied with usually provides us a general time. It doesn't take into account life-saving efforts, though. That's why I spent the last hour watching eight people try to breathe life back into Don White, age eighty-eight.

His soul detached from his body about fifteen minutes into the effort. I should have just collected it then, but I was curious. And, truth be told, I didn't want to return to the condo and face Jerry just yet.

So, I watched.

Once time of death was called, Don remained standing next to his body, watching it with a detached curiosity, as all of the nurses and doctors left the room. When it was just the two of us, I slipped the ring off and approached him.

"Mr. White?"

"I felt you," he said.

"You felt me?" I was confused.

"You're an angel, aren't you?"

"Kind of," I replied.

"Am I going to Heaven?"

I had read his file in the parking lot before entering the building. "Yes."

"Will my wife be there?"

That was a difficult question. "I hope so."

He turned to me, his knobby knees poking out from the hospital gown. "You don't know?"

I shrugged. "Was your wife a good person?"

"She was the best."

"Then I'm sure she'll be there waiting for you."

"Good," he said. "I wouldn't want to be in a place where she wasn't."

"So, you're ready?" I pulled the scepter out of my pocket.

"I've been ready for twenty years."

That was sad. I pushed it out of my mind, though. "This won't hurt."

"It doesn't matter," he said, shrugging. "Let's just go. I'm ready to see my hereafter. I'm ready to see my family again."

I wish they could all be this easy.

Don was watching me expectantly. He was old and resigned, but he was still curious. He wanted to see every aspect of the process.

I smiled reassuringly. I turned my head to the door when his gaze unexpectedly shifted there, mentally cursing myself for taking the ring off. How was I going to explain my presence here?

It wasn't a doctor or a nurse, though. It wasn't an orderly coming to collect the body. What walked through the door was seven feet of pasty hell wrapped in a black cloak. It was a wraith.

"What are you doing here?"

The wraith didn't bother looking at me. I couldn't see his face under the cloak – not that I wanted to. I took a step protectively toward Don.

"I thought you said I was going to Heaven," he squeaked.

"Don't go with him," I warned before focusing all of my attention on the wraith. I had never seen one up close before. "This is my soul."

The wraith acted as though he didn't hear me so I took another step toward him. "He's not for you."

The wraith finally reacted to my presence. He turned to me and I could see the horror under the cowl up close and personal. I opened my mouth to yell before realizing how fruitless that endeavor would be. It didn't matter anyway. The wraith cast his arm out, catching me with it, and tossing me toward the window behind me.

The window was large. A nurse had closed the blinds when Don coded, so no one could see what was happening unless they were looking through the small window in the door.

I didn't expect the wraith to be so strong. He was tall, but he looked frail. I thought he would have to put some effort into moving me from my spot. I was wrong. He barely touched me. I could feel evil crawling all over my skin, spreading from the point of origin on my abdomen where his arm caught me, before I realized that I was in real trouble.

Then, I was flying through the air and crashing through the observation window – glass shattering in an explosion as I hit it.

The last thing I saw was Don's terrified face as the wraith moved toward him. Then everything went black.

21

TWENTY-ONE

"She looks dead."
"She's not dead."
"She might be dead. How would we know? We're not doctors."
"She would show up on the list, you idiot."
"You're all idiots. Shut up."

I fought to open my eyes, but they felt glued shut. It was too bad I couldn't say the same thing about my ears. "You guys are giving me a headache," I groaned, reaching up to feel whether my forehead was unusually large. For some reason, my head felt really big.

"I think that was flying through a plate glass window." I recognized Aidan's voice.

I finally managed to wrench my eyes open and five concerned faces swam into view. Despite their jovial words, there was a tense vibe slumping far too many sets of broad shoulders.

"How are you feeling, kid?" Redmond asked, rubbing my hand, worry etched across his face.

"Not so great. What happened?"
"We were about to ask you that."

My mind was a jumble of memories. "I'm not sure. Where am I?"
"You're in the hospital," Aidan said.
"She's knows that, dummy," Braden griped. "Even with a scrambled brain she can recognize a hospital. She's not you."

"Then why did she ask?"

"Because she was making conversation. She's a girl. She likes to talk."

"Shut up," Dad growled. "You're all giving me a headache."

"How long have I been here?"

"A couple of hours," Dad said. "They called us when they found you."

"When they found me?" My memory was still fuzzy, although a vision of a terrified face managed to cut through the fog. I bolted upright in bed, immediately wishing I hadn't. "Don White."

"He was the soul you were here to collect," Cillian prodded. "Do you remember?"

"It took forever," I said. "They did CPR on him for more than a half hour. Once they were finally gone, I remember taking off the ring so I could talk to him."

"You took off the ring?" Redmond asked, his eyes flashing. "Why?"

"So he could see me."

"Why didn't you just absorb his soul?" Dad asked, working to keep his tone neutral.

"Because he was confused and he had a few questions," I said, picking at a few nubs on the blanket across my lap in an effort to avoid Dad's probing gaze. "I only talked to him for a few minutes."

Since I was in the hospital, Dad was fighting the urge to wring my neck. "And then what happened?"

"He was ready to go," I said. "I had the scepter out and then something caught his eye by the door. When I turned, there was a wraith."

Redmond sucked in a breath. "A wraith? Here? In the hospital? How is that even possible?"

"He was probably cloaked," Cillian replied.

"How?"

"The same way we can cloak if we want to," Cillian said.

"But she could see it," Aidan pointed out.

"She's supernatural," Cillian reminded him.

"Barely."

Dad pointed at Cillian and Aidan and then held his index finger to his lips to silence them. "What happened then?"

"I told it to back off, that Don was my soul. Then I took a step toward it …."

"You took a step toward it?" Redmond looked incredulous. "Why would you do that?"

I shrugged. "I have no idea. It seemed like the thing to do at the time."

"Well, for future reference, if you're in a small room with a wraith, don't walk toward it," Redmond said.

"Good to know. Now."

"I'm still unsure how you ended up thrown through a window," Dad pressed.

"The wraith just kind of ... flicked his arm out ... and the next thing I know I'm flying through the window."

"It touched you?" Braden was incensed.

"Kind of," I said, mimicking the wraith's actions for their edification. "It's more like it just kind of swept me aside. Like I wasn't even there."

Redmond fixed his eyes on Dad. "They're not usually that strong, are they?"

"Not generally," he replied, choosing his words carefully. "The whole thing about wraiths is that they're supernatural, but they're not really here. They're straddling the line between life and death – living only by absorbing souls. They usually can't get their hands on enough souls to gain real strength. They're more like ghouls than anything else."

"So this wraith has been eating his Wheaties and is stronger than he's supposed to be?" Aidan obviously wasn't thrilled with the prospect.

"What if they all are?" Braden asked.

"All are what?" My pounding head was making it hard to keep up with the conversation.

"All of them are bulking up on souls," Braden continued. "What if they're trying to make themselves stronger for a reason?"

"What reason?" I asked.

"That's the question, isn't it," Dad said, rubbing his chin thoughtfully. "We have to find out why the wraiths are here – and what they're doing."

"That sounds like an easy task," I grumbled.

"We have a bigger problem right now," Redmond said, pointing outside the window of my room. We all turned to see what he was talking about, and I groaned as I did because my back was so sore.

"Oh, crap," Aidan said. "What is Detective Taylor doing here?"

"What do you think?" Cillian replied. "He's tracking Aisling's name. The minute she was tossed through that window and the hospital staff went through her stuff to find out who she was, it was only a matter of time."

A flicker of panic ran through me. "What are we going to tell him?"

As though sensing we were talking about him, Griffin looked up and met my gaze through the glass. It was almost as though an electrical current shot through me, lasting a few seconds before he broke the connection. Griffin nodded to the nurse behind the desk and then started moving toward my room.

"Just let me handle this," Aidan said calmly. "I'm the best under pressure."

"You are not," Braden scoffed. "I am."

"Neither one of you are," Dad corrected them. "I'm going to do the talking, and you guys are going to pretend you lost your tongues in an industrial accident."

"That's going to seriously affect my love life," Braden grumbled.

"Don't be obnoxious," Dad ordered.

Griffin knocked on the door before opening it. He glanced at my brothers and father in turn and then focused his attention on me. "How are you feeling?"

"Sore."

"I bet." Griffin moved to the side of my bed where Redmond and Braden stood. "What happened?"

"She's having trouble remembering," Dad answered for me.

Griffin raised his eyebrows. "And you are?"

Dad was affronted. "Cormack Grimlock. I'm her father."

Griffin tipped his chin up in acknowledgement. "I guess I should have guessed that. You all have a few family traits that are hard to deny."

"Good looks," Aidan suggested.

"I was going to say black hair and purple eyes, but we can go with good looks if that makes you feel better," Griffin replied, his tone flat.

"I'm going with good looks," Aidan said, glancing at Cillian for support.

Cillian wasn't impressed. "Why don't you fall down under the sheer weight of your ego more often?"

"I'm ripped," Aidan replied.

"You're a moron," Dad shot back.

"In other words, just sit there and look pretty," Redmond offered.

"All of you sit there and look pretty," Dad growled.

Griffin smiled, but the expression didn't make it all the way up to his dark eyes. "You still haven't told me why you were here," he prodded.

"I said she doesn't remember," Dad said.

"Why don't you let your daughter answer my questions, sir," Griffin said. "She was the one involved in the incident."

I clasped my hands in my lap as I considered what to say. "It's really a jumble."

"Maybe you're being distracted by all your family," Griffin said. "Why don't you guys go out and wait in the hall. That will make my questions go that much quicker. The nurse said that Aisling suffered a concussion and multiple contusions, but that they were going to cut her loose on your promise, Mr. Grimlock, that you would have a private physician check her over at your home. I'm not sure taking her out of the hospital so quickly after an accident of this nature is a good idea, but if you plan on following through with your plan I suggest letting me ask my questions to move things along."

I was stunned by Griffin's bluntness and, one look at my father's face told me he was, too. No one talks to Cormack Grimlock like that. When you have money, people kiss your ass. When you have a temper, people cower in fear. When you have both? Clear the room, folks, things are about to get ugly.

"Are you trying to kick me out of my daughter's room?"

"I'm telling you it would probably behoove you to remove yourself from the situation, yes," Griffin said.

"Under what authority?" Dad's voice was booming , his chest puffed out like a tomcat protecting his turf against another furry invader. I was waiting for the hissing and claws to come out.

"The authority of the City of Detroit," Griffin responded, his voice even and cold. "Ms. Grimlock was in a closed hospital room with a dead body, and she ended up flying through a window and getting knocked unconscious. Someone needs to explain that."

"She doesn't remember," Dad seethed.

"I'd like to hear that from her."

"You just did."

"No, I didn't. What I've heard is you answer questions for her and her brothers talk about how good-looking they all are. That leads me to believe you're hiding something," Griffin said.

Crap on toast.

"I'm calling my lawyer," Dad announced.

"That's certainly your prerogative," Griffin said. "It seems a little heavy-handed for this situation, but if you feel it's necessary, go ahead. Since Aisling isn't under arrest ... yet ... a lawyer really has no purpose in these proceedings, though."

"Dad," I mumbled. "I'll be fine. Just wait outside."

Dad looked uncertain. He glanced down at me, taking in the set line of my jaw, and then ran his hand over the back of my head and dropped a quick kiss on my forehead. "I'll be right outside if you need me."

"I know."

Dad moved toward the door, stopping at the foot of my bed to shoot a look of derision in Griffin's direction, and then snapped his fingers. "She'd better not need me, Detective Taylor. Let's go boys."

"What are we, dogs now?" Aidan grumbled as he followed Dad out into the hallway.

Once they were gone, Griffin grabbed one of the chairs from the corner of the room and pulled it closer to my bed. "Your family is a trip."

"They're just protective," I replied, trying to keep my voice even. "I think they were worried I wouldn't wake up."

"I can see that," Griffin said, focusing on my face. I hadn't seen my reflection yet, but I had a feeling I wasn't going to like what I eventually saw. "Getting a call that your daughter has been thrown through a window could probably be a little jarring."

I nodded, unsure of what answer I should supply.

"So," Griffin pressed on. "Why were you here?"

"I was supposed to meet the daughter of a client here," I replied.

"In the hospital?"

"Her father was sick and they were looking for money to pay for his health care," I said, warming up to my lie. "They had two antique pieces – a lighter and a set of candlesticks from the Revolutionary War – and they said they had them locked in their car."

"What is the name of your clients?"

"You'll have to check that with my father," I said. "We promise anonymity. I can't really remember now anyway."

"It wasn't the family of Don White, though?"

"I don't know who that is," I lied. "That name doesn't sound familiar, though, so I think I can honestly say he wasn't our client."

"Then what were you doing in Don White's room?"

I shrugged, the motion causing pain at the base of my neck. I leaned forward and ran my hand over my upper back cautiously, fingering a few shallow cuts as I did. Great. I guess I wasn't going to sleeveless for the next few weeks. "I don't know."

"You don't know why you were in the room?"

"No," I shook my head. "I can't remember."

"What is the last thing you do remember?"

I ran my hand over my lips as though deep in thought, committing to my performance. "Walking down the hall," I said finally.

"The hall outside Don White's room?"

"I don't know where this Don White's room was, let alone why I was in it."

"Don White was an elderly gentleman who had been in a coma for ten years," Griffin supplied. "He coded this evening and died in a room around the corner. The emergency personnel tried to save him but, after they called time of death, everyone left the room and notified the orderlies that he should be moved down to the morgue."

"That's sad."

"All the hospital personnel say that the room was empty when they left," Griffin continued. "Then, all of a sudden, you flew through the window and landed on the other side. When they rushed back into the room, they said it was empty."

"That's weird." Really? What else am I supposed to say? An invisible seven-foot-tall soul sucker tossed me through the window? I don't think that will go over well.

"And you don't remember any of this?"

"No," I said, forcing my eyes to meet his. "I have no idea."

Griffin looked disappointed, which sent a jolt of guilt straight to my stomach – although I have no idea why. Lying comes with this business. It's not like I have a choice – or Griffin could do anything about the situation even if he knew. I felt guilty all the same, though. I need some ice cream.

Griffin blew out a sigh and then got to his feet. "Okay."

"Okay?" He was just going to let this go?

"I have no reason to hold you," he said. "You didn't technically do anything illegal. Maybe you'll have more answers after a good night's sleep."

"Maybe," I murmured.

Griffin instinctively reached over and patted my hand. "Feel better."

"Thanks."

He turned and moved toward the closed hospital room door. I could see my family standing on the other side, waiting to see what would happen next. Griffin paused and glanced back at me. "I don't know what you're up to," he said. "You can tell me, though. I might be able to help."

That wasn't an option – no matter how much I wished otherwise. "I wish I could tell you more."

"Me, too," Griffin said, shaking his head. "Me, too."

TWENTY-TWO

"I can't believe no one called me."

Despite my firm assertions that I felt fine – raging pain coursing through my back notwithstanding – my father insisted that I spend the night at Grimlock Manor. So, here I was, snuggled up in my childhood bed, with Aidan laying on one side of me while Jerry paced back and forth on the other.

"We didn't have a lot of time," Aidan offered. "When we got the call, everyone panicked. Then Dad started screaming at everyone because they panicked. Then there was an argument over who would drive. Then we finally got to the hospital. We didn't think to do anything else."

"Who won?"

"Who won what?"

"The driving argument?" I was genuinely curious.

"Redmond won," Aidan said.

"Dad let Redmond drive?" I was surprised.

"He was a little worked up," Aidan admitted. "In fact, I haven't seen him that flustered since ... well, you know."

Unfortunately I did. The only time I had ever seen a crack in Cormack Grimlock's armor was the day my mother died. This was an interesting, if somewhat frightening, development.

"I still don't understand why no one thought to call me," Jerry complained. He had arrived at Grimlock Manor thirty minutes earlier – a duffel bag in hand – and he hadn't shut up since.

"Maybe they didn't think you'd take it well," I suggested, leaning carefully back on my pillows. The bed was queen-sized but it fell small with Aidan and Jerry gobbling up all the oxygen in the room. I didn't want them to get any ideas.

"Why wouldn't I take it well?" Jerry shrieked. "I'm good in a crisis."

"Obviously."

Jerry glared at me and then bounced on the bed, causing me to cringe when the reverberations traveled up my back.

"Hey, chill out, dude," Aidan warned. "Her back is a mess."

Jerry looked contrite. "I'm sorry, Bug. I would know these things if I had been called to the hospital like a proper best friend should be."

"It's fine," I said through gritted teeth. "I'm fine."

"You don't look fine," Jerry countered.

"Thanks."

"You know what I mean."

"Detective Taylor didn't seem to care how rough she looked," Aidan teased.

I pinched his wrist viciously. "You have a big mouth."

"Griffin? Griffin came and visited you in the hospital?" Jerry was intrigued. "That sounds promising."

"He didn't come to visit me," I corrected him. "He came to find out what I was doing in a dead guy's room and how I ended up getting thrown through a window when no one else was in the room. He was a little confused, not that I blame him."

"Oh." Jerry's face lost some of its initial excitement. "Oh! How did you explain it?"

"She lied like a pro," Aidan said, clearly proud.

The knot returned to my stomach at his words. My frown wasn't lost on Jerry. He knew me too well.

"I don't think Aisling likes lying to Griffin."

"Why wouldn't she?" Aidan can be oblivious when he wants to be. "I can't believe she came up with such a great lie. Dad is trying to figure out a client he can offer up to Griffin if he shows up tomorrow."

"Because she likes him, you idiot," Jerry said, reaching over and flicking Aidan on the ear. Even that minimal contact was enough to make me uncomfortable.

"I do not like him," I argued.

"Yeah, that's written all over your face," Jerry said. "Your poor, puffy face. You're just lucky you didn't go through the window face first. You need to catch Griffin with your looks and then reel him in with your personality when he gets to know you. He's not going to get caught by your personality without a little help."

"Hey!"

"It's a little abrasive, Bug," Jerry brushed off my righteous indignation. "When people get to know you, they end up liking you. It takes a while, though."

"Thanks."

"I'm not telling you anything you don't already know," Jerry said, patting me on the hand. "So, how did you leave things?"

"I told him I didn't know why I was in the room," I said. "I said my mind was a blank – no jokes, Aidan, I'm not in the mood. He said maybe I would remember more after a good night's sleep."

Jerry looked disappointed. "And he didn't try to kiss you or anything?"

"No."

Aidan smirked. "If he tried to touch her with the five of us standing on the other side of the door – watching his every move – he would have the biggest balls in the world."

"I'm betting he does," Jerry said, his eyes twinkling. "That's why he keeps hanging around even though Aisling is ... difficult."

"I'm not difficult," I grumbled. "And can we not talk about his balls?"

Aidan chuckled. "Fine," he acquiesced. "What do you want to talk about?"

"I want to know why the wraith was there in the first place."

"Redmond, Cillian and Braden are on that," Aidan replied.

This was the first I was hearing about this. "How?"

"They're going to Panorama tonight," Aidan replied.

Panorama was a local paranormal bar in Ferndale. A coven of area witches had placed a spell on it that gave normal humans a "push" away from the building. So, even though they couldn't understand why, if a human came into proximity with the establishment they felt an overwhelming urge to stay away. That's how Panorama managed to keep the clientele so specific.

"What do they think they're going to pick up there – besides women?" I asked.

"What's Panorama?" Jerry asked, confused.

I ignored the question and fixed Aidan with a hard stare.

"If anyone knows anything about the wraiths, they'll probably be at Panorama," Aidan said. "It makes sense to go."

"And will Braden, Cillian and Redmond be able to ferret out this information before they're distracted by something with big boobs and low-waisted jeans?" I asked.

"You'll have to ask them that," Aidan said, although he didn't look convinced himself.

"Why haven't you ever taken me to this Panorama?" Jerry asked.

"Because you can't go in," I replied. "You're normal."

"You've clearly never seen me with my shirt off," Jerry said, flexing his bicep for emphasis.

I caught Aidan staring at the movement out of the corner of my eye. Great. This little flirtation clearly wasn't going away soon.

"I mean you're not paranormal," I clarified. "You can't go in unless you are."

"Well, that's discrimination," Jerry sniffed.

"I'll take it up with management next time I'm there," I sighed, stifling a yawn.

Aidan noticed my fatigue, despite my best efforts to hide it. "What movie do you want to fall to sleep to?" He climbed off the bed and rummaged through the desk for the remote control to the television.

"I don't care."

Aidan and Jerry exchanged a look.

"No *Pretty Woman*," I growled.

"How about *The Avengers*?" Jerry suggested, snuggling in next to me.

I could handle a little Thor. "Fine," I said. "No commenting on their bodies, though. I'm hurt, and I don't want you guys making it worse by getting all animated and reenacting the fight scenes like you usually do."

"Don't think you can handle it?" Aidan teased, climbing carefully back onto the bed in an effort not to jostle me.

"I don't think I can tolerate you two arguing about who has the better body, Captain America or Thor," I admitted.

"I like Mark Ruffalo," Jerry said. "He's like a cute little bear."

Whatever. I had serious doubts I would be able to stay awake long enough for Thor to even make his entrance. Oh, look at that, I was right. I dropped off to sleep before the opening scene even blinked on the screen, letting Jerry and Aidan's murmured movie observations lull me into dreamland.

TWENTY-THREE

"Why don't we have pancakes?" Cillian whined at the breakfast table the next morning, rubbing his head and reaching for the bottle of aspirin in the middle of the table.

"Because Aisling wanted an omelet," Dad replied, never looking up from the newspaper he was reading at the head of the table.

"But I have a hangover," Cillian said.

"And she was thrown through a glass window and can barely walk," Dad countered. "You always have a hangover; Aisling almost never gets thrown through a window. You're not the one in pain here."

"I'm fine," I announced, shoveling a forkful of eggs, tomatoes and onions into my mouth. My pain meds had kicked in twenty minutes ago. I was beyond feeling anything but joy at the moment.

"Since when did I become your least favorite child?" Cillian complained.

"You're not my least favorite child," Dad replied. "That honor goes to Aidan this morning."

"What did I do?" Aidan asked, surprised at being singled out.

"I'm sure you did something," Redmond grumbled, draining a glass of water and immediately reaching over to the pitcher to refill his glass. "You always do something."

"Rough night?" I asked him.

Redmond merely growled in response.

"I still want to know why I'm the least favorite child in this family," Aidan said. "I am nothing if not delightful."

"I think it's the way you dress," Braden said, rubbing his forehead.

Aidan glanced down at his silk pajamas. "These are monogrammed."

"That doesn't make them any less weird," Cillian said.

"They are weird," Dad agreed. "That's not why he's my least favorite child today, though."

Okay, I'll bite. "And why is he your least favorite child?"

"Because, at two in the morning, I was awakened by the sound of something breaking," Dad explained. "I was worried, since it was outside your bedroom. I thought maybe you had fallen or something on the way to the bathroom."

"You were going to help her go to the bathroom?" Redmond looked scandalized. "That's not weird or uncomfortable at all."

Dad ignored him. "Instead of Aisling, though. I found Aidan and Jerry pretending they were superheroes in the hallway – complete with towels tied around their necks."

"How do you know we were superheroes?" Aidan asked.

"Because my only other option was flying nuns," Dad replied. "And I could hear the movie playing in Aisling's room so I had a pretty good idea that you thought you were Captain America."

"Captain America can't fly," Aidan countered.

"I'm surprised you weren't trying to pretend you were Black Widow," Braden said, shooting Aidan a smirk. "You would look great in that outfit."

Aidan flipped him off in response.

"I didn't hear anything," I admitted.

"You were out like a light," Dad agreed. "That's the only reason I didn't beat the two of them with a belt."

"What did they break?" Redmond asked.

"A very rare statue."

"That ugly lion?" Cillian asked. "Good. That thing was creepy."

"It was a family heirloom," Dad corrected. "It was priceless."

"Well, now it's junk," Aidan said. "I was trying to do a kick and I missed."

"How much did you guys have to drink?" Braden asked. "You don't seem to have a hangover."

"We didn't have anything to drink," Aidan replied. "We were just high on life."

"I told you that would happen," I said. "Watching *The Avengers* turns them into horny little devils with delusions of grandeur."

The sound of a throat clearing on the other side of the room caught everyone's attention. Jerry was standing there – in his own set of silk pajamas – but he wasn't alone. Griffin was a few feet behind him.

"Look who I found waiting in the foyer." Jerry looked both excited and concerned.

"Good morning," I greeted Griffin brightly. For some reason, my meds were making me giddy.

"You look better," Griffin said after a beat. "Kind of."

I ran a hand through my hair, my fingers snagging on a few snarls, and then shrugged. "I'm eating breakfast."

Griffin couldn't hide his smile. "Pain meds?"

"Either that or she found some pot when we weren't looking," Redmond said.

"I don't think you're supposed to say pot to a police officer," Braden said.

"I told the maid to keep Detective Taylor waiting in the foyer until we were done with breakfast," Dad said.

"You knew he was here? That doesn't seem very polite."

Dad shook his head, still refusing to put the newspaper down. "Eat your omelet."

"And drink your juice," Jerry ordered, motioning to the open seat on my left. "Have a seat, Griffin. What do you like in your omelet?"

Griffin looked uncertain. "I'm not here for breakfast."

"You don't know what you're missing," I said, shoving another forkful into my mouth.

"It would be rude not to offer him breakfast," Jerry said, directing the comment at my father. "He's a hardworking civil servant, after all."

Dad sighed. "Fine, he can have an omelet."

"Yay!" Jerry clapped his hands together. "Sit here," he instructed and moved toward the end of the table where Aidan and Redmond were sitting. "So, what were we talking about?"

Griffin still didn't look sure about eating breakfast with us, but he pulled a chair out and slid into it.

"Dad was telling us how you and Aidan thought you were superheroes last night," Braden offered.

"Or flying nuns," Redmond snickered.

"We didn't think we were superheroes," Jerry corrected Braden. "We were imagining what it would be like to be Thor."

"And you broke a priceless statue," Dad said.

"An ugly statue," Cillian shot back. "That thing was creepy."

Dad finally lowered the newspaper. "They were still being immature when Aisling was trying to sleep."

"Please," Redmond scoffed. "Those pills knocked her out before we even left the house. The house could have burned down and she wouldn't have noticed."

"That still doesn't change the fact that they were acting like idiots when your sister was hurt," Dad replied, not bothering to hide his irritation.

"At least they weren't being the Hulk," I offered. "Jerry says he's like a cuddly little bear. That would have been a disaster if the Hulk decided to smash."

"Don't encourage them," Dad ordered.

"Yeah, Aisling," Redmond smiled. "You'll be Dad's least favorite child today if you continue to encourage them."

"She can't be my least favorite child today because you're all much more annoying," Dad countered.

I stuck my tongue out at Redmond. He returned the gesture.

"So, you do this often?" Griffin asked.

"Act like we're still in middle school? Yeah," Braden said, picking at his omelet. "I agree with Cillian; we should have had pancakes. My stomach can't take eggs right now."

"Whose fault is that?" Dad challenged.

"Sergio."

"Who is Sergio?" I asked.

"He was the bartender last night," Braden replied. "We tipped well so he poured well."

"Isn't that the story of your life?"

"Drink your juice," Braden ordered.

I did as I was told.

"You guys went to the bar last night? It doesn't exactly sound like you were prostrate with worry over Aisling's little predicament," Griffin pointed out.

"She had Aidan and Jerry," Cillian said. "There isn't enough room in that bed for six of us."

"You slept with your brother and your best friend?" Griffin seemed mildly creeped out.

"It wasn't dirty," I said. "Besides, I could have slept with an entire football team and not noticed." Yes, I realize how that sounded, but it was out of my mouth before my mind had a chance to catch up.

Redmond broke out into a hearty laugh. "So, we've moved on from middle school to high school."

I wrinkled my nose at him.

"That is not funny," Dad said.

"Gang bangs are never funny," Jerry agreed.

"Gang what?" Dad furrowed his brow, perplexed.

"No one answer that," Redmond ordered. "We'll all be locked in our rooms without food for the rest of the day if someone explains that."

"Not Aisling," Aidan said. "She's Dad's favorite today."

That was a new development. I can't remember ever being Dad's favorite.

"She certainly is," Dad agreed.

Griffin looked surprised when a maid slipped a full plate – omelet, hash browns and toast – in front of him. "Thank you."

"It's good," I prodded him. "We spare no expense on food preparation."

Griffin smiled and tentatively took a bite. "This is good."

"I told you," I said. "See, Griffin is glad we have omelets."

"Well, bully for him," Braden grumbled. "You know I don't like eggs."

"So eat the hash browns and toast," I suggested.

"How long do those happy pills last?" Braden asked. "I prefer Aisling grumpy and sexually repressed."

"Hey!"

Griffin's shoulders shook with silent laughter. Dad didn't seem to appreciate his reaction.

"Why are you here, Detective Taylor?"

Griffin swallowed. "I just wanted to see if Aisling remembered anything else," he said. "I'm guessing, thanks to her meds, that's probably not going to happen today."

"No," Dad agreed.

"I was wondering if you could verify the clients she was meeting at the hospital, though?"

"Of course," Dad replied, not missing a beat. "David and Cynthia Braxton. I was in contact with them this morning. They don't mind me passing their name and contact information over to you."

Dad must have been busy with some finagling this morning.

Griffin looked surprised at how gracious my father was being. "Um, great."

"Isn't it?" Dad said, his eyes bright with faux innocence. "Stop it, you two."

I glanced down the table and saw Aidan and Jerry sharing food from each other's plates.

"We're not doing anything," Aidan complained.

"Well, stop doing whatever it is you're not doing," Dad ordered.

"He's such a killjoy," Aidan muttered.

"I heard that."

When breakfast was over, I managed to get to my feet – even though my equilibrium was clearly off – and I walked Griffin to the front door. "I'm sorry you had to sit through that."

"It's fine," Griffin said, reaching over and pushing a strand of hair from my face. The small gesture caused a flood of heat to rush to my cheeks. "I like seeing you with them, even if you are a little high on life this morning."

"Why? They're idiots."

"Idiot is a strong word."

"You have a better word?"

"Family," Griffin said, shrugging. "You're a family. Even Jerry."

"Yeah, Jerry might be actual family before it's all said and done," I grumbled, my eyes narrowing at the thought.

Griffin chuckled. "Something tells me that's going to be all right."

Something told me that, too – even though I didn't want to admit it out loud.

"I'm sorry I don't remember anything," I said.

"I am, too," Griffin admitted. "Maybe you will, though, in time."

"Maybe." Probably not.

Griffin opened the door and moved to step through it, stopping before I could shut the door behind him.

"I know there's something going on here you don't want to tell me," he said. "I have a feeling your whole family – and probably Jerry, too – is in on it. I just want you to know that, when you're ready to tell me, I'm ready to listen."

It was a nice offer – and part of me really wanted to take it – but it wasn't an option.

"Um, okay, thanks."

Griffin took a step back in my direction, his lips hovering a few inches from mine. Instead of pressing them together, though, he brushed them against my forehead before pulling back. His face was flushed with color and he looked embarrassed at his own brazenness. "So, uh, feel better."

I had lost all rational thought, so all I could do was wave goodbye. *What is going on here?*

TWENTY-FOUR

When I got back to the dining room, I found it empty. I followed the sound of voices until it led me to Dad's office. Everyone, including Jerry, was congregated inside. Since my mind was still mulling the near-kiss, Jerry's presence didn't strike me as particularly odd.

"What are we talking about?"

"Is your friend gone?" Dad asked.

"Yes."

"Did he kiss you?" Jerry asked, barely containing his excitement.

"He better not have," Dad said.

Jerry shot a disappointed look at my father. "Why not?"

"Dad doesn't like him," Redmond said.

"Why not? He's hot." Jerry wasn't going to let this go.

"I'll let you be the judge of that," Dad replied. "He's still a police officer. A police officer investigating Aisling and Aidan in conjunction with a murder, I might add."

"So?" Jerry really can be clueless sometimes.

"So, it's not like she can be honest with a cop," Dad said.

"Why not?"

"That's what I said," Aidan interjected. "He'll probably be a little put off at first, but I think he can handle it."

"Why would he?" Now Dad was the one being oblivious.

"Because he's warm for Aisling's form," Jerry replied.

"Stop saying that," I snapped.

"I agree," Dad said. "In fact, if I hear that come out of your mouth again, I'm banning you from this house. We have bigger problems right now."

"Yeah," I agreed, wedging myself between Braden and Cillian on the couch. "What did you guys find out last night? Besides the fact that alcohol and information gathering don't mix?"

"I'll have you know that we had a very successful information hunt last night," Redmond countered. "We found out a ton of stuff."

"Were any of them real blondes?"

Redmond narrowed his eyes. "If you don't want us to start talking about Griffin again, I'd be very careful."

"I'm injured," I reminded him. "You can't be mean to me."

"That's right," Dad said "Let's get back to what you guys learned last night."

"Well, what we learned wasn't good," Redmond admitted.

"Not good how?"

"There have been at least seven wraiths sighted in the area," he said.

"How can they be sure? It's not like they look different from each other."

"No," Redmond agreed. "Two different people have seen them in a group, though."

Uh-oh. "I thought wraiths didn't like each other."

"They don't, under normal circumstances," Dad said. "These are clearly not normal circumstances."

"Why don't wraiths like each other?" Jerry asked. "I would think that if you're a soul-sucking Dementor, like these guys, you would want someone to hang out with. Someone who understands the issues associated with being a soul sucker. Someone who knows makeup tricks to hide pale skin."

"What's a Dementor?" Dad looked confused.

"They're from Harry Potter," I explained. "They're ... well, they kind of are like wraiths."

"And Harry Potter is a book?"

"And movies," Aidan said. "Pretty great movies, actually. You should watch them. I think you'll find you have a lot in common with Voldemort."

"Aren't they for kids?" Dad asked, the Voldemort reference flying over his head.

"And kids at heart," Aidan replied, tapping the left side of his chest for emphasis.

"Maybe, when this little disaster has passed, I will."

"Can we come back from movie hour?" I griped. My meds were clearly wearing off.

"Right," Redmond said. "Anyway, at least two people have seen seven of them in a group. That means there could be seven of them, or there could be more."

"What do they want?" Aidan asked.

"I don't know," Redmond said. "I do think it has something to do with Brian Harper's missing grimoire, though."

"What makes you say that?" I asked. I didn't doubt him, but it seemed like a big leap.

"Well, that's where I come in," Cillian said. "I managed to find out exactly what grimoire Brian Harper had in his possession."

"How did you do that?" Dad asked.

"I found him on a buyer's list from an auction house in England last night, right before we got the call about Aisling," Cillian explained. "The name of the grimoire was in the auction catalog."

"Why do I think this is going to be bad?" I asked.

"Because your meds are wearing off," Braden said, rubbing my knee.

"It's the Torth Grimoire," Cillian announced.

That name meant absolutely nothing to me. A glance around the room told me it didn't mean anything to anyone else either. Maybe this wouldn't be so bad.

"The Torth Grimoire belonged to a seventeenth century witch named Genevieve Torth," Cillian continued. "She lived in Salem, Massachusetts."

"Was she burned at the stake?" Jerry looked excited at the prospect.

"No," Cillian said. "She was never suspected of being a witch until after her death. In fact, she was the one naming names to the witch hunters in Salem. Also, not to be a pain, but the witches in Salem were hanged, not burned at the stake."

"That's not nearly as exciting," Jerry grumbled.

"So she was hiding her identity by pointing a finger at others," Redmond mused, turning the conversation back to the point. "Nice lady."

"Exactly."

"That sounds evil," Jerry said.

I had to agree.

"Anyway, Genevieve Torth left Salem just as the witch trials were dying down," Cillian said. "That in itself is not particularly interesting. What is interesting is that once she was gone, Salem residents claimed they had made the accusations against these supposed witches because they were under a spell. They also said that Genevieve had three demons in her employ – seven-foot-tall demons that bear a striking resemblance to what we now know are wraiths."

"Wait a second," I interrupted. "When we initially were talking about the grimoire, you said it was an eighteenth century book."

"I'll get to that," Cillian said. "Anyway, nothing much is known about Genevieve Torth in the decade following her departure from Salem. She seems to have just fallen off the face of the Earth."

"I'm guessing recordkeeping wasn't that great back in the day," Aidan said.

"No," Cillian agreed. "However, in 1708, a Jennifer Torth appeared in London, England. She was believed to be the daughter of Genevieve Torth, even though Genevieve Torth never had any children, according to anyone who knew her in Salem."

"So Jennifer Torth was Genevieve Torth? How does that work?"

"It wasn't exactly hard to change your identity back then," Cillian said. "Jennifer Torth lived in London for ten years and the historical anecdotes about her time there seem to signify that she didn't age. When people started to question her about it, Jennifer Torth moved from London and disappeared like her supposed mother."

"Where did she go?" Jerry asked, clearly enthralled by story hour.

"She disappeared," Cillian said, his voice lowering as he played to his audience.

"Is that the end of the story?" Braden looked disappointed.

"Not even close," Cillian said. "In 1822, a Sarah Torth surfaced in the New Orleans area."

"Another descendant?" I asked.

"That was the assumption, even though Jennifer Torth was also childless. Sarah Torth became entrenched with some locals, creating a religion that has some striking similarities with modern voodoo."

"But it wasn't voodoo?"

"No," Cillian shook his head. "It was a religion that Sarah Torth invented – but she managed to amass more than a hundred followers, many of whom disappeared under mysterious circumstances during her years in the city."

I could see where this was going. "She was feeding them to the wraiths."

Cillian frowned. "You're ruining my story."

"Sorry. Continue." He's so touchy sometimes.

"After more than twenty of these religious followers disappeared, a bunch of people banded together and went to Sarah Torth's house," Cillian said.

"They were going to burn it to the ground. Five tall figures in robes, though, stopped them. A lot of people were left dead and those who survived swore that they were attacked by demons."

"More wraiths," Redmond breathed.

"Yes."

"So, what happened after that?" I asked.

"No one knows," Cillian said. "Sarah Torth, Genevieve Torth and Jennifer Torth were never heard from again – at least that I can find mention of, that is."

"Then how did the grimoire get out there?"

"That's a really good question," Cillian ceded. "All we know is that the Torth Grimoire first went public in 1920, when a housewife in Detroit, of all places, discovered it in the basement of her home. A local historian dated the book to the eighteenth century, which I think we all can agree was an error, not that it matters now."

"So we have no idea what happened to Genevieve Torth?" I asked.

"No," Cillian said, but I could tell he was holding back.

"What do you suspect happened to her?"

Cillian rubbed his hands together. "I think, and I have no proof of this mind you, but I've been thinking about it all morning and I think I have an answer."

"We're hanging on your every word," Redmond prodded him.

"I think that Genevieve Torth discovered how to control wraiths," he said. "Not only that, but she fed them people to keep them in her servitude."

"I think we all figured that out."

Cillian shot me a dark look. "I also think, as part of the endeavor, that Genevieve Torth managed to utilize the immortality of the wraiths, thus keeping herself young for decades."

Well, that was more impressive. "But we have no idea how she finally died? Or how her grimoire ended up in Detroit?"

"No."

"So, what does all this mean?" Jerry asked, his gaze wandering from drawn face to drawn face.

"It means we're in trouble," Dad said. "It means that someone here has gotten their hands on the Torth Grimoire and they're trying to continue what she was doing. They're amassing wraiths in an attempt to gain immortal life, although I'm not sure how that works. That seems like the best supposition with the facts in front of us, though."

"Up until now," Cillian said, bobbing his head up and down. "The wraiths have slid under the radar because they've been sucking souls that weren't on our lists, so we weren't aware of what was going on."

"They're getting bolder," Aidan said.

"Yeah," Cillian agreed. "Either they don't care that we've found out, or that was part of their plan all along. We really have no way of knowing."

"The question is why," Dad said, running his hand through his hair. "If they do want us to know – and I find it hard to believe that they don't – what is their ultimate goal?"

"Is there any way we can find that out?" I asked.

"I have no idea," Dad said. "I honestly have no idea."

I turned to Cillian, but he merely shrugged in response. "I don't know either."

Well, this isn't good.

TWENTY-FIVE

"I'm sorry, what are we doing?"

Redmond had informed me about Dad's way of distracting us from our current dilemma, but I thought he was playing a joke on me.

"Dad wants to go golfing," Redmond said, matching me shrug for shrug.

"Golfing? I don't golf. It's a stupid sport. It's really just whacking a ball and walking after it."

"You can drive the cart," Redmond offered.

"Is that legal on the meds I'm on?"

"At least it will be entertaining."

"Don't any of us have to work today? I know I'm off the schedule for a few days because of my little incident, but the rest of you should have to work," I said.

"Thanks."

"You know what I mean."

"I guess there were only six names to deal with today," Redmond explained. "Dad contacted the Grimaldis and they've agreed to cover for us."

"So Dad is actually organizing an event that encourages us to shirk our duties? Has he been possessed?"

"Funny," Redmond poked me in the ribs, making me cringe because of my back. "And I'm a little worried, too."

"I don't think it's a good sign," I said. "It means he thinks we're all going to die or something."

"God, you're so dramatic."

"Am I wrong?"

Redmond swished his lips as he considered the question. "Let's just humor him."

"So, you think we're going to die, too?"

"We're not going to die," Redmond laughed. "Is it so wrong that he wants us to go out as a family?"

"He's taking us to the country club," I reminded him. "That means we have to dress properly."

"So?"

"So? So I don't have any short pants here." Or anywhere, for that matter.

"Yes, you do," Jerry said, breezing into the room. "I went to the store and picked some up for you."

"You did? When?"

"When you were in the shower."

"I don't like those little short pants. I don't have any shoes that will go with them."

"Your golf shoes are in the foyer," Aidan said, only a few feet behind Jerry, two shopping bags in his hand.

"I threw those shoes away when I was a teenager," I said. "They made me look all bow-legged."

"The maid saved them," Aidan replied.

"Which maid?"

"Marcella," Aidan answered. "And don't even think about retribution. Dad ordered her to get them out of the trash. It's not her fault."

When we were students, Dad had insisted we all join the high school golf team. The boys had been fine with it – even when it interfered with their football schedules. Since my hand-eye coordination was lacking, I had taken to insulting the golf coach until she kicked me off the team. It had taken less than two weeks.

Jerry took the shopping bags from Aidan and handed them to me. "Get dressed, Bug. It's going to be fun."

Jerry always did have a weird sense of fun.

Forty-five minutes later, the seven of us were standing outside the pro shop and debating cart assignments.

"I'm deciding who is riding together," Dad announced.

"That doesn't sound like any fun," Aidan complained.

"It sounds like the most reasonable way for me to keep the lot of you from embarrassing me."

If he thought that was a genuine option, he had been drinking all morning when I wasn't looking. Maybe that's why he is always hiding behind his newspaper. Hmm, food for thought. Speaking of food … .

"Okay," Dad said after a second. "Redmond and Aidan are together. Cillian and Jerry are together. That leaves Braden and Aisling. That sounds like a good combination."

"I want to ride with Jerry," Aidan complained.

I openly glared at him.

"After the superheroes extravaganza last night, that's not even a remote possibility," Dad replied. "You two are grounded from each other for the day."

"I notice you get to have a cart all to yourself," Redmond grumbled.

"I'm the patriarch. I need time to myself," Dad replied.

"How do you figure?" Cillian asked.

"I have to live with you idiots," Dad shot back. "I've earned it. Plus, I'm paying."

"Can we at least grab a hot dog or something before we go? I'm starved," I said.

"You ate a dozen eggs for breakfast this morning," Cillian pointed out.

"They don't serve hot dogs here," Dad scoffed. "We'll eat after we're done with our round. In the dining room, like proper golfers."

"I thought golf was all about getting drunk and staying out of the rough," I said.

"Ruff. Ruff." Aidan started to bark, snapping his mouth shut when Dad's glare landed on him.

"This is why you're riding with Braden," Dad said. "He can teach you a few things."

"I guess you're not his favorite anymore," Braden laughed.

"My back hurts," I announced. It was a little late to get out of golfing, but I figured it was worth a try.

"Then just sit in the cart," Dad ordered.

I glanced over at Braden. "I'm driving."

"I'm driving," Braden corrected me.

"If I have to be here, I'm driving," I shot back.

"Let your sister drive," Dad said. "Make sure she's behind me, though."

"Is that another comment on my driving?"

"You drive fine," Dad said. "You're a woman. You can't help yourself."

Jerry snickered.

"You're not allowed to drive," Dad turned on Jerry. "Cillian will drive your cart."

"Why?"

"I've seen you drive."

"I THOUGHT YOU WERE SUPPOSED TO STAY OUT OF THE SAND."

Braden shot me a dirty look. "If you're not going to play, then shut your mouth."

"I'm injured," I reminded him.

"How long do you plan on playing that card?"

"Until my back doesn't feel like I got caught in a tent with thirty angry cats."

Braden looked properly chastised. "I'm sorry," he said after a minute. "You were really hurt and I'm glad you're all right."

"I know."

"Then why are you needling me?"

"I'm bored."

"Well, at least you have a reason."

"Sonofabitch!"

I glanced to our left, where Aidan was caught in a different sand trap.

"Use your sand wedge," Dad ordered.

"Thanks, I never would have figured that out myself," Aidan deadpanned.

"Maybe you should have tried staying out of the sand trap," I suggested.

"Shut your trap," Aidan grumbled.

"Don't be mean to your sister," Dad said. "She's injured."

I shot a triumphant look in Braden's direction. He was too busy swinging to notice. When the ball popped up and landed on the green, rolling to a stop two feet from the hole, Braden raised his fist. "Yes!"

"You're still going to bogey," Redmond said. Since he was winning, he looked rather pleased with himself.

"My whole day has been a bogey," Jerry complained.

"You look great, though," I offered, sending him a thumbs up from my spot in the cart.

"I do," Jerry agreed.

"Can we play faster?" Dad asked. "We're starting to hold people up."

I glanced back to the tee, where a foursome was standing and waiting for us to move on. "We could just quit here."

"It's only the eighth hole," Dad countered.

"It feels like the hundredth," I grumbled.

"We can get something to drink after this," Redmond said. "There's a refreshment stand just over there."

"I thought golf courses were supposed to have cute women in short shorts delivering beer," Cillian mused.

"There are no beverage carts here," Dad replied. "They're tacky. This is a classy place."

"And boring," Cillian muttered.

"I heard that," Dad said.

"I meant for you to."

Dad was angry now. "Why can't we do anything nice as a family?"

"We can," I replied. "It should just be something we all want to do."

"Therapy?" Redmond suggested.

Dad ignored him. "And what is that?"

"We could have gone to the zoo," I replied.

"Oh, I love the zoo," Jerry said. "That polar bear exhibit is awesome."

"I love the zoo, too," Aidan said, sending Jerry a saucy wink. "We'll have to go some time."

"That sounds like a good idea."

"The zoo is for children," Dad argued.

"What do you think we are?" I pointed out.

"Hit your shot," Dad ordered to Aidan.

"Fine."

Aidan whacked at the ball and missed. "Do over," he shouted.

"It's called a mulligan," Redmond corrected him.

"Why?"

"I don't know," Redmond shrugged.

"Will you just hit the ball?" Dad looked about ready to explode.

Aidan tried again, this time making contact with his little white nemesis and knocking it up onto the green. Jerry applauded while I rolled my eyes.

"I'm bored," I said.

"Take a nap," Dad instructed.

"I can't sleep outside, you know that. That's why I can't camp."

"I still think that's an excuse," Braden said. "You just don't like the great outdoors. You're scared of bugs."

This was true. "If we were meant to sleep outdoors, God wouldn't have created houses."

"Which God?" Redmond teased.

"Any of them."

"Will you all shut up and play?" Dad was close to his limit.

"Can't we just declare Redmond the winner and go eat?" I asked. "I'm hungry."

"No!"

"I need to take my pain meds," I tried again.

"So take them."

"I can't take them on an empty stomach. They'll make me sick. Are you saying you want me to get sick?"

"We'll get you a snack in a few minutes," Dad said.

Braden knocked a putt in, with Aidan following suit a few minutes later. Dad wasn't the only one at his limit, though.

"I'm bored," I announced again.

Dad sighed. "Why couldn't I have fathered grateful children?"

"We learn from your example," Redmond said.

If red were a natural color for a man's face, I would say Dad looked marginally relaxed. I'm not that stupid, though. On the other hand, I was definitely hungry.

"We're eating soon, right?" I prodded again.

Dad sighed, the sound akin to an irritated lion.

"You're definitely not the favorite anymore," Braden laughed.

TWENTY-SIX

"I can't believe they're making you go back to work so soon. You almost died."

Jerry and I were eating muffins at the kitchen table – Jerry is in the middle of a new recipe-tasting extravaganza – and my work plans for the day were sending him into a tizzy.

"I didn't almost die," I corrected him. "I hurt my back."

"And your back is fine now? Because you still seem to be favoring your right side and you're hiding under some big shirts."

"My back is a little colorful," I admitted. "It's getting better, though."

"So, your dad decided to reward you by sending you out into another dangerous situation?" Jerry's face was filled with unspoken vitriol. "He makes me mad – and sad. I'm smad."

"I only have one assignment," I replied, ignoring Jerry's attempt at coining a new word. "It's at an old folks home in St. Clair Shores. They don't get much safer. Unless one of them attacks me with knitting needles, I think I'll be fine."

"Still." Jerry huffed. "I think you need another week off. And, for the record, knitting is a viable hobby."

Jerry was taking a knitting class. Of course he would say that. "You were the one who said I had to find a job and thought working for my family was a good idea," I reminded.

"That's before I knew there were soul-sucking wraiths and eternal evil witches running around trying to kill you," Jerry said.

"To be fair, I don't think it was trying to kill me," I said. "In fact, the wraith barely seemed to register I was in the same room with it. And we don't know what happened to Genevieve Torth. Odds are, she's dead."

Jerry rolled his eyes and dropped his mouth open in mock horror. "And how is that different?"

I blew out a sigh. "Can we argue about this later? I'm going to be late." I got up from the table and leaned over to drop a quick kiss on Jerry's forehead. "You're a good friend. It's going to be fine."

"It doesn't feel that way," Jerry grumbled.

"I like the blueberry, if that helps," I offered.

"Does that mean you didn't like the lemon ones?"

"I don't like lemon."

"You like it fine when vodka is mixed with it," Jerry pointed out.

"That's different."

"Fine, whatever," Jerry waved me off. "I can't focus on food when you're about to walk in to imminent peril and probably die."

I cocked an eyebrow. "Imminent peril?"

"What? I know things."

"Was there another *Law & Order* marathon on last night?"

"That's a great show," Jerry protested.

It's no wonder he's so dramatic. He lives his life according to television.

An hour later, I was standing outside of Summer's Dream Ultimate Living Center. It didn't look like a bad place – it even had a view of the lake – but, in general, these places always leave me depressed.

I walked through the front door – an excuse to explain my visit on my lips – but the secretary merely waved at me and continued to chatter on her cell phone. I moved through the double doors that separated the lobby from the rest of the center.

My list told me that Evelyn Pratt was in Room 116, so I followed the plaques on the wall until I found her room and poked my head around the corner. I believed what I told Jerry – that the wraith wouldn't come here – but I had no problem being overly cautious.

"Frank?"

The ravaged voice took me by surprise. I moved the entire way around the corner and found Evelyn resting in her bed. I had brought the ring – in case I needed to cloak myself – but I was playing it by ear right now.

"Can I help you, ma'am?"

"Frank, is that you?"

Maybe Jerry was right and I did need to start branching out with my shoe choices. "No, ma'am, my name is Aisling."

"I'm ready to go, Frank. I'm ready to come home."

She must be delirious. "Ma'am, I'm not Frank."

"I'm ready, Lord."

Great. If she was talking, that must mean she wasn't close to shuffling off her mortal coil. I moved inside the room and sat down in the chair opposite Evelyn's bed. Once I saw her up close, I realized my knee-jerk reaction might be a little off. If her shriveled body and sallow skin were any indication, she'd really died yesterday and no one had noticed. Seriously. I don't want to get old. It freaks me out.

"Frank, I want you to know that I forgive you."

I decided to let Evelyn babble. If anyone questioned my reason for being in the room I would tell them that I was worried about leaving her alone and then slip out when no one was looking. I could come back later with the ring – if it became necessary.

"I know you were running around with Aida," Evelyn continued. "You didn't know I knew, but I knew."

I felt sort of bad for Evelyn. Here she was, missing her husband, and the bastard had cheated on her – and with someone she obviously knew. Men are scum.

"That's why I cut her brake lines," Evelyn admitted.

I frowned. Evelyn's file said she was going to Heaven. Maybe no one was hurt and she told someone before anything bad happened.

"When she died, I saw how crushed you were," Evelyn prattled on. "It made me happy."

Wait, she killed someone and she's going to Heaven? And she was happy about it? That can't be right.

"God forgives me, though," Evelyn said. "Father Henry told me so. I told him what I did and he gave me my penance – and he agrees that she was fat so he has no idea why you cheated on me with her. He gave me a pretty stiff penance, though. I did it all, too. Two hundred rosaries and five hundred Hail Marys. I did every single one."

That didn't sound like much of a penance for murder, but that Catholic confession thing has always been an interesting loophole.

"I thought it was a bit much, but I did it," Evelyn said. "Now, I'm ready to come home. So, come get me."

She seriously didn't sound as though she's dying within the next few minutes. Maybe I should try to find a vending machine? Twizzlers sound good. I got to my feet and started to move out of the room, but something about Evelyn's body stilled me.

Evelyn let loose with one long, rattling breath and then her chest stopped moving up or down.

"Oh, seriously?" I grumbled. "I had my heart set on Twizzlers."

I sighed and took a step toward the bed. None of the machine alarms had sounded yet, so I was hopeful I could collect my soul and go. That would be a nice change of pace. Evelyn's soul started to rise from her body and I made a decision. I whipped the scepter out and absorbed it before it even had a chance to achieve ethereal form. What? She cut a woman's brake lines and still gets to go to Heaven. She's had enough breaks.

I let myself out of Evelyn's room, releasing a relieved breath when I saw a nurse was wandering up and down the hallway and would find herself at Evelyn's bedside in a few minutes. I plastered a smile on my face as I passed her, but she didn't even bother to look up.

I started moving back through the home but stopped when I heard a familiar sound. I made a quick decision and headed in the direction where the noise originated from and pulled up short when I caught sight of Aidan sitting with three women around a small table on the patio.

Aidan looked up when he caught sight of me. "Hey. How's it going?"

"Are you eating?"

"Yeah, they have really good pie here," Aidan said, sending me a saucy wink.

"Is this your girlfriend?" One of the elderly ladies sitting at the table with Aidan patted his arm to draw his attention. He clearly was a hit with the Geritol set.

"That's my sister," Aidan corrected.

"And you still don't have a girlfriend?" The woman asked again. "I have a granddaughter. She's not very pretty, but she has a lovely personality. You might like her."

"Dorothy, you know you're my only girlfriend," Aidan flirted shamelessly.

"And he likes boys," I added.

Dorothy's eyes widened as she glanced between Aidan and me. "He's a poof?"

Aidan frowned. "That's not a nice thing to say, Dorothy."

I sent Aidan a rueful frown and shrug. How was I supposed to know he was in the closet here?

Dorothy patted the open seat to her left. "Sit here, dear. Tell us all about your brother."

Not seeing the harm, I did as I was told. I smiled at the other two women at the table, but neither looked happy with my interruption.

"This is Edna and Dolores," Aidan introduced them. "And you've already met Dorothy."

"It's nice to meet you," I said.

"She looks like a tramp," Edna whispered to Dolores. Since she had a hearing aid in her ear, I had a feeling that her idea of a whisper and my idea of a whisper were vastly different.

"That's just how the young girls dress now," Dorothy chided Edna. "Don't be rude."

"She looks like a skunk," Dolores said. "What's with her hair?"

I reached up and patted my head subconsciously. "They're highlights." I have no idea why I was suddenly defensive, especially at a table where muumuus were the obvious trend.

Aidan smirked. "I like her hair," he said. "The streaks give her some street cred."

"You are a poof," Dolores said after a beat. "I don't see how we never noticed before."

I met Aidan's churlish smile with one of my own. "You spend a lot of time here?"

"Aidan visits us every month," Edna said. "He always has the most fascinating stories."

"For a poof," Dolores interjected.

"He can't help it," Dorothy said, her eyes flashing. "The television says they're born that way."

"The television also says you can find love in two weeks in a roomful of strangers," Dolores countered. "I prefer it the old way, where poofs pretended they weren't and women didn't wear jeans so tight their business was on display for everyone to see."

I risked a glance down to see what jeans I was wearing today and then bit my lower-lip. Hey, I don't like super-low-waisted jeans either. You try finding something else in stores these days. Plus, they make my butt look great.

"You're a real peach," I muttered.

Dolores sneered. "I'm not the one who's hard of hearing," she said.

I rolled my eyes and fixed my attention on Aidan. "So, what are you doing here? Besides eating pie and picking up women, I mean."

Aidan stuck out his tongue. "I had an assignment in the area and I thought I would stop in and see my girls."

"In this area? In this immediate area? Why would Dad send me then?"

Aidan suddenly seemed interested in the painting on the wall behind me. Since it was a kitten in a toilet, I figured something else was up besides art appreciation.

"He didn't think I could handle it, did he?" It shouldn't surprise me, but the realization still hurt.

Aidan shrugged. "You'll have to ask him that."

"I am so pissed."

"Watch your language," Dolores ordered. "You already dress like trash, you shouldn't talk like it, too."

"How has someone not stabbed you in your sleep yet?" My patience was short today and Dolores was on my last nerve.

Dolores raised her eyebrows – which were drawn on – and puckered her lips. "I could say the same thing about you."

I ignored her retort. "I want to know why Dad sent you here."

Aidan's head lolled to the side. "You know why."

"Well, I'm already done, so this was completely unnecessary."

"You're done with what?" Dorothy asked.

"Yeah, Aisling, what are you done with?" Aidan's question was a challenge. He was clearly trying to remind me that we were supposed to remain under the radar.

"I just can't believe this," I muttered. "It's because I'm a girl. He's never trusted me because I'm a girl. This is total crap."

Dolores snorted. "Welcome to the real world, dear," she said. "Men are assholes and, even if you are a tramp, you never have any real control."

Despite myself, I was starting to come around to Dolores' way of thinking. "I'm on Dolores' side," I announced.

Aidan looked surprised. "She called you a tramp."

"Maybe she's right," I growled, standing up to make my dramatic exit, holding on to the lip of my pants to make sure they didn't dip too low when I did. "She's right about these pants, too. They're indecent. No one should wear them. They're dangerous. I could flash someone at any time. And, just for the record, he's a total poof."

With those words, I left Aidan -- his mouth agape and his eyes wide with frustration -- and flounced out of the patio area. This was certainly not the end of this argument and, just as soon as I peeled these pants off and set them on fire, I was going to start complaining. Loudly.

27

TWENTY-SEVEN

I was so caught up in my mental retribution I didn't notice another familiar face as I stalked through the dining room. It wasn't until Aidan practically tackled me from my left, forcing me behind a small partition, that I returned to reality.

"What the hell?"

Aidan slapped his hand over my mouth, furrowing his brow and focusing his purple eyes on mine. It was like he was trying to send me a silent message. We had tried to read each other's minds when we were kids. It never worked. I have no idea why he thought it would suddenly start working now.

"I can't read your mind," I hissed.

Aidan held his finger to his lips in an attempt to silence me. I rolled my eyes, but mimed drawing a zipper across my mouth. When Aidan was sure I was going to be quiet, he slowly withdrew his hand.

I widened my eyes to express my irritation.

Aidan silently pointed to a table in the far corner of the dining room. I rolled my eyes but looked. My heart instantly started hammering. Griffin was sitting at a small table, smiling as he talked to a woman with orange hair – no joke. I couldn't hear what he was saying, but whatever it was the woman was tickled to hear it. She cackled, grabbing Griffin's arm as though he was the funniest man in the room. A further glance told me he was practically the only man in the room. Wow, I guess that myth about women outliving men isn't really a myth.

"What is he doing here?"

"How should I know?" Aidan whispered. "He's here, though. We got lucky at the hospital. If he sees us here, we're going to have a lot of explaining to do."

"He didn't believe the hospital story," I countered.

"He let it go, though. He won't let this go."

"What are we going to do?" I asked. "You still have a soul to get. I knew I should have just left when I took Evelyn's soul. She cut a woman's brake lines, by the way, and she's still going to Heaven."

Aidan smirked. "Catholic?"

"Yeah."

"That's always fun."

"That doesn't help us right now," I reminded him.

Aidan breathed in heavily, considering. "Okay," he said finally. "My charge is in Room 102. We'll go hide down the hall until she goes. It shouldn't be long now. We'll just be really careful."

"How are we going to get out of here without him seeing us? We could use the rings, I guess."

Aidan shook his head. "Someone might see. We can't explain disappearing into thin air. Those rings only work when there's no chance of someone seeing us putting them on."

"So, how are we going to do it?"

"We're going to move really quietly and carefully."

"Yeah, because we're stealthy spies," I griped.

"Do you have a better idea?" Aidan looked as though he wanted to shake me.

I blew out a sigh. "No."

"Just follow my lead."

Aidan moved toward the edge of the partition and then tiptoed out into the room. I had to fight the urge to laugh when he plastered himself against the far wall and sidled down it. When he managed to turn the corner without Griffin looking up, he sent me a thumbs up and motioned for me to follow. Like I was going to do what he did. Instead, I just ambled out from behind the wall and made my way in Aidan's direction, refusing to look across the room to see what Griffin was doing. Once I hit the corner, Aidan latched onto my wrist and yanked me. Hard.

"I told you to do what I did," he said, his voice full of recrimination.

"I'm not a poof," I replied.

Aidan smacked me upside the head. "Thanks for that, by the way."

"How was I supposed to know that you're Johnny McStraight when you're at an old folks home?"

"They're old; they don't know any better."

"And you like the attention," I said.

"They love me here."

"We need to talk about your self-esteem."

"We need to talk about your trashy pants," Aidan countered.

I frowned. He wasn't wrong.

"So, where is Room 102?"

"It's near the entrance," Aidan said.

"And where are we going to hide until she dies?"

Aidan mulled the question. "We could hide in the room."

"What if she has a roommate?"

"Then I'll charm her like I do everyone else."

Aidan was already halfway down the hall before I decided to follow. He's not half as charming as he seems to think he is.

Luckily for us, Aidan's charge not only had her own room, but the door was shut. We sneaked inside and found Addie McHale asleep, resting peacefully. Her white hair was spread around her pillow – like a halo – and she looked as though she could slip away at any moment.

"She looks a lot more accommodating than mine was," I said.

"The brake line-cutter? That's a little freaky. Did she tell you that stuff?"

"She kept calling me Frank," I said, sinking into one of chairs at the edge of the room.

"It's the shoes," Aidan offered, going for levity.

"She kept saying she knew he cheated on her but she still wanted to see him," I said. "Then she mentioned cutting the brakes. She said she confessed to her priest and he gave her some rosaries and Hail Marys and she was good to go."

Aidan snickered. "Catholics."

"We're Catholic," I reminded him.

"Barely."

"Dad has crosses on the wall in his office," I said.

"That's just for show."

"So, where do we go when we die?" The question was a lot more serious than I initially intended.

Aidan settled himself in the chair next to me and thought about the question. "Where do you want to go?"

"I like the idea of reincarnation," I said finally. "I think it would be cool to be able to come back and do it all again."

"Really?" Aidan raised his eyebrows. "You don't want to spend eternity with me?"

"Not really."

Aidan poked me in the ribs. "What's so bad that you want to be reincarnated and try to do it over again?"

"Nothing," I said. "It's just ... we see death all the time. Every day. It's nice to think of there being something else."

"And you can't physically see Heaven or Hell," Aidan replied. "So, if you can't see them, how do we really know they exist? That's what you're really thinking, isn't it?"

"Of course not," I scoffed. "We know those souls go somewhere."

"True," Aidan said. "We only have some guy's word, though, or several guys, actually, that these souls are going to a better place."

"Do you ever think about it?"

"Dying? I try not to."

"You know what I mean."

"I think that it's important to live your life for what it is," Aidan said. "I'm not really worried about the afterlife. At least not yet."

"When will you worry?"

"When my looks start to go," Aidan said with a wink. "And that won't be for at least fifty years -- if ever."

I coughed to hide my laugh. "You're nothing if not optimistic."

Aidan's face sobered. "Aisling, you can't worry about death when we're in the business of death. Besides, look what we've learned about everlasting life over the past few weeks. Do you really want that?"

"Reincarnation isn't everlasting life," I countered. "I don't want to be a wraith. I just like the idea of a do-over."

"What would you do over?"

I shrugged.

"Griffin?" Aidan had a knowing look on his face.

"I don't like Griffin," I growled.

"Yes, you do."

"I do not."

"You do, too."

I decided to change the subject. "Do you like Jerry?"

Aidan looked uncomfortable and shifted in his chair. "Why do you ask that?"

That wasn't a denial. "Because you seem to."

"I told you, what happened after the police ball was because of alcohol and *Pretty Woman*."

"That's not what Cillian and Braden say," I hedged.

Aidan's eyes flashed. "What did they say?"

"They said that I should stop being against you and Jerry and embrace it," I answered honestly. "They said that they thought you and Jerry would get together years ago, and I was the one holding the two of you back."

"Ais, you're my sister. You're my twin. I love you."

"I love you, too," I said, "even if you're a total tool most of the time."

"I don't love you so much that I would put my own happiness aside," Aidan said, ignoring my jab. "It was just an accident."

Why didn't I believe him? I opened my mouth to tell him that I would be fine if he dated Jerry, but I didn't get the words out. The door to the room opened. Crap. How were the two of us going to explain our presence?

One look at our new visitor told me that wasn't going to be a problem.

Aidan was on his feet, putting himself between the wraith and me, before I could even register what was going on.

"Oh, shit."

"Double shit," Aidan agreed.

"What do we do?"

"I have no idea."

"So, why did Dad send you?"

"He didn't," Aidan said, his jaw grim. "Jerry called, he was worried. I traded Cillian for this charge."

My heart swelled for my brother – and then plummeted. "You didn't think I could do it myself either."

Aidan's eyes darkened with irritation as he glanced at me – and then immediately focused back on the wraith. "Is now the time to focus on that?"

"Fine," I grumbled. "We're not done talking about this, though."

"Great."

"Awesome."

Aidan took a lateral step, cutting the wraith off from the woman in the bed but not lessening the distance between himself and our ghastly visitor. "There's nothing for you here."

The wraith ignored him, splaying its long fingers out and twitching at the sight of Addie. The wraith didn't speak, but a low rumble emanated from its body.

"Oh, gross," I muttered. "Was that its stomach growling?"

Aidan wasn't listening to me, though. His face was drawn and his arms were tense. "You need to leave."

"No leave," the wraith hissed.

This was the first time I heard one speak. I wasn't a fan of hearing it again. I glanced around the room, looking for a weapon. My eyes fell on the dresser at the edge of the room. I shuffled away, hoping the wraith would be distracted by whatever Aidan was about to do, and slipped to the edge of the dresser.

There wasn't a lot there. A few books, a newspaper, a picture frame and a hairbrush were my only options. I shifted the newspaper and saw that there was something beneath it – an antique letter opener. Score.

I grabbed the letter opener, wrapping my hand around the end of it, and pulled it toward me. I didn't know a lot about wraiths. Killing them was a mystery, at least for me, but I thought I remembered something about silver hurting them. The letter opener looked like real silver. It was certainly tarnished.

Aidan seemed unsure of himself something I wasn't used to seeing. "You can't have her."

"Mine."

"No," Aidan said, shaking his head and wagging his finger as though talking to a naughty child. Like that was going to help.

The wraith reached a hand out to touch Aidan. I was just about to warn him when he moved to the side. He then lifted a leg and kicked the wraith in the ribs for emphasis. The wraith, caught off guard by Aidan's quick movement, tumbled into the wall next to the bed.

"I said no," Aidan said, puffing his chest out as though he had accomplished something.

The wraith regained its footing and turned from Addie. This time, the wraith wasn't so slow. When it reached for Aidan its hands were so fast all I saw was a blur.

The wraith's fingers were around Aidan's neck. Aidan gasped, reaching up to try to release the grip, but he was having trouble breathing.

His face turned red as he fumbled with the fingers closing off his airway. He was struggling, trying to keep from passing out.

I strode toward them. "Stop!"

The wraith didn't acknowledge my presence.

"I said stop!"

Still nothing.

Aidan's eyes started to roll into the back of his head. I had no other options. I reared my arm back and plunged the letter opener into the left side of the wraith's chest – where I assumed its heart (if there was one) still existed. There was initial resistance, but I had enough momentum to push past it.

The door to the room flew open, but I didn't move my eyes from the wraith. We would have to deal with the fallout after Aidan's neck was free. Maybe we could convince a psychotic nurse that she imagined all of this?

The wraith howled – a sound that reminded me of an animal dying more than a human being – and then staggered back.

I didn't have the strength to pull the letter opener back out and try again. Instead, the handle slipped from my grasp.

The wraith reached for the letter opener, trying to dislodge it from its chest. Something weird was happening, though. The wraith's body seemed to be disintegrating. It started in its fingertips and then traveled up its arms, the edges turning to dust as the phenomenon traveled.

Within seconds the wraith crumbled and completely disintegrated, leaving a pile of black dust where it had stood.

"Holy crap."

"You can say that again," Aidan gasped, dropping to his knees.

"What the hell?"

I swiveled to the door to see who had joined us, trying to think of an appropriate lie. As bad as I thought our guest would be, I couldn't really fathom the truth.

"Griffin," I groaned.

28

TWENTY-EIGHT

"Oh, well, this really sucks."
I rolled my neck as I fixed my gaze on Aidan. "You think?" Despite my anger, I dropped to my knees and wrapped my arm around his waist, placing my other hand on his heart to find the faithful beat that always gave me strength. "Are you okay?"

"I feel a little ... flustered," Aidan admitted.

"Like you're wearing-the-same-shirt-as-another-guy-at-a-gay-bar flustered or your-heart-might-fall-out-of-your-chest flustered?"

Aidan smirked. "Neither."

Well, that was something at least.

Griffin strode into the room, his face a mask of disbelief and fear, and let the door swing shut behind him. "What was that?"

I ignored him and kept my focus on Aidan. "Can you stand?"

"Help me."

I wrapped my arm around Aidan's waist, letting him put his weight on my shoulders, and helped pull him to his feet. I ran my hand over his neck and the red welts that were starting to appear on his skin, and frowned. "You're going to look like you're into some freaky bondage stuff for a couple weeks."

"That should improve my love life."

"Are you two deaf? What just happened here?"

Griffin's face was now as red as Aidan's welts. He was shifting his toe into the pile of dust – as though worried the wraith would suddenly materialize out of it again – but his eyes busily traveled from the floor to us. My stomach roiled at the accusation – and betrayal – reflected in the dark depths of his eyes.

Aidan plastered a bright smile on his face – although I had no idea where he found the energy. "We're doing community theater. What do you think about our special effects?"

Crap.

"Community theater?" Griffin was one snide comment away from exploding. "That's your story?"

Aidan shifted his head, grimacing when the movement reached his neck. "Not buying that? Good for you. I don't blame you."

"Aidan," I warned.

Griffin managed to regain some form of control, but it was minimal. "I am not joking with the two of you."

I glanced at Aidan, but I knew we were at a crossroads that only I could traverse. "Why don't we go outside?"

"Outside? What about the dead ... thing?"

"We need to clean that up," I admitted. "Aidan can do it."

"Oh, Aidan can do it," Aidan muttered. "It's not like Aidan didn't just almost die."

"You were nowhere near close to dying," I retorted. "I was in a lot more danger when it tried to kill me than you were just now."

"You were in a lot more danger?" Griffin looked momentarily confused. "Is this what threw you through the window at the hospital?"

"Maybe," I said. "Probably."

"We have no idea," Aidan admitted. "It could be, though."

"There are several in the area," I said, trying to explain. "They all look alike, though. We have no way of being able to tell whether it's the same one."

Griffin ran a hand through his hair and then placed his hands on his hips. "I want an explanation."

"What are you even doing here?" Aidan asked.

Griffin was flabbergasted. "What?"

"Why are you here?"

"Why are the two of you here?"

"We have a reason," Aidan replied.

"Aidan likes pie and my dad thinks I'm incompetent," I griped.

Yeah, now Griffin looked furious. That comment pretty much tipped him over into outright rage. "You have three seconds … ."

"We're reapers," Aidan supplied.

That wasn't enough of an explanation for Griffin. "Reapers? What does that even mean? Are you monsters?"

I took a step forward, causing Griffin to take a step back. I tried to pretend his reaction wasn't a knife to my heart – but it was hard. "We're grim reapers," I clarified.

"Like angels of death?"

"Kind of," Aidan said. "We're better – and much better looking, though."

I pinched Aidan's ribs. "That's not helping."

Griffin's hands tightened into fists. "Someone better start some explaining."

Next to us, still in her bed, Addie's breath started rattling in her chest. I glanced over at Aidan, asking for silent permission, and he nodded. "Show him."

I pulled the scepter from my pocket, glancing at Griffin to try to reassure him, but since overt fear was the only emotion I could feel rolling off of him I focused on Addie.

When she ceased breathing, I held up the scepter and waited. The second I saw her soul detaching I sucked it into the scepter and then turned back to Griffin. Unfortunately, since he was human, he had no idea what had just transpired.

"She's dead?"

"She's gone," I agreed.

"Did you kill her with that stick?"

"No."

"What did you do with the stick?"

"I absorbed her soul," I said, rubbing the bridge of my nose to ward off the headache that was building in my temples. "That's what we do."

"You're soul thieves?"

"No," I said. "We're … couriers."

Griffin remained silent, his face immovable.

"We're like UPS for souls," Aidan supplied.

"You're not helping," I growled. "Find a dustpan and broom or something."

Aidan looked nonplussed. "We're just going to sweep it up and put it in the garbage?"

"Do you have a better idea?"

Aidan shifted his gaze to Griffin. "What about him?"

"I'm going to talk to him."

"What if … ?"

"He's not going to hurt me," I said. "You know that."

"Are you sure? Because I'm not sure. He looks … broken."

One look at Griffin's face caused a river of doubt to rush through me, but I nodded. "I'll be fine."

Aidan was doubtful, but he slipped around Griffin and exited the room.

Once we were alone, Griffin finally started moving again. "This? This is what you've been hiding? You're some sort of magical … I don't know … mailman?"

"I'm a woman."

Griffin's face reddened further, something I didn't think possible. "So, you're a dead mailwoman?"

"I'm not dead," I replied. "I'm alive."

"But you collect souls?"

"Yes."

"Then what do you do with them?"

"We help them move on," I said, tamping down the irritation starting to encompass me.

"Move on where?"

I considered how to answer him. The whole story would take too long. I had to simplify this. "Wherever they're supposed to go."

"I don't know what that means."

I hated how helpless he looked. "It depends on what they believe," I said. "If they're Catholic, they follow Catholic rules. If they're Muslim, they follow Islamic law. If they're Jewish, well, Jewish law applies."

"So they go to Heaven?" Griffin still looked confused.

"It depends," I said, choosing my words carefully. "How you live your life depends on how you spend your afterlife."

Griffin didn't look convinced. "For all I know, you just waved a stick around and pretended it was magic."

He had a point, which brought up another question.

"You saw the wraith, though."

"What?"

"You shouldn't have been able to see it," I said. "You're human. To you, it should have looked like Aidan and I were fighting air. How is that possible?"

"You're asking me?" Griffin's voice was bordering on shrill now.

"What did you see?"

"I saw a seven-foot-tall freak in a cloak," Griffin exploded. "He had his hands around your brother's neck until you stabbed him with a knife and then he turned into a big pile of dust."

"It was a letter opener," I corrected.

"What was?"

"It wasn't a knife, it was a letter opener."

"Do you think that's a salient point?" Griffin was not getting any less angry.

I guess not. "I don't understand how you could see the wraith and not the soul transfer," I said. "I guess it wasn't cloaked, but that doesn't make a lot of sense to me. Why would it come into a retirement community uncloaked? If it was cloaked, though, you shouldn't have been able to see it. I'm confused."

"What?" I don't think I was the only one confused.

"That shouldn't be possible," I said, trying again.

"What shouldn't be possible?" Griffin asked through gritted teeth.

"Well, if you're human, you shouldn't be able to see either," I explained. "If you're something … other … you should be able to see both."

"That's an explanation?"

I sighed. There was no way I was going to convince him without the whole story. I motioned to one of the chairs. "You might want to sit down."

"Why? Are you going to suck me into that thing, too?"

My heart clenched. I tried to keep my face impassive, though. "Do you think I want to hurt you?"

Griffin's eyes met mine, searching. Finally, he moved to the chair and sat down. "Go ahead. Wow me."

So I did.

I told him a story. It was a long story. It was a story about my family. It was a story about faith. It was a story about religion and the beginnings of humanity. It was a story about love, forgiveness and forever. It was a story about paranormals living in a human world. It was a story about moving on, moving up and, sadly, moving down. It was a story about evil sucking souls to survive. I told him the history of the reapers – at least as much as I dared. The whole story would take longer than either of us had to spare right now. As it was, the story took a long time – and a lot of fought-off tears.

When I was done, Griffin's face crumbled as he dropped it into his hands. I wanted to move toward him, run a hand through his hair, and offer him whatever limited comfort I could. I didn't, though.

"I can't believe this," he said.

"I'm sorry." I meant it. My heart ached at his pain. "I'm so sorry."

"I thought … I always thought that God was real. I have seen horrible things. Terrible things. Rape. Murders. Hate. I still thought God was real."

I dropped to my knees, shuffling toward him, only stopping when he flinched at my movements when I got too close. I swallowed the knot in my throat. "God is real," I said. "He's real to you, and he's real to your faith."

Griffin lifted his head, hope streaking across his face. "So, if I die, I'm going to Heaven?"

I didn't have his file. I couldn't be sure. My heart told me the answer, though. "Yes."

"And you? Do you go to Heaven?" Griffin asked.

"We go wherever our beliefs lie when we die," I said, swallowing hard to keep the tears at bay.

"And what are your beliefs?"

I shrugged. "We're Catholic." The truth was, I wasn't sure what I believed. Now certainly wasn't the time for that admission, though.

Griffin reached a hand toward me, as though he wanted to capture my chin in it. He stopped himself, though. He cleared his throat and got to his feet instead. "I'll handle this."

I was surprised, but I followed suit. When I was on my feet, I searched his face for clues, but there was nothing there for me to find. "We can handle this. It's our responsibility."

"I think you've done enough." His voice had gone cold.

"Griffin … ."

"Detective Taylor," he corrected me. "I'll handle this from here."

Tears were threatening to spill from my eyes. If he could be cold, though, so could I. Did I really think this would end any other way? "Thank you."

Griffin didn't bother to meet my eyes. "Have a nice day."

I had been dismissed. I took the hint.

TWENTY-NINE

When I opened the door to the condo, I knew what I looked like: A broken-hearted idiot.

If Jerry were a worse person, he would have commented. My hair was a mess. My eyes were red and puffy from crying. My face was drawn and pale -- easy fodder for someone like Jerry.

Instead, he was on his feet and his arms were around me before I could shut the door.

"What happened, Bug?"

"A wraith attacked," I said, finally allowing myself to feel what I wanted to feel. "I killed it."

"You killed it?" Jerry pulled back so he could see my face. "Shouldn't that make you happy?"

"Griffin saw," I sobbed, burying my face in Jerry's broad chest. "He saw and he hates me."

"How? I thought you were at an old folks home?"

"We were," I said, wiping my nose in Jerry's paisley shirt. "It should have been easy. It was supposed to be easy."

"But a wraith showed up?" Jerry led me to the couch, never removing his arms from my shaking frame.

"Not on my job," I sniffed, settling myself in the crook of his arm.

"It killed an old person? That's terrible." Jerry loves old people.

"No," I shook my head. "Aidan was there. Apparently he hangs out with the old women so they can boost his ego whenever he's in the area."

"Maybe he just likes them?"

I glanced up at Jerry. "Now is not the time."

"I'm sorry," Jerry said, rubbing my back. "So Aidan was there."

"You know he was there," I practically exploded. "You called him."

"I told him not to tell," Jerry complained. "I didn't want to look bad."

I pulled my head back. "Really? You're worrying about you now?"

"I'm sorry, Bug. You have to tell me what happened, though. I'm going to freak out if you don't."

"Griffin was at the home visiting someone – I still don't know who – and when the wraith attacked he walked into the room."

"And you killed it?"

"I stabbed it with a letter opener and it turned into a big pile of dust. It was horrifying – and kind of cool."

"That's good, right?" Jerry is a glass half-full kind of guy. "You can kill them."

"Jerry!"

"Right, we're talking about your almost boyfriend." Jerry centered himself. "Tell me."

"Griffin walked in right before I stabbed it and it turned to dust," I said.

"What did he say?"

"What do you think he said? He had a few questions."

"What did you do?"

"Well, Aidan started by telling him it was a community theater project," I complained. "When that fell flat, Aidan told him we were reapers."

Jerry's breath caught in his throat. "What did he say?"

"What do you think he said? Are you trying to kill me?"

"Hey," Jerry said, holding up his hands in mock surrender. "I'm trying to help you. I don't know how to handle this situation. Sue me. I just want to help."

"Well, you're not doing a very good job of it," I complained.

"I'm all confused," Jerry admitted.

"Confused isn't the right word," I said. "I think dumbass is."

"Well, you know what I mean. Don't leave me hanging, Bug."

"Short story? I made Aidan leave the room and I told Griffin the truth."

"The whole truth?"

"This story is going to take a lot longer if you keep interrupting me," I chastised.

"Fine, tell me the story."

When I was done, Jerry's eyes were wider than saucers. "He told you to call him Detective Taylor?"

"That's what you're upset about?" I love Jerry, but the things he deems important baffle me sometimes.

"Well, Bug, he obviously is going to keep your secret."

"What makes you think that?" I pulled a Kleenex sheet out of the box Jerry waved in front of my face.

"He said he would handle it," Jerry said. "If he was going to arrest you, he would have done it there."

"With what proof?"

"Your magic glow stick of death? The dead body in the room? The big pile of dust?" Jerry was serious.

"What was he going to tell the cops? He would have looked crazy," I complained. "He really didn't have a choice."

Jerry was silent for a minute, clearly considering how to continue. ""I think it's more than that, sweetie."

"How?"

"He's confused right now," Jerry said "Who could blame him? I remember when you first told me what your family did for a living. I thought you were making it up – and I had a lot more time to love you before I found out."

"You said you believed me!"

"I just didn't want to upset you." Jerry's hands rubbed a lazy trail on my back.

His words made sense. Dammit. "When did you believe?"

"I don't know," Jerry shrugged. "At some point, I just realized you were telling the truth."

"How?"

"I asked myself if you were really a liar," Jerry said. "I knew you weren't. When I searched my heart, I knew you were telling the truth. So, I just believed what you said."

"I still don't understand why," I sniffed.

"Neither do I," Jerry admitted. "Bug, when I met you, I just knew you were my forever. Not my wife. Not my partner. Just my forever. When I believed what you were telling me – I mean, really believed – things fell into place."

"How?"

"Your family was never normal and you were always so secretive," Jerry said. "Once you told me, though, things just made sense."

"I don't think they're going to make sense for Griffin," I said. "Detective Taylor, I mean."

"He needs time, Bug," Jerry pressed his lips to my forehead. "Just give him time."

"Time is not going to fix this."

"You don't know that," Jerry said, pulling from me. "Besides, I thought you didn't like him."

Crap. "I don't."

"You are a terrible liar."

"I'm a great liar," I countered.

"You're a terrible liar," Jerry said. "I love you anyway."

I rested my head on Jerry's chest, closing my eyes as I tried to wipe the events of the day from my mind. "What if he doesn't understand?"

"Then he never deserved you, Bug."

I considered his answer, ultimately lifting my lips and brushing them against his jaw line. "You're my favorite person in the world."

"Right back at you, Bug. Right back at you."

I WASN'T SURE WHEN BUT, AT SOME POINT, I FELL ASLEEP. JERRY shifted his body from beneath mine, trying to make me comfortable on the couch, ultimately waking me. "Where are you going?"

"I have a date," Jerry hedged.

I glanced at the clock on the DVR. "It's ten at night."

"I'm late," Jerry admitted.

"I'm sorry." I forced myself into a sitting position. "I've ruined your night."

"Never, Bug. Never."

We were interrupted by the sound of a knock on the door.

"Is that your date?"

"I don't think so," Jerry said, moving toward the door. When he opened it, his whole body tensed. I couldn't see who was on the other side. "You're an ass."

I was stunned at Jerry's words. "Who is it?"

"Detective Taylor," Jerry said, his words precise, cold, and dripping with disdain.

My heart started pounding. "What does he want?"

"You know what I know, Bug."

I couldn't see Griffin, but I could hear his voice. "Can I come in?"

"It's late," Jerry said.

"You're obviously up."

"Actually, Aisling was sleeping. I woke her when I was leaving. Come back tomorrow."

Silence.

"Is he still there?" Part of me hoped this was a dream. A terrible, terrible dream.

"I'm still here. Can I come in?"

I bit my lower lip. Jerry glanced at me, shrugging to emphasize his helplessness. "It's up to you, Bug."

I sighed. "Let him in."

I don't know what I was expecting, but the man who appeared in the doorway was not the man I had met two weeks before. His face was drawn, his skin pale, his features uncertain. He shuffled in the open doorway, glancing between Jerry and me. "Can we talk?"

"About what an ass you are?" Jerry was full of righteous indignation.

Griffin shrugged. "Maybe."

Jerry's face softened. "Are you here to apologize for being a bad man? See, I knew you weren't an ass."

Griffin mustered the energy to roll his eyes. "I'm here to talk to Aisling."

Jerry bit his lower lip. "I can stay."

"Go on your date."

"Are you sure?"

"Yes."

Jerry fixed his eyes on Griffin. "If I come home and she's crying, I'm going to … ."

"What? Beat the crap out of me?"

"No," Jerry shook his head. "I'm going to really be mad at you, though. I'm going to call you names that would make your mother blush."

"Good to know."

Jerry shot one more glance in my direction. "Are you sure?"

"Have a good date."

Once Jerry was gone and the door was closed, Griffin looked unsure. "I'm … I … are you upset?"

I ran a hand through my hair and rubbed under my eyes. There wasn't a mirror near – which is shocking when you live with Jerry – but I had no doubt that my eyeliner was dipping into the leftover rouge on my cheeks. "I'm fine."

"You don't look fine."

"Thanks for the compliment."

Griffin lifted his hands. "I don't want to fight."

For lack of something better to do, I got to my feet and skirted around the coffee table. Only a few feet separated us. I was relieved to see that he didn't step away from me when I closed the distance between us. "I don't want to fight either."

"I'm just … it's a lot to think about."

"I understand."

"I knew there was something about you, I just didn't know it would be this big."

"I know," I said. "I don't blame you. If I were you, I would run the other way and pretend that what you saw never happened."

"You live with this," Griffin said. "Every day, you live with this."

"It's a different life," I admitted.

"And you're not a monster?" Griffin was still unsure.

"You'll have to ask my brothers," I shot back. "When I have PMS, they'll all swear on a Bible that I'm the Devil."

Griffin smirked. "Is the Devil real?"

"We send a lot of people to Hell, although, there are a lot of different hells. I guess it depends on what you believe."

"But you've never seen the Devil?"

"Our part of the job stops when we put the scepter into an urn," I said. "We've never seen anything beyond that."

Griffin chewed on his bottom lip. "Then how do you know you're doing the right thing?"

I held up my hands. "We don't, I guess. It's been this way forever, though. We do what we do. It is what it is."

Griffin took a step toward me. "And you're not a monster?"

"Are we going to go over that again?"

"And you're a real person?"

I sighed. "I'm a real person."

"Good."

Griffin traversed the distance between us in a second. His lips were on mine – hot with need – before I realized what was happening. I thought about fighting the kiss, but I didn't have the energy – or the want. His hands were suddenly tangled in my hair – his tongue in my mouth – and his desire

171

was pressed firmly against my thigh. I answered his kiss with my own pent-up need, matching him tongue thrust for tongue thrust and moan for moan.

I could have stopped it.

I could have made him leave.

Instead, I gave into the emotion and ... fell.

30
THIRTY

A typical woman would ask a man what sex meant the morning after. I was determined not to be that woman.

"So, now what?"

So much for not being that woman.

I felt Griffin shift beside me. We had left a trail of clothing between the living room and the bedroom – and neither of us had gotten more than two hours sleep between very enthusiastic rounds. After the initial coupling, things were slower, more sensuous. Now that it was seven in the morning, though, I was starting to see the harsh light of day – and the problems ahead of us.

"I don't know," Griffin admitted. "When I came here last night I didn't think ... ."

I didn't believe him. He knew what would happen. Now he was backtracking. I shifted my body away from his, immediately missing his warmth. "It's fine."

Griffin must have read the coldness in my voice. "I don't regret last night."

"It's fine," I repeated. "It was just ... hormones."

Griffin snorted out a laugh. "Hormones were definitely a factor."

My heart solidified; I was already distancing myself.

"They weren't the only factor, though," he added.

Hope soared in my chest, and I immediately hated myself because of it. "I have to work today."

"You mean you have to suck souls."

"No. I mean I have to collect souls to help them move on."

Griffin sighed. "I didn't mean ... ."

"I know what you meant."

"Aisling ... I don't know what this means."

I knew he was trying to be honest, but his words burned all the same. "It's fine." I moved to get out of the bed, but Griffin's hand was on my arm before I could finish the trek.

"It's not fine," Griffin said, his voice firm. "I'm sorry. I shouldn't have come here last night."

I knew he regretted it, hearing it come from his mouth sent a dagger through my heart, though.

"I'm not a child," I said. "I know how this goes."

Griffin rubbed my arm with his index finger – twice – before pulling it away. I glanced over at him. With the morning light filtering through the blinds, he looked godlike. I immediately hated myself for thinking that.

"It's fine."

"You keep saying that," Griffin said, struggling to a sitting position. Without his shirt on, he was more than I ever imagined. He clearly worked out. A lot. His chest was chiseled, but not bare. He wasn't into the whole manscaping thing, which was a relief. There was a smattering of brown hair spreading across his chest, tapering down his six-pack, leading to ... well, we all know what it was leading to.

Crap.

"I don't know what this means," Griffin said, brushing his hand through his hair to tame it. "I'm still ... confused."

"Of course you are." My attempts to rein in the tears were making my voice go icy. Griffin's sigh of disgust finally gave me the courage to meet his eyes. "I don't expect anything from you."

"You know, you're really starting to piss me off." That's always what you want to hear when you're in bed with a guy.

"Sorry."

"Don't take that tone with me."

"What tone am I taking?"

"You're not the victim here," Griffin exploded. "You're not the one who was wronged here."

"And you are?"

Griffin shrugged. "I don't like to think of myself as a victim, but in this scenario I don't know how to cast myself. You lied to me. I knew you were lying. I even knew you were hiding something big. I just didn't realize that you were hiding this. This is beyond all ... I still don't even know what to think of it."

I scowled. It's hard to be mad with a guy when he's right. Hard, but not impossible. "You could have just let it go," I said. "You could have just handled the mess at the retirement center and pretended you never met me. You could have walked away."

"No, I couldn't."

"Why? It's not like you can tell anyone what you saw," I said. "If you try, they'll drum you out and you'll lose your job. You'd be the crazy ex-cop.."

Griffin was on his feet, the morning light playing havoc with my imagination when I saw his ass up close and personal as he paced. Dammit! Why did he have to be so hot?

"You don't think I know that? You don't think I've run every scenario through my head? You are impossible!"

"Oh, like you're some bowl of cherries."

Griffin paused. "What does that even mean?"

"I don't know," I shrugged. "I don't even like cherries."

Griffin barked out a laugh. "You are infuriating."

I focused on the blanket covering me, picking at it to keep my hands busy. "I've been told."

"I need to think."

That's always what you want to hear a guy you just slept with – four times – tell you. "I figured." Actually, I figured he would just walk out and I would never see him again.

"I ... I am intrigued by you," Griffin admitted.

I glanced up at him, trying to keep in check the hope building inside of me.

"I find you fascinating and annoying every time I'm within twenty feet of you," Griffin continued.

"Thanks?" I wasn't sure how to respond to that.

"I need to think."

I put myself in his shoes for a second and then grimaced. "So, think."

TWO HOURS LATER I WAS ON EIGHT MILE AND FURIOUS.

"Think? He needs time to think? He had four orgasms last night. Who needs to think after that?"

"Did you say something, honey?"

Eight Mile is a mess. Drug dealers. Homeless People. Prostitutes. It was the latter speaking to me now.

"I'm sick of men," I announced.

The hooker smiled. "Join the club, honey. Join the club."

I had already collected two souls today – no muss, no fuss – and was waiting for the final assignment. I was in a particularly bad part of town – which fit my mood – and I was waiting for a gangbanger to meet his untimely fate. Still, the presence of a professional got my intellectual juices flowing.

"You've been with a lot of guys, right?"

The hooker glanced down at her tube top and thigh-high boots, and shrugged. "You think?"

I ignored her sarcasm. "What do you do when a man sleeps with you – four fricking times, for crying out loud – and then says he has to think the next morning?"

The prostitute smiled. "Thank the heavens that I demand money upfront?"

Of course. "Don't you date … what's your name?"

"Epiphany."

And I thought strippers had imaginative fake names. " Do you date, Epiphany? I mean, you can't work every night."

"Not according to my pimp."

I frowned. "Is he a dick?"

"All men are dicks, honey. That's why I have a profession in the first place."

"Does he beat you?" What? I've heard stories.

Epiphany laughed, waving off my concerns. "That's a movie thing, honey. If he beat me, I wouldn't make much money."

"But he still takes your money?"

Epiphany shrugged. "It's like a corporation," she said. "I need the corporation to find clients. They know where the clients are. When I find those clients, they get a share. That's just how it works."

Men are scum. "But you do all the work."

"It's not really work," Epiphany hedged. "I just kind of lay there."

"Don't they want blow jobs and stuff?"

"I'm lazy."

That was probably why she still needed a pimp. Still, I kind of liked her. "You should probably find another corner."

"Are you claiming this one?" She looked surprised.

I glanced down at my outfit: Simple jeans, my new Justice League Converse, a hoodie and lilac tee. "No."

"Then why do you want me to leave?" Epiphany looked annoyed.

I considered lying, but that seemed like too much effort. "Because there's going to be a shooting here in about three minutes and you don't want to be in the crossfire – or questioned by the cops."

Epiphany raised her eyebrows. "You a gang ho?"

"Yep."

Epiphany nodded her head. "'Thanks for the heads up."

Once she was gone, I waited. I heard the screech of tires from two blocks over before I realized the door of the house behind me was opening. I glanced behind me; the guy on the porch already had a semi-automatic in his hand and was waiting. He knew something bad was coming.

"This isn't going to end well for you," I warned.

"Shut your mouth, bitch."

"Darnell, that's your name, right? Darnell, you're going to get shot in a few seconds." I don't know why I was talking to him. It wasn't as though I was trying to save him or anything. It just seemed the right thing to do.

"Shut your mouth!"

"You've been a bad guy. You can still fix your life."

"Shut up!"

"You're going to Hell."

Darnell faltered. "Do you want me to kill you?"

"Not particularly."

"Then stop telling me I'm going to Hell. I'm in the right here."

"Something tells me you deserve it," I continued. "You've got 'dick' written all over you. You could still … ."

It was too late. The 1975 Chevy was already on the street, the windows down. I slipped the ring in my pocket on my finger – moved a few feet away -- and waited. It didn't take long. Darnell opened fire first, but the two guys in the Chevy were more accurate. As Darnell fell, I saw his eyes search the spot where he had last seen me standing before I disappeared.

I wanted to feel remorse. I wanted to feel sympathy. All I felt was annoyed. Men are really stupid – and this one deserved what was coming to him.

31

THIRTY-ONE

"I know I don't have to tell you this, but men suck!" I threw open the front door to the condo in dramatic fashion.

I had expected Jerry to be on the couch waiting for me, Blue Moon ice cream in hand, a stack of sappy Blu-Rays on the coffee table, and open arms and ears to listen to my crappy, crappy day.

Jerry was on the couch all right, he just wasn't alone. I couldn't see his friend's face – it being pressed against Jerry's as they rolled around on the couch – but I recognized the figure all the same. Aidan.

"You have got to be kidding me!"

Aidan and Jerry scattered, both seeking opposite ends of the couch and – if their heaving chests were any indication – huge gulps of oxygen.

"I ... um ... it's not what it looks like," Jerry said, rubbing his hand through his hair and trying to straighten his shirt.

"Yeah," Aidan agreed, mirroring Jerry's movement as he tried to put himself back in order. "It was an accident."

"An accident? What, did someone trip and accidentally stick their tongue in someone else's mouth?"

"Don't be crass," Jerry chastised. "It was just one of those things. I was watching television, waiting for you because I knew you were still upset about what happened. Where were you, by the way?"

"Working," I snapped. "I've had a really crappy day."

"You already said that, Bug."

"Why?" Aidan asked, instantly alert. "Did you run into another wraith?"

No, I had sex and then got jilted before the sun was barely up the next day. "No," I shook my head. "It's just been a bad day."

"She was upset about the whole Griffin thing," Jerry said. "She thinks he's gone for good." Jerry raised a hand to his heart. "It's really sad. I think she really liked him."

Something occurred to me. "Where were you last night?"

Jerry blinked, the change in conversation jolting him. "What?"

"Where were you last night?"

"I told you, I had a date."

Jerry refused to meet my eyes, so I shifted my attention to Aidan. "Was it with you?"

Aidan shifted uncomfortably. "No."

He was lying. "Oh, man! I just … I can't … I am so pissed off!"

"Take it down a notch," Jerry cautioned. "The last thing we need is the neighbors calling the cops. With our luck, Griffin will show up and things will get really ugly."

He had no idea. "You know what?" I pointed at Jerry for emphasis, biting the inside of my lip to rein myself in. It wasn't working. "You know what?"

"What?" Jerry asked, his eyes wide.

"I was going to tell you two to go for it," I admitted. "Yesterday, when Aidan and I were waiting for Addie to die – before the wraith, before Griffin, before it all went to hell, figuratively not literally – I was going to tell him to go for it."

"You were?" Aidan looked hopeful.

"I was."

"And now?" Jerry looked worried.

"Now? Now I just don't care," I said, flapping my arms in an effort to calm down. "I've had a really, really crappy two days. My head feels like it's going to explode. And why? Why?"

Aidan's face was blank. "Why?"

"Because of men," I replied. "You all suck. You're just big piles of muscles and … suck. You two couldn't wait two weeks for me to get my head around this. No. You had to sneak around. And that just makes it worse."

"Bug, you're really worked up. Did something else happen?"

Aidan looked intrigued by the question. "He's right. You're dramatic, and annoying on a normal day, but you're really out there right now. Like crazy out there. Is it that time of the month?"

Jerry shook his head. "Not for two weeks."

Why is it whenever a woman gets worked up, men naturally assume PMS is involved?

"What happened?" Aidan asked, his voice level.

Now I was the one playing defense. "I have no idea what you're talking about."

"You're a terrible liar," Aidan said. "Now, what is this whole man diatribe about? Generally, I would agree with you about men, but something else is going on here. I know you too well to think otherwise."

I placed my tongue in my cheek and shook my head. There was no way I was going to tell them.

"It's about Griffin," Jerry said finally.

"How do you know that?" I countered.

"Because, that's what you were really upset about yesterday," Jerry replied. "It wasn't the wraith. It wasn't killing the wraith. It was Griffin treating you like a leper. That's what really upset you."

"What makes you think that?"

Aidan arched an eyebrow. "Answering a question with a question is a dead giveaway," he said. "You really like him, don't you?"

"No," I shook my head. "I'm just worried he's going to tell someone what he saw."

"And risk being locked up in the loony bin? I don't see that happening," Aidan said. "Neither do you. Something else happened."

Jerry's eyes sparked. "What happened after I left last night?"

"Nothing," I replied. "I fell asleep on the couch, woke up and then moved to my bed. You would probably know that, though, if you'd bothered to come home."

Guilt flooded Jerry's cheeks. "I should have come home," he said. "I knew you were upset."

"She's trying to derail you," Aidan interrupted. "It's a family trait. When in doubt, divert. What happened last night, Aisling?"

"Oh, fine," I blew out a sigh. "I had a guest after you left last night."

"Griffin," Aidan said.

"Griffin," I agreed.

"I almost forgot," Jerry said. "He was at the door when I was leaving last night."

"And you left her alone with him?" Aidan was ticked.

Jerry waved off Aidan's anger. "Did he want to tell you all was forgiven? He looked upset when I saw him at the door."

"Not exactly," I said. "He wanted to know more about what we are, why we exist at all. He was curious. Wouldn't you be?"

"If that's all that happened, you wouldn't be this angry," Jerry said. "Something else happened."

I rubbed my hands over my hips, trying to decide what to do. It didn't matter, Jerry could read my indecision.

"You slept with him," Jerry guessed.

Aidan smirked. "You did, didn't you?"

"No," I fibbed. "What? That's just preposterous."

"Then why do you look like you just swallowed a bug?" Aidan asked.

Oh, well, great. "Fine," I spat out. "I slept with him."

"How was it?"

Perfect? "I'm not giving you sex details while my brother is in the room, the brother you were just making out with, by the way."

"Aidan, go in the other room," Jerry ordered.

"No way," Aidan argued. "I want to hear, too."

"This is beyond belief," I growled. "I need some air."

Aidan was on his feet. "Wait a second," he said. "If you finally bagged your cop, why are you so upset?"

"Because the first thing he said to me this morning was that he needed to think," I snapped. "Then he practically ran out of here like I had the black death or something."

Aidan's face colored with an emotion I didn't like: Pity. "Oh, man, I'm sorry." He reached for me, but I took a step back, fleeing from the comfort he wanted to offer.

I could feel the tears threatening to spill over so I refused to let Aidan touch me. The minute he did, I would start to cry, and I wasn't certain I would be able to stop. "I'm going to take a walk."

"It's late, Bug," Jerry said. "Why don't you just stay here and talk to us."

I didn't meet his eyes, turning so my back was to them. "Maybe, in a little while," I said, hearing the tremble in my own voice and hating myself for it. "I just need some time to myself."

I was already out the door, not bothering to shut it behind me, when I heard Aidan's voice. "Let her go, Jerry. Just give her a few minutes. She doesn't want to cry and if you go after her right now, it's just going to make things worse. Give her a few minutes."

I was down the steps and on the front walk within seconds, inhaling deeply to calm myself. It wasn't Jerry's fault, I reminded myself. He hadn't made this situation. It was easier to be angry with Aidan, but it wasn't his fault either. Griffin was my problem, and they couldn't deal with it for me. I was the idiot here. It was rare that I found myself wishing I listened to what my father said – but now was one of those times.

There was nowhere to go – even if I wanted to. So, instead, I started pacing. Up and down the front walk, stopping when I got the street and then turning around and ambling back. My mind was busy, so I let it wander.

What was my problem? Was it really Aidan and Jerry? Sure, I was angry with Jerry for leaving me the previous evening, but I wasn't angry because he sneaked away to see Aidan. My brother and Jerry seemed inevitable at this point; I had already readied myself for it. In fact, the more I thought about it, the more I liked it.

So, what was I really angry about? The petulant part of me knew I was angry because if Jerry hadn't left last night, I wouldn't have slept with Griffin and then had my heart crushed this morning when he walked away.

"Crap," I grumbled. Jerry isn't the bad friend. I am. I guess I had some apologizing to do.

I moved toward the front door to the building, every intention of making up with Jerry and Aidan propelling me forward, when two figures moved from the nearby shrubbery and cut me off from the door.

For a second – just a second – I thought they were Jerry and Aidan coming to find me after all.

I was wrong.

The figures were too tall. They were wrapped in dark cloaks, the only hint of skin visible coming from their unhuman white hands.

Wraiths.

I opened my mouth to yell, immediately thinking better of it. If I drew a crowd, the wraiths were likely to hurt anyone who crossed their path. I considered my other options.

I could run, but where? The wraiths knew I would circle back. They would just wait me out.

My keys were in my coat pocket and my car was in the parking lot. That seemed a safer bet.

"So, are you guys lost or something?" I asked the question and took a step back.

The wraiths remained still.

"There's a great karaoke bar about two blocks over. You guys would really fit in there. You should give it a try."

The only sound coming from the wraiths was a low hiss. Maybe that's how they communicate? Maybe I don't really care. Another ten feet and I'll be in the parking lot.

"If karaoke isn't your thing, I think they still do drag queen bingo downtown," I offered. "It's proven to be a big hit. The waiting list is like two months long, but they'll probably just let you guys in because of your ultra-cool outfits."

I was only five feet away now. Oh, screw it.

"Or you could just crawl back into whatever holes you crawled out of and die like you should have from the beginning."

My keys were out of my pocket now and I pressed the button to disengage the car's locks. The wraiths must have realized what I was doing, because they were moving toward me now. I didn't know anything could move that fast. They were on me before I could open the door, one set of hands gripping my left arm and jerking me in the opposite direction from the car.

The minute the hands were on me, I felt the same draining sensation I had in the hospital. I hit the ground, my arm sliding across the cement as I fought to keep my head from taking the brunt of the blow.

It took me a second to collect my wits, but when I did I managed to roll over onto my back. The wraiths were standing above me, like horror movie ghouls readying themselves to descend on their prey.

My arm was sore from the fall, but I pushed the pain out of my mind. "What do you want?"

The wraiths didn't answer. Instead, they both took a step closer to me, in tandem, as though they shared the same mind. It was eerie.

I wanted to screw my eyes shut so I couldn't see what was about to happen. My mind traveled to Aidan for a second, because I knew he would be the one to find my body. I don't know how I knew, I just knew. It was something that would haunt him forever. My heart clenched in my chest. There was no way I was going to give these … things … the satisfaction of showing fear. They may kill me, but I wouldn't let them scare me before they did it.

Instead, I braced for whatever was about to come – knowing it wouldn't be good – and waited.

Everyone has to die. I wonder whose list I'm on?

THIRTY-TWO

When you accept your inevitable death, it's the waiting that becomes tedious. So why, after moving so fast, were the wraiths now moving slower than senior citizens at a Rihanna concert?

I almost jumped out of my skin when I saw the point of a knife slip through the chest of the wraith on my right and then disappear. For a moment, I thought I imagined it. Then the wraith howled and started to disintegrate – just like the one at the retirement home.

"What the … ?"

Once it was gone, and I saw a familiar face materialize in the dark, I realized what had happened. Aidan was there with one of Jerry's large cooking knives clenched in his hand and a look of absolute loathing on his face.

The other wraith turned from me and focused on Aidan – the more serious threat. The hiss it let loose sounded like a cry of mourning – but that could be my imagination running wild.

Aidan didn't look particularly perturbed.

"I think you're going to find that coming to my sister's home was your first mistake," he growled, pulling the knife back and slamming it into remaining wraith's chest. He didn't pull it out right away, though. Instead, he used it to pull the wraith closer to him. "I think you're going to find that your second mistake was touching my sister. Putting your filthy, stinking hands on her."

Aidan wrenched the knife out of the wraith's chest, watching with disinterest as it staggered to the ground before pieces started flaking off. Aidan kicked the wraith, causing it to explode into a poof of black dust, which started to dissipate on the wind.

Aidan fixed his concerned eyes on me. "That's right, who's the boss now?"

I rolled my eyes, but I couldn't tamp down the sense of relief rushing through me. Aidan reached down, wrapped his hand around my wrist, and then tugged until I was on my feet and his arms were around me.

"You scared the shit out of me," he said, burying his face in my hair. I could feel his heart pounding in his chest.

"I scared the shit out of myself," I admitted.

"Are they gone?"

I glanced over Aidan's shoulder and saw Jerry standing on the front porch, a tennis racket in his hand and a baseball helmet sheltering his head.

"They're gone," Aidan confirmed.

"It's good for them," Jerry said, rushing toward us. "I was just about to go medieval on their asses."

Aidan couldn't hide his smile. "It's a good thing I got to them first then."

Once Jerry got to us, he pushed Aidan out of the way and enveloped me in a huge hug. "Thank God I was here," he said. "You could have died."

I exchanged a wry look with Aidan, but patted Jerry's back all the same. "I don't know what I would do without you."

Aidan glanced around, but – surprisingly – we hadn't managed to draw a crowd. "I think we should get you inside and get you cleaned up."

"What about this?" Jerry asked, pointing to the twin piles of ash on the ground.

"What about it?" Aidan asked. "No one is going to know what it is. Hopefully it will just blow away."

He didn't seem concerned, so Jerry merely shrugged. "Sounds good to me. I don't really want to sweep it up anyway."

When we got back upstairs, Aidan helped me pull my coat off and handed it to Jerry. "Go get some peroxide and bandages."

Jerry took the coat, holding it between two fingers, and frowned. "Well, this is ruined."

"What's wrong with it?"

"It's ugly."

I scowled.

"And there's a big hole in the sleeve," Jerry said, waggling his fingers through it so I would believe him.

"Fine," I sighed. No matter what Jerry said, I loved that coat. It was a simple, lightweight canvas accessory, but it was easy to move in, and it made my hips look smaller. That was a win for me.

Jerry shoved the coat in the trash and then disappeared into the bathroom. Once he was gone, I risked a look at Aidan's face. He had been angry when he killed the wraiths – and a little hopped up in the minutes after it happened. Now, though? He seemed calm. Looks could be deceiving.

"Are you all right?" I asked him.

"I'm fine," Aidan replied, running his hands over my arms and shoulders as he looked for other injuries. "What hurts?"

I didn't think everything was an appropriate answer, so I shrugged. "My arm."

Aidan wrinkled his nose as he took a closer look at the shredded skin on my elbow. "I can see that. Once we clean it out it should be okay. It's going to hurt for a few days, though."

That was better than the alternative.

"What else hurts?" Aidan asked.

Since I had been running on adrenaline, I didn't have time to think about it before. Now that he mentioned it, though, some definite aches and pains were starting to make themselves known.

"My knee," I admitted.

"This one?" Aidan moved his hands down gently, making sure he wasn't about to cause me undue pain. Once his hands hit a sore spot, though, I couldn't help but yelp. "Sorry," Aidan said. "You need to take your pants off."

"Um, no."

Aidan held his hands up. "I'm your brother – and I'm gay. Trust me, I don't want to see anything you have to offer."

He had a point.

"Fine," I grumbled. "This is still all kinds of weird."

"We could go to the hospital," Aidan offered. "Unfortunately, once your name is flagged in the system – looking like someone beat the crap out of you, by the way – that's probably going to show up in whatever little database Detective Dinglefritz is using to monitor you."

I couldn't help but laugh as I pulled my pants down – silently thanking the gods (yes, all of them) that I had worn boy short panties instead of a thong today. "Detective Dinglefritz?"

"That's his new name," Aidan growled.

It fit.

Aidan helped me pull the jeans off the rest of the way when fatigue forced me to sink back down onto the couch. There was an ugly red welt growing across my right knee. The skin wasn't broken, but it was going to hurt in the morning. Aidan's face was almost as red as my knee when he saw it – but I could tell it was rage fueling him.

"I'm going to beat that guy to within an inch of his life," he said.

"Who? You already killed them."

"Not them," Aidan said. "Detective Dinglefritz. This is all his fault."

I wasn't Griffin's biggest fan right now, but even I couldn't fathom how this was his fault. "How so?"

"If you hadn't been mad at him you wouldn't have yelled at me and stormed out into a big wraith trap," Aidan replied.

That sounded reasonable.

"Fine, we'll go with that."

"I TALKED TO DAD," AIDAN SAID THE NEXT MORNING. HE HAD insisted on spending the night, so all three of us had slept in my bedroom because Aidan refused to leave my side and Jerry didn't want to be alone in case wraiths infiltrated the condo in the middle of the night.

The three of us were now sitting at the kitchen table eating breakfast.

"What did he say?"

"He's not happy," Aidan replied.

One look at his face told me that was an understatement. "Well, we've killed three wraiths in less than forty-eight hours; that's got to make him happy."

Aidan cocked his head to the side. "Yeah, I don't think that's the way he sees it."

"What else did he say?"

"We have to be there for dinner tonight because he wants to talk about things," Aidan said. "Oh, and you're excused from work for the next few days."

"I'm fine," I protested.

"It took you five minutes to walk the twenty feet from your bedroom to the kitchen this morning," Aidan pointed out. "And you stopped drinking liquids last night because it hurt too much to go to the bathroom."

"Oh, God," Jerry said, smacking the side of his face with his hand. "Does it burn when you pee? Did Detective Dinglefritz give you the clap?"

It wasn't funny, but I couldn't stop the laughter from bubbling up.

"Not because of that," Aidan snapped. "Because it hurts for her to sit down on the toilet. She's a girl, they don't go standing up."

Realization – and relief – washed over Jerry's face. "Well, that's good to know."

In what world? I was uncomfortable with the conversation thread, though, so I changed it. "You didn't tell him anything else, did you?"

Aidan looked confused. "Like what? If you're asking whether I told him about Jerry and me, that would be a big, fat no. It's none of his business. It's none of any of their business. And, quite frankly, I'm going to be pissed off if you tell them. I'll tell them when I'm ready."

I raised my eyebrows. "That's not what I meant."

"Then what did you mean?"

I was really close to hating men again – even when the man presently irritating me was acting like a woman.

"I think she's talking about Detective Dinglefritz," Jerry supplied.

"Oh," Aidan said. "No, of course I didn't tell Dad about that ass sleeping with you and then ditching you the next morning. He'd have a heart attack."

Well, that was a relief.

"I told Redmond, though," Aidan added. "He's planning revenge even as we speak."

Crap.

THIRTY-THREE

"Can I get you anything?"

The minute I walked through the door of Grimlock Manor my brothers were on me, offering to help me sit down, bringing me drinks and trying to force feed me finger sandwiches every time I turned around.

It was sweet – and annoying.

"I said I was fine," I said.

"She looks cold," Dad said from behind his desk. "One of you get her a blanket."

Cillian immediately grabbed the afghan off the back of the couch he was sitting on and brought it toward me.

"I'm not cold," I said.

"And that blanket is ugly," Jerry said. He had insisted on coming to dinner. He said it was because he wanted to protect me, but it was far more likely he was uncomfortable being alone. At least he left the tennis racket at the condo.

Dad cleared his throat. "My mother knitted that blanket."

Jerry looked momentarily flummoxed. "Well, I'm sorry."

"It's okay," Dad waved him off. "She was a wonderful lady, though, and that blanket is a family heirloom."

He thinks everything in this house is a family heirloom.

"Was she colorblind?" Jerry asked.

"Who?"

"Your mother."

"No." Now Dad was the one who looked confused.

"Well then, someone should have told her that orange and blue don't make up a pleasant color pattern – even for a blanket."

Dad pursed his lips and turned back to me. "You're very lucky, young lady."

"How did this become my fault?" I shifted, trying to flex my knee. It hurt. Braden was on his feet and moving a footstool in front of me, gently placing my leg on it, before I could even register his movement.

"You were the one that went out by yourself after dark," Dad explained. "You're obviously on the radar of whoever is amassing these wraiths. Try using your brain next time."

"Hey!"

Redmond was angry. "Leave her alone," he said. "It's not like she could have guessed this would happen. Until now, we've only seen the wraiths when we were out collecting souls. How could she know they'd follow her home?"

"Well, since wraiths have only shown up on her jobs, it wasn't that foregone of a conclusion," Dad countered, "but we should have anticipated it."

Huh, that was weird. I hadn't even thought about that. Apparently, no one else in the room had put it together either.

"Wait, so you think that the wraiths are following Aisling?" Cillian asked.

"Have the rest of you run into a wraith?"

Everyone shook their heads.

"Then we have to assume, for now at least, that they're keyed into Aisling somehow."

"That's not right," Aidan said suddenly. "Addie was my charge. Aisling just happened to be at the retirement home."

"Yes, but she was originally on Aisling's list," Dad pointed out. "I didn't want to overtax her, though, so I gave her only one charge that day and assigned one of you to do the other as backup."

Aidan's face fell. "Yeah, and I traded Cillian for it when Jerry called me all freaked out."

Why do I feel like I'm being infantilized here? "Why would the wraiths only be sent out on my assignments?"

"Maybe because you're new," Braden said. "Maybe whoever is in charge thinks that a new reaper is an easy reaper?"

"See, I'm not the only one who thinks you're easy," Aidan teased, immediately regretting his words when my face fell. "I didn't mean that. I'm sorry."

"You didn't mean what?" Dad asked, clearly behind the gossip curve.

"Nothing," I replied hurriedly.

"When I get my hands on Detective Dinglefritz, I'm going to wring his neck," Redmond growled.

Clearly that nickname was catching on.

"Who is Detective Dinglefritz?" Dad asked.

Crap.

"Detective Taylor," Braden supplied. "He's on our list. He's at the top now. He might be the only name on it for the foreseeable future actually."

"He's always been on my list," Dad said. "Not that I'm complaining, but why are we especially mad at him now?"

I glared at Aidan. "Thanks."

"I'm sorry," he said.

"What is going on?" Dad asked.

"Aisling had sex with Griffin – sorry, Detective Dinglefritz – and he bolted the next morning," Jerry explained. "Sorry, Bug, this could take forever and you guys are terrible liars. It was going to come out eventually, and I'm hungry."

I tried to swallow my upper lip when color started creeping up Dad's neck. This wasn't going to be good.

"What did you just say?"

"He said he and Aidan are a couple now," I said. What? If I'm going down I'm taking everyone else with me.

"Oh, nice," Aidan exploded.

"Aisling," Jerry chided. "That was not nice."

"Congratulations," Redmond offered, slapping Aidan on the back.

"It's about time," Braden agreed.

"Jerry is definitely a better choice than Detective Dinglefritz," Cillian added.

Dad held up his hand for silence. "We'll get to Jerry and Aidan in a second," he said. "I want to know – wait, I don't want to know, but now I guess I have to know – what happened with Detective Taylor?"

I frowned. I was not talking about my sex life with my father. This is the man who found my birth control pills when I was a teenager and accused me of being on drugs. This couldn't end well. I was just going to pretend this wasn't happening. Is he still looking at me?

"Detective Dinglefritz showed up at the apartment after that whole wraith thing at the retirement home," Jerry explained. "I guess things got heated – in more ways than one – and then he bolted the next morning."

Besides, I don't have to say anything when I have Jerry the Mouth to do it for me."

Dad looked as though he was hoping for a hole to open up and swallow him. "I see."

I glanced at Redmond, who was having trouble keeping a straight face. "This isn't funny."

"I agree," he said after a beat. "I'm going to kill that guy. I'm laughing at Dad. I think he honestly thought you were still a virgin."

"He didn't think that," I scoffed. "He just pretended that was the case. Why is it that when you guys get laid he gives you a pat on the back and an 'atta boy' but when it happens to me the world suddenly ceases turning on its axis?"

"Because men are considered studs when they get some and women are considered sluts," Redmond replied. "I don't make the rules."

"Who are all these women that these studs are getting laid with?"

Redmond shrugged. "Sluts?"

"That seems really misogynistic."

"That's life."

"Life sucks," I said.

"And then you die."

Everyone jumped when the doorbell rang.

"Are we expecting someone?" Braden asked.

"No," Dad said. "Maybe it's just a delivery. I ordered some books. Let's get back to the conversation at hand."

"Let's not," I argued.

"Aisling, this is a serious issue."

"Wait a second," Aidan interrupted. "I don't think this is fair."

"I agree," Cillian said. "I don't think it's fair to jump on Aisling."

"Yeah," Jerry said. "Detective Dinglefritz already did that and look how that turned out."

Dad's face was now beet red. "Jerry, you're a part of this family and I love you."

"Thank you." Jerry looked pleased.

"If you don't shut your mouth, though ... I can't be responsible for what I'm going to do to you."

"What did I say?" Jerry turned to me, his eyes wide.

I leaned back on the couch, stretching my knee across the footstool. This night was turning into a mess. And since I was almost killed by two wraiths the night before, that was saying something.

"I want to get back to you ... doing things with the cop," Dad said, trying to pretend this was a normal conversation.

"What things?" Braden pressed.

"You're not funny, young man," Dad yelled.

"I just need clarification," Braden said. "Were they knitting? Reading a good book? Playing Monopoly?"

"She's your sister," Redmond pointed out. "How much clarification do you need?"

Braden considered the question. "Point taken. As far as I'm concerned, Aisling is sexless."

"Thanks."

"You're welcome."

Thankfully, the conversation was interrupted by a knock at the door. One of the maids – I think her name was Steffi – poked her head in. "There's a police officer here."

Uh-oh.

"Tell him we're busy," I ordered.

"No," Dad said, his smile slight and grim. "By all means, show him in."

No. No. No. It was too late, though. Griffin was already in the room and all four of my brothers were on their feet, their hands clenched into fists.

"Is this a bad time?" Griffin asked, refusing to look me in the eye.

"Oh, no," Redmond said. "We're really happy to see you, Detective Dinglefritz."

Oh, good. This will end well.

34

THIRTY-FOUR

Griffin must have sensed he was walking into a room where he was the most unpopular occupant, but to his credit he didn't turn and flee.

Dammit!

"I'm glad you're all here," he said, clearly nervous. "I have something I want to discuss with you."

"Good," Redmond agreed. "We have something to discuss with you, too."

Griffin's eyes finally found mine, even though my brothers were trying to build a wall between us with their bodies. The minute he caught sight of me his face moved from grim to concerned. "What happened to you?"

"You happened to her," Jerry said.

Griffin attempted to push his way between Braden and Redmond to get to me. "What are you guys doing? Is she okay?"

"She's fine," Redmond growled. "No thanks to you."

Griffin looked momentarily taken aback. "What's going on here?"

"Well, Detective Dinglefritz, my sister was attacked outside her condominium last night," Aidan said.

"By one of those things? One of those things from Summer's Dream?"

"It's called a wraith," I said.

"And she was attacked by two of them," Aidan said. "If I hadn't been there, she would be dead."

"We all know you're a hero," Braden deadpanned. "This isn't about you, though."

"Are you all right?" Griffin ignored my brothers.

Concern was evident on his face, but I wasn't feeling overly conciliatory. "I survived."

"Her jacket was ruined," Jerry said.

Redmond hit him in the arm. "You're not helping. Go sit down."

Jerry huffed. "Everyone in this family is mean, especially today."

"That's what happens when our sister is almost killed twice in two days," Cillian said.

"And it's all Detective Dinglefritz's fault," Aidan grumbled.

"How is it my fault? And why are you calling me that?"

"It seems to me you've earned it," Dad said, speaking for the first time since Griffin walked into the room. His voice was so low it bordered on evil. I had to fight the urge to shudder.

"Listen," Griffin said. "I understand you're all worried that I'm going to spill your big family secret. I'm not going to."

"Don't act like it's because you're doing us some big favor," Braden said. "You're doing it because no one would believe you."

"You're right," Griffin conceded. "I wouldn't tell even if that wasn't the case, though. I promise."

"Forgive me if I find your promises empty," Dad said.

Griffin's gaze bounced around the room, not settling on any one face for too long. "I think I'm missing something. Does anyone want to enlighten me?"

Jerry's hand shot up.

Griffin sighed. "Jerry, do you want to enlighten me?"

"Everyone knows you had sex with Aisling and then bolted the next morning," he said. "They're pissed."

Man, I wish I still had some of those happy pills from the first wraith attack about now.

Griffin's jaw tightened and he risked a look in my direction. "You told your father? Really?"

"No," I shook my head, beyond embarrassment at this point. "I told Jerry and Aidan. Aidan told the rest of my brothers and … here we are."

Griffin nodded his head, wrinkling his nose as he did. "Well, that makes perfect sense."

"Hey, it's not my fault," I said. "I was upset. Aidan is the one with the big mouth."

"Aidan is the one who saved you from being sucked dry by two wraiths on the front lawn last night," Aidan reminded me. "Detective Dinglefritz here is the reason you were out pacing the front lawn, putting yourself in danger."

"Thanks, I forgot."

I'm going to wake up any second now. I just know it. This dream is even worse than the one where Great White sharks are living under my carpet trying to eat me.

"I think my relationship with Aisling is between the two of us," Griffin said. "That's not why I'm here."

"What relationship?" Jerry asked, his hands on hips. "I don't consider a one-night stand and morning-after jilting a relationship."

"He has a point," Aidan said. "And I was on your side, dude."

"You're a bad, bad man," Jerry said.

This was getting out of hand.

"Detective Taylor, why don't you have a seat," Dad said.

Griffin looked unsure.

"Sit down, Detective Taylor."

Griffin looked unhappy at being talked down to, but he did as he was told, opting for one of the wingback chairs in front of my father's desk.

Dad turned his attention to everyone else in the room. "Boys, sit down."

Redmond, Cillian and Braden all shuffled to the couch I was sitting on, sandwiching me between them as they scrunched in. The message was clear: If Griffin wanted to get near me he would have to go through them.

Aidan settled on the other couch with Jerry, but he didn't look happy about it. I think, if I wasn't so sore, he would have tried to settle on my lap to make the Grimlock wall complete.

"Detective Taylor, I'm not going to lie to you," Dad said. "I'm not thrilled with what I've just heard about you."

Griffin opened his mouth to speak but Dad silenced him with a look.

"Raising boys isn't easy, but it's certainly easier than raising a girl," Dad continued. "One minute they're rosy-cheeked little moppets with dolls and stuffed animals and your biggest concern is that they want to curl your hair and put makeup on you."

"That was Aidan," I protested.

Dad shot me a hard glare.

"Then, practically overnight, they turn into these giggling little phone-obsessed aliens in your house," he said. "That's when your worries begin. And why, you may be asking yourself? Because you know what dogs men are."

I couldn't argue with that.

"The last thing you want for your daughter is to get caught up with the kind of man who isn't going to treat her right," Dad went on. "At a certain point, though, you realize that no man is going to treat her right because it isn't possible."

"Does anyone know where he's going with this?" Cillian whispered.

"I think he's saying we're all dogs," Redmond said.

"I got that," Cillian said. "Why is he telling this to Detective Dinglefritz, though?"

Griffin shifted his eyes in our direction. His face was unreadable.

"I'm telling this to Detective Dinglefritz, I mean Detective Taylor, because I want him to be aware of where he stands in this family," Dad said.

"Last time I checked, I'm not a part of your family," Griffin said.

The jab hurt.

"Just be aware that if you hurt my daughter again, this family is going to bury you," Dad said. "And we're reapers, so we know how to hide a body. I want to make sure that you're clear that when I say bury, I mean in the literal sense of the word."

The chill in the room was unmistakable.

"Now, with that out of the way, what is it that you wanted to talk with us about?"

Griffin pulled his phone out of his pocket, fiddling with it for a second, and then handing it over to my father. Dad took the phone without saying a word and glanced down at the screen. His frown deepened. "What am I looking at?"

"It's a symbol," Griffin said. "It was found burned into Brian Harper's body. We've had people researching the symbol, but we can't find anyone who knows what it is. I figured since you guys seem to know a little bit about things that other people don't know exist, you might be able to tell me what it is."

"It looks familiar," Dad admitted. "I'm just not sure. Cillian?"

Cillian took the phone and looked at it, furrowing his brow. "This does look familiar."

Cillian handed the phone to Redmond so everyone could pass it around. When I finally saw it, I felt a stirring in my memory, even though I couldn't quite hold on to the thread.

"It looks like a Celtic symbol, or Greek," Braden said.

"I think it's Greek," Cillian agreed. "It's got that little eye thing. I see that a lot in Greek mythology."

We're so scholarly sometimes.

"May I ask, how was it burned into the body?" Dad asked. "Was it a brand?"

Griffin shook his head. "The medical examiner says that if it were a brand there would be bits of skin missing when the brand was pulled away. So, no, it's not a brand."

"It looks as though this was on the victim's shoulder," Aidan said when he got a chance to look at the photo.

"Right above the heart," Griffin said.

"Well, the question is, how did it get there?" Dad mused.

"Well, do those wraith things burn it there with their minds?" Griffin asked, searching the room for an answer and finally landing on me. "And if these wraiths can suck the life out of people, why are they stabbing them?"

That was a good question.

I shrugged. "We haven't actually had a wraith problem until the last two weeks," I said. "They're supposed to be rare. Maybe someone else stabbed Brian Harper and they sucked his soul after the fact."

"Why would they be here then?"

"That's what we keep asking ourselves," Braden sighed, shifting on the couch and jarring my knee. "Sorry," he said, rubbing my shoulder. "I keep forgetting how banged up you are."

Griffin frowned. "Should she be in the hospital?"

"And how do we explain that?" Aidan asked. "Oh, yeah, two ghouls jumped her in downtown Royal Oak?"

Griffin rubbed his jaw. "I guess you're right. If you say she was mugged, then they would have called us and you would have had to file a false police report."

Aidan rolled his eyes. "Yeah, that's why we didn't do it."

"I thought we didn't take her to the hospital because we didn't want Detective Dinglefritz showing up?" Jerry asked.

"Jerry, it's quiet time for you," Dad admonished him.

Griffin got up from the chair and moved toward me, ignoring the rumbling emanating from Redmond's chest. He knelt down in front of me, searching my eyes for a second. "Do you think you should go to the hospital? I'll take you."

"I'm fine," I said. "It's just a sore knee and a torn up elbow – and my face is a little bruised."

"And that huge bruise on your ass," Aidan said.

Redmond shot Aidan an incredulous look.

"What? I was there and she had to take her pants off so I could get a look at her knee," Aidan protested. "It's not as though I looked."

"You obviously looked," Redmond said. "She's your sister."

"Dude," Braden muttered.

"Hey, you weren't there," Aidan said. "You didn't see her two seconds from death and you didn't shove a knife into the chest of two soul-sucking asshats to save her. Don't judge me."

"Leave him alone," I said.

Griffin hadn't moved. "Are you sure you're all right?"

If I weren't so angry with him, his concern would have touched me. "I'm fine."

Griffin got back to his feet and turned. "So, what happens now?"

"Now?" Dad looked nonplussed. "Now we have the same problem we had a week ago and no answers to solve it. The only thing we know is that Aisling and Aidan have managed to kill three of them and that, for some reason, they're focusing on Aisling."

Griffin's eyebrows shot up. "What makes you say that?"

"Because they've only appeared on her jobs," Braden said.

"None of the rest of you have seen them?"

"No."

"Well, then she can't go out on any more jobs," Griffin said.

"Since when are you the boss of me?" I asked.

Griffin ignored me. "I'm not joking."

"She's right, you're not in charge," Dad said. "That being said, she's not going out on any jobs until we know what's going on here."

My mouth opened to argue but, who am I kidding, I'm too sore to care.

"If the numbers we got from the club the other night are right, that means there are only four left," Redmond said.

"We don't know that, though," Aidan said. "We just know that at least seven of them were sighted together. We have no idea whether that means there are only seven or at least seven."

"They're not the big worry either," Cillian said. "Not that they're not something to worry about."

"No," Dad agreed. "The big worry is whoever is controlling the wraiths."

"And we're still thinking it's a witch?" I asked.

"A witch?" Griffin's face drained of color. "Now there are witches, too?"

"There are lots of things out there," Jerry said. "Just go with it."

"What makes you think a witch is behind this?" Griffin said, recovering slightly.

199

I glanced at Cillian. "You're on."

Cillian repeated the story of Genevieve Torth – not shortening it, even a little – and, when he was done, Griffin looked more confused than he had when Cillian started.

"You all believe in this?"

"We're reapers," I replied. "You'd be surprised at what we believe."

"And what we've seen," Redmond added.

"Oh, well good." Griffin's face went from disbelieving to weary as he sank back down in the wingback chair.

"I say we have some dinner," Dad said. "After that, we'll form a plan."

THIRTY-FIVE

"That's the plan?"

Dad focused on his cherry cobbler – my least favorite dessert – and pretended he didn't hear me. "This is really good tonight."

"You know I hate cherries," I grumbled, pushing my plate to the center of the table. You would think, after two near-death experiences in a row, that I would have warranted a blueberry pie or something.

Braden and Cillian both reached for my uneaten dessert.

"I want it," Cillian said, his mouth full.

"You've had enough," Braden countered. "You'll get fat."

Griffin was still at the table, picking at his own dessert. I had risked a few glances at him over the meal, but never caught him looking in my direction. I'm guessing his "thinking" wasn't going so well. Well, no matter, I never really liked him anyway.

"I'm still not clear on the plan," I said.

"What part confuses you?" Dad asked.

"The part where I go home and do nothing," I replied.

"You're injured," Redmond said.

"That won't last forever," I countered.

"It will last for the next week or so," Aidan said. "Besides, if we keep you away from jobs, that might force the wraiths to show up when we're covering.

If everything goes as planned, we can pick them off one at a time. By the time you get back on the job, things will hopefully be more settled."

"And you're big, strong men," I muttered.

"What?" Braden raised an eyebrow, challenging me to say more.

"And you're big, strong men," I repeated. "You can handle the wraiths while I lie on the couch and watch soap operas. That's what you have in mind, right? That's what you're really saying."

Redmond blew out a sigh. "You have got to get over this boys-against-girls thing. That's not what this is about."

I crossed my arms over my chest. "Then why does it feel like that is exactly what this is about?"

"Because you're all hopped up on estrogen and ... PMS," Redmond shot back.

"Not for two weeks," Jerry said.

I wanted to crawl across the table and strangle him.

From his spot on the other side of the table, I couldn't miss Griffin's smirk as he silently laughed. Great.

Cillian wrinkled his nose as he regarded Jerry. "How do you know that?"

"I live with her," Jerry said, nonplussed. "It's pretty obvious when it's going on."

"How?" Braden looked mildly curious – and majorly grossed out.

"The garbage can," Jerry said.

"Eww," Aidan said.

"Can we not talk about this while I'm eating my cherry cobbler?" Cillian asked.

"Can we not talk about this ever again?" Redmond chimed in.

"I wish I was an only child," I said.

Dad rubbed his forehead wearily. "On days like today, so do I."

ONCE DINNER WAS OVER, GRIFFIN ANNOUNCED HE WAS LEAVING. He leveled his gaze on me, forcing a tingle to course from my head to my toes. "Do you want to walk me out?"

Well, that was a loaded question. I could feel every set of purple eyes in the room boring into my back, causing my neck to heat up as I considered an answer. "Um, sure."

"I'll show him out," Redmond interjected. "You need to rest."

"I can show him out," I protested. "I'm not a child. It's not like he's going to jump me in the bushes in front of the house."

Dad cleared his throat but didn't offer an argument. I met Redmond's eyes, challenging him to offer further complaint, but he wisely stepped back.

"Fine," Redmond said. "If you need me ... ."

"I'll yell," I finished.

I turned to Griffin, moving toward the dining room door and leading him away from the overt anger emanating from the men in my life. Once we got to the door, I opened it and let him walk out in front of me. I shut the door behind us, making sure my brothers couldn't interrupt whatever sterling conversation Griffin and I were about to embark on.

I expected Griffin to yell at me for spilling about our tryst, but he seemed uncertain when we were finally alone.

"Well, what do you want to talk about?" I prodded.

"I'm not sure," Griffin admitted.

I bit my lip, fighting the urge to smack him across the face and then jump his bones while he was still reeling from the blow. Seriously, what is wrong with me? I sighed. "I'm sorry I told Aidan and Jerry what happened," I said. "I didn't plan to; it just kind of spilled out when we were fighting last night."

Griffin shrugged. "It's not like I'm ashamed."

His comment surprised me. "It's not? You couldn't get out of my place fast enough. Shame had to be involved in that decision somewhere." Do I sound bitter? I feel bitter.

"Not shame," Griffin corrected. "More like guilt and worry."

"Guilt?"

"I didn't go over to your place with the intention of, well, doing that."

I laughed, the sound hollow in my ears. "It's not like I think you're some sort of sexual predator."

Griffin shook his head, running a hand through his hair as he tried to gain control of his emotions. "Good. I just don't ... this is all really strange to me."

I tried to put myself in his place. "I understand that," I said. "I've turned your whole world upside down, challenged your belief system and made you rethink everything you thought you knew about the nature of life and death."

Griffin chuckled. "That's a little heavy-handed, don't you think?"

I shrugged. "My family says I'm the dramatic one."

"Your whole family is dramatic," Griffin replied. "I don't think you're on the top of the Grimlock list when it comes to drama."

I smiled ruefully. "Yeah, I guess not."

"Aisling, I don't want you to think that I don't find you attractive," Griffin

203

said, trying not to choke on the words. "I do. That's why what happened the other night happened. Since the minute I saw you, I couldn't help but be drawn to you. It's been building inside of me."

That was nice to hear. I think.

"I also don't want you to think that I can just accept this all in a matter of days and sign up for the Grimlock crazy parade," he continued. "I need to sort this all out."

His words hurt, even though I don't think that was the intent behind them. "It's fine," I said, trying to project an air of breeziness. "It's not like I'm sitting in my bedroom crying about you while listening to sappy love songs."

Griffin inclined his head. "I would be okay with that if you were," he said.

"How so?"

Griffin puffed out his chest. "If you were pining for me, I would be okay with it."

I shook my head, trying to hide my smile. "Typical man."

"I have a feeling you're used to being around men and the strange ways they think," Griffin said. "At least I have that going for me."

He wasn't wrong.

"Still, I don't know how this is all going to go," Griffin said. "I just want to get through this and then we'll see ... we'll see where things are when I can wrap my head around everything, when I've had a few days to breathe."

Something about his statement hit a nerve. "I'm not going to sit around waiting for you," I challenged. "You're not that good in bed, no matter what you may think."

Griffin's eyes widened, surprise and hurt warring for control. "That's not what I meant."

"I know what you meant," I said, taking a step away from him. "You need to think. No one is stopping you. I'm not asking for anything from you. I'm a big girl. It's not like I'm looking for wine and roses."

It was pride talking. I knew that. I didn't know how else to handle the situation, though. Being close to him was doing weird things to my head – and my heart – and things were getting jumbled.

"So, you don't want ... you just want to forget the other night happened?" Griffin looked pained.

That was the exact opposite of what I wanted. I couldn't tell him that without laying myself bare, though, and I couldn't bear the thought of being vulnerable and letting him have all the power. Still, I couldn't bring myself to say the words I knew I should.

"I think you should take some time and think," I said finally. "When you figure things out, when this is all over, we'll see how we both feel."

Griffin's eyes searched my face for a moment. "I need you to be careful," he said.

"I am careful," I said. "It's not like I go out looking for this stuff, no matter what my brothers say to the contrary."

"No," Griffin agreed. "It seems to find you, though. It's like you're a magnet for trouble, and that scares me. Even with all this stuff going on, the one thing I'm sure about is that I don't want anything bad to happen to you."

His words warmed me. "We can both agree on that."

"That we don't want anything to happen to you?"

I nodded, smiling despite myself. "Absolutely."

Griffin reached out, taking my hand in his. "Just be careful."

I tried to tamp down the warmth creeping up my body at his touch. "You, too."

"I don't think I'm the one in danger," Griffin said.

"You're a cop," I replied. "Aren't you always in danger, especially in Detroit?"

"I guess," Griffin agreed. "Somehow, I think the danger I'm in on a day-to-day basis is a little different than the danger you're in."

"Not usually," I countered. "When wraiths aren't around, being a reaper is pretty boring. It's kind of like being a travel agent – without the free first-class upgrades."

Griffin smirked. "That's an interesting way of looking at things."

"I'm nothing if not interesting," I teased.

Griffin, still holding my hand, reached up with his other and brushed a strand of hair from my face. "This is all going to be okay, right? Your family will be able to handle this and things will be fine."

I didn't know who he was trying to convince, himself or me. I didn't have the heart to tell him that I had no idea how this would end so I did what came naturally: I lied. "It's going to be fine."

Griffin pulled my hand up and pressed a quick kiss into my palm before turning and moving down the front walk. "Don't forget what you promised," he called back.

"And what did I promise?"

"That you will be careful."

"I won't forget."

Griffin was almost to his car, which was parked at the curb in front of the house. "Oh, and Aisling," he said, turning back to face me. "You turned my world upside down before I knew what you were. Don't forget that."

My heart flip-flopped as I watched him drive away.

Crap. I'm in so far over my head here.

36
THIRTY-SIX

Once back at the condo, I left Aidan and Jerry to watch a movie – and whatever else they had planned (which I didn't want to know about) – and climbed into bed. My body was still sore from the wraith attack, but for the first time in days I felt a sense of hope.

Unfortunately, that hope was wrapped around Griffin, which made me feel a little pathetic. When you grow up in a family of men, you learn at an early age that you don't want to give a man the power in a relationship. Where Griffin was concerned, I felt utterly powerless. And, while that's exciting in some ways, it's terrifying in others.

Despite my busy mind, I dropped off to sleep relatively quickly. At some point in the night, though, something woke me. I bolted to a sitting position, my heart racing, and wracked my brain to remember what I had been dreaming about.

Then it hit me: The symbol. The symbol burned into Brian Harper's body. I knew where I had seen it before.

I tossed the covers off and climbed out of bed, pushing the pain in my knee out of my mind. Aidan and Jerry weren't in the living room. A quick look at the clock told me it was almost 2 a.m. They were probably in bed. I could only hope they were sleeping.

I made my decision quickly. I would go and check my hunch. It wouldn't take long and, if I was right, I could tell Aidan about it in the morning.

I dressed quietly, climbing into simple yoga pants, a tank top and a dark hoodie to ward off the cold. I grabbed my keys from the hook on the wall and let myself out of the condo carefully, making sure not to make any noise as I exited.

Once in the car, I jumped on the freeway and headed toward Detroit. It took me fifteen minutes – the roads were mostly empty at this hour – before I finally got to my destination: Eternal Sunshine Cemetery.

The gate was locked, so I had no choice but to park on the street and slip through the gate bars. It was a tight fit. For the first time tonight I was glad dessert was so gross that I hadn't eaten any.

You would think that a reaper has occasion to spend a lot of time in cemeteries. You would be wrong. By the time bodies get to cemeteries their souls are long gone. So, no, I wasn't familiar with this cemetery because of my work. I was familiar with this cemetery because this is where my mom was laid to rest.

Eternal Sunshine is big – one of the biggest cemeteries in the area – but I knew exactly where I was going. The ambient light from the streetlights on the road surrounding the cemetery allowed me the ability to navigate the cobblestone paths without tripping.

My mom was in the family mausoleum, located in one of the older sections of the cemetery. Grimlocks have been laid to rest in it for more than a century, but I visit only on my mom's birthday to leave her a bouquet of lilies. They were her favorite, and that's not just because she was named after them.

It took me a few minutes to find what I was looking for: the Olivet mausoleum. It was two spots away from our mausoleum, and I had seen it so many times that I couldn't believe that the symbol etched on its door didn't jog my memory when Griffin was passing around his phone earlier.

I pulled my cell phone out of my pocket and tapped the flashlight app just to be sure. As soon as the light fell on the door I felt a chill rush through me. I turned the flashlight app off – it drains your battery pretty quickly – and considered my options.

A smart person would turn around and go home, I told myself. She wouldn't go into that mausoleum – in the dead of night – and snoop around. I reminded myself of my promise to Griffin, forcing my body to reluctantly turn and walk away. I was a smart person, no matter what the rest of my family thought.

I was twenty feet down the path when another thought gave me pause. It couldn't do any harm to look. Maybe if I saw some other occult symbols inside the mausoleum I would be able to help Cillian with his research.

What? That's a valid reason to look in that mausoleum. I'm certainly not doing it to prove something to anyone, especially my brothers.

Yeah, I don't believe it either.

Still, I'm not a complete idiot. I pulled the phone out of my pocket again and sent a short text to Aidan.

I found the symbol. It's on the Olivet Mausoleum – in the same row as our mausoleum. Going to check it out. Be home soon.

I flicked the button on my iPhone so it wouldn't alert me to any incoming texts or phone calls and then slipped it back into my pocket. There. I covered my bases. Odds are I'll be back home, in bed, before Aidan even sees the text.

I strode back to the mausoleum, took a deep breath and turned the door handle. It was locked.

I shouldn't have been surprised. People break into these things to steal all the time, especially in a city as economically depressed as Detroit. Still, I couldn't quite swallow my disappointment. I shouldn't have sent the text. I could hear Aidan howling about my stupidity now.

I tried the door again – not that I was expecting a different outcome – and then blew out a frustrated sigh as I turned to leave. Well, at least I had found the symbol. That was something. Unfortunately, that wasn't all I found. When I turned, I realized I was no longer alone – and in a lot more trouble than I initially thought possible.

"Hey guys," I greeted the two wraiths with faux enthusiasm. "Nice night, huh?"

The wraiths stood like twin pillars of dark death. I guess when you start sucking souls in an attempt to hold on to a life that is no longer yours the sense of humor goes first.

I bit my lower lip, considering my options. If I fled in the opposite direction I would be heading deeper into the cemetery. I had never been to the far end of it, but I was pretty sure the same brick walls that covered the front surrounded the back. Otherwise, the gate wouldn't be necessary – and locking it would be a moot point.

On the flip side, even if I had a weapon – which I didn't think to bring (so much for being smart) – I couldn't guarantee my ability to fight off two wraiths in the dark. I could try to track a wide circle and get behind them, but I wasn't feeling all that comfortable with that scenario either.

Well, crap.

"So," I tried again. "I don't suppose you guys are just out for a midnight stroll and I can just be on my way?"

No answer, just that airy hiss that was starting to invade my dreams nightly.

"How about a truce," I offered. "We all can just agree that it's late, we're tired and we'll pick this up tomorrow. We can even set up a meeting time and place and the fight will be so much more interesting after a full night of rest." What? It might work. Wraiths aren't admitted to Mensa membership on a regular basis.

Still nothing.

"Okay," I held up my hands in surrender. "Take me to your leader."

The wraiths remained where they were, not a hint of movement or understanding emanating from them.

Maybe they're confused? Maybe they don't know who I am? Maybe I'm deluding myself? That sounds more likely.

I took a step to my right. The wraiths remained immobile so I took another step, and then another. I almost convinced myself that I was going to be able to get away, that they were going to just stand there while I moseyed out of the cemetery. That's when I noticed another pair of wraiths standing beside a large willow tree about twenty feet down the path.

Well, double crap.

"Did someone forget to send my invitation to the party?" The fear in my voice was evident despite my feigned bluster.

I glanced around, peering into the dark to see whether I could find more hidden wraiths. After a few moments, I was fairly sure that it was just the four of them. That was still four too many.

I was out of options. I could run or I could die. Maybe, if I was lucky, I would be able to hide in the cemetery until it opened the next morning. The wraiths would be less likely to show themselves once the groundskeepers and visitors started to arrive. Plus, once Aidan got the text, he would call the rest of our family and they would come. I just needed to hide for a few hours.

I edged over to my right, making sure I had a clear shot around the mausoleum. It was now or never.

That's when someone else joined the party.

"Freeze!"

37

THIRTY-SEVEN

"Griffin?"

Relief washed over me – followed closely by a new wave of terror. What was he doing here? How had he found me? Did Aidan call him? No, that wasn't possible, I had sent the text just a few minutes ago. Even though I wasn't alone now, that didn't mean I was safe. All that it meant was that Griffin would probably die, too.

"Aisling, stay where you are," Griffin ordered.

It was hard to see his face in the dark, but the tone of his voice told me he was deadly serious.

"There are four of them," I said. "There are two more under the tree over there."

"I saw them."

Griffin's arms were locked and, even though I couldn't see him clearly, I knew he had a gun in his hand. I had no idea, though, whether a gun would have any effect on the wraiths. I had never really thought about it before.

"You should run," I said. He still had a chance. He could get out of the cemetery. He wasn't surrounded. "Go and get help."

"You think I'm going to leave you?" Griffin's voice was steady, but his anger obvious.

"If you stay we'll both die," I said, trying to be pragmatic. "If you go, there's a chance you can get help."

"If I go you'll be dead," Griffin replied.

"If you stay I'll probably still be dead." I hated the hitch in my voice.

"Well, I guess we'll just have to find out then, because I'm not leaving you."

The wraiths closest to me hadn't turned their attention to Griffin despite the gun in his hand. The two other wraiths, though, were starting to edge closer.

"Do you have any ideas on how to get out of this?" I didn't expect an answer; I just wanted to hear the sound of his voice. It was the only thing keeping me sane.

"Not particularly," Griffin admitted. "If I shoot these things will it hurt them?"

"I don't know," I admitted. "If you do shoot them, aim for the heart. That's how we killed the others."

"Does it have to be silver, though?" Griffin sounded worried. "Didn't you have to use silver when you killed the one at the retirement center? That's what you said after, when we were talking in the room."

"Yeah, but the knife Aidan used wasn't silver," I said. "I think it just has to be a direct wound to the heart."

Griffin grunted. "Great. And where is the heart on a seven-foot freak?"

"Just guess," I suggested.

"I can't just shoot them," Griffin argued. "I have to give them proper warning."

"They're not people," I said. "And I think that you've given them proper warning. They're not deaf."

"Didn't they used to be people?"

"A long time ago," I said. "Now they're ghouls. They don't have souls and they're not alive. Just shoot one and see what happens."

"I don't know if I can," Griffin said, his voice strangled.

He was in an untenable situation. I knew he would rather be anywhere but here. I also knew that we didn't have a lot of choices. "This isn't much of a rescue."

"You wouldn't have needed a rescue if you had stayed home and safe like you were supposed to," Griffin shot back. "I knew you wouldn't, though. How do you think I found you?"

"You followed me? What, were you parked outside my condo?" Men, I swear.

"I wanted to make sure you were safe," Griffin replied.

"It's still an invasion of privacy."

"And where would you be now if I hadn't done it?"

"The same place I am now." What? It's the truth.

"Are you trying to piss me off?"

"Is it working?"

"Yes," Griffin growled.

"Then shoot something," I said. "It will make you feel better."

"Just be quiet," Griffin ordered. "I need to think."

"Is that your answer to everything?" I grumbled.

"I heard that."

"Good."

Apparently the wraiths weren't entertained by our banter because they started to move. The two closest to the mausoleum were on me before I could warn Griffin about the two moving in on him.

The wraiths tumbled me onto the ground, my breath trapped in my chest, as the white hands of death closed around my throat. I bucked up, trying to dislodge the wraith from my chest, but I was drained already. Obviously a wraith has the ability to suck a soul from a living person with its hands – no scepter required. That little tidbit might have come in handy earlier. I fought against my captors, jolting when I heard Griffin's gun go off. I couldn't see him, though, so I had no idea whether he hit anything.

I was starting to lose consciousness. From the lack of oxygen or the wraith's hands, I had no idea. I reached up, wrapping my own fingers around the wraith's claws, trying one last time to push them from my neck.

Griffin's gun went off again. I registered the sound, but my mind was drifting. My last thought was of Griffin – and then everything was black.

I HAVE no idea how long I was out. Consciousness reclaimed me in a slow and painful trickle, gradually building to a fast-moving river and then crescendoing with a waterfall of agony.

"Sonofabitch!"

"Are you okay?"

It took me a second to regain my senses. When I did, I found myself in a small room, marble statues on each wall and memorial plaques in every direction. We were in a mausoleum – the Olivet one, if I had to guess.

I was on the floor, my back propped against one of the marble walls. Griffin was at my side, his leg pressed against mine and his arm around my shoulders. I risked a glance at his face, the left side already coloring with what was sure to be a world-class bruise – if we lived long enough for the color to set, that is.

"What happened?"

"Well, we didn't win."

"I figured that out." We appeared to be alone. The wraiths were gone and the mausoleum was empty. "Where are they?"

"One of them is gone," Griffin said. "The other three are somewhere outside. I heard a woman's voice talking to them when I came to."

"A woman's voice? You're sure?"

"Yeah, I'm sure."

I reached a hand to my temple, touching it experimentally. When I pulled my fingers back I saw blood. "How did this happen?"

"I don't know," Griffin admitted. "I couldn't see you. When they got their hands on me it was like … it was like I couldn't breathe. I managed to get one in the heart and it just kind of blew up in a dust bomb or something. I winged the other one, but it wasn't enough to take it down."

"You should have … ."

"Don't even say I should have listened to you," Griffin said. "I already know that. Those things aren't human. It's just hard to kill something without giving them a chance to surrender."

"Wraiths don't understand surrender," I said. "They understand eating and nothing else."

"Well, next time."

I knew he was going for levity, but I couldn't join in. "Why haven't they killed us?"

"I have no idea," Griffin said. "I thought when I lost consciousness that was it. I figured one of your brothers would show up and collect my soul and that would be it."

He had a point, although I don't think he realized it.

"You're not on a list," I said after a second. "I'm not either. If we were, my brothers would have been tipped off that something was going down and they would have locked me in the manor and kept me under armed guard."

Griffin looked confused. "Is that a good thing?"

"That we're not a list? Yeah."

"Does that mean we're not going to die here?"

Now wasn't the time to lie. "I don't know," I admitted. "If a wraith sucks us dry, there's no soul to collect."

"So we might not show up on the list," Griffin mused.

"Still, if our deaths are ordained, we should show up on the list." I was trying to make both of us feel better.

"So, we might still get out of this?" Griffin was hopeful.

"If we're lucky."

"Any idea how?" Griffin wasn't going to rely on hope. He was the sort of man who needed a plan.

"I have one idea," I said.

"And that is?"

"Aidan."

"Aidan? He doesn't know you came here, does he?" Griffin's face flooded with anger. "How could he let you come here in the middle of the night after everything that's happened?"

"I didn't tell him before I left," I explained. "I texted him before I tried to get in the mausoleum."

"Which was stupid."

"Why didn't you try to stop me earlier then?"

"Because I wasn't sure what you were doing," Griffin admitted. "Then, when I saw you came to a cemetery in the middle of the night, I wanted to follow you and find out what you were doing."

Realization dawned on me. "You were spying on me. You thought I was hiding something from you."

Griffin bit the inside of his cheek. "I wasn't sure."

"You thought I was lying."

"I didn't think you were lying," he hedged. "I thought maybe you knew something and you didn't want to tell me."

How is that different from lying? "I am insulted."

"Well, great, that should help the situation," Griffin replied.

"Sarcasm isn't going to help either."

"Really?"

He wasn't so cute anymore. Oh, who am I kidding? He's still hot. He's just a royal pain in the ass, too.

"We just have to remain calm," I said. "The wraiths were obviously ordered not to kill us."

"Why?"

"Because whoever is in charge wants something else."

"And what would that be?"

I remained silent, but Griffin knew.

"You," he breathed. "She wants you."

"That would be my guess."

"Why?"

"I have no idea," I replied honestly.

"So, basically, we're at the whim of a crazy woman who is trying to use wraiths to keep herself alive," Griffin said. "We have no idea whether your brother even knows he has a text from you, but we have a good idea you're the prize in this scenario and I'm just cannon fodder."

I knew he was thinking out loud, but Griffin's tone chafed. "Aidan sleeps with that phone by his head. He knows. He's on his way."

Under normal circumstances that would be true. Jerry and Aidan's new relationship wasn't normal, though. Still, he was my best hope – my only hope, actually.

"Do you really believe that?"

"I have to," I said. "He's never let me down before. He won't start now."

Griffin sighed. "I hope your faith in your family isn't misplaced."

"My faith in my family is never misplaced," I countered. "They're good people. They're good men."

Griffin tightened his arm around my shoulder. "It's going to be okay, Aisling."

"How can you be so sure?"

"I'm not," Griffin admitted. "That's just what you say in situations like this."

"Have you been in a lot of situations like this?"

"No," Griffin shook his head. "I have faith in you, though. If you believe in them, I believe in them."

I rested my head on Griffin's shoulder, taking strength from his belief. "It's going to be okay."

"It's going to be okay," he repeated.

We both jumped when the door to the mausoleum opened. Part of me expected Aidan to be standing there, eyes blazing, churlish remark about my stupidity on his lips. Instead, a red-haired woman in a purple cloak and velvet dress – totally tacky, by the way -- walked into the crypt.

Her skin was chalky, her lips bright red and her eyes – well, they were as black as coal.

I don't know how I knew. I didn't really know – it was more of a guess really. I said it anyway. "You're Genevieve Torth, aren't you?"

The woman smiled, revealing a row of teeth that harkened back to the days before dentists began working their magic.

"Hello, Aisling Grimlock," she said. "I've been waiting for you."

THIRTY-EIGHT

I tried to wrap my brain around our predicament. I decided to go with snark and sarcasm. They were my best defense.

"Well, you know women, we're always late."

Griffin grunted next to me, but kept his thoughts to himself.

"Yes, that is a particular weakness of our gender," the woman agreed. "Still, I'm betting you're worth the wait."

I wasn't sure how to take that statement, so I ignored it. "So, are you Genevieve Torth?"

The woman nodded, smoothing her dress as she leaned against the wall. She hadn't brought the wraiths in with her – which meant she didn't fear us – but she was keeping her distance. "I see my reputation precedes me."

"Reputation, urban legend, horror story," I said. "None of them are particularly flattering."

"And what is it you think you know about me, my dear?"

"I think you've been sacrificing people for centuries as a way to prolong your own life," I replied. "I think you've changed your identity multiple times, but some things can't be changed." Like narcissism and a God complex.

"And yet you had no idea I was still alive," Genevieve said. "I guess I must have been doing something right."

"Yeah? What was that?"

"I am 362 years old," she replied. "That should earn some measure of respect, even from a girl such as you."

"Respect is earned," I countered. "You haven't earned squat."

"I've earned the right not to be talked down to by a child," Genevieve warned. "I would be careful with your tone."

"Why? You're either going to kill me or you're not. I don't see how my tone is going to change the outcome."

Genevieve smiled again. It was eerie. She tilted her head to the side, considering. "You have a point."

"Great," I said. "Now that we agree on something, I don't suppose you could just cut to the chase. Why are you here? And how are you still alive?"

"Here in this mausoleum? Or here in Michigan?"

"Both, actually."

"Well, we're in this mausoleum because this is where my family is," she said. "And, despite all I've seen, I still have a certain … love for my family."

Now I was confused. "You're an Olivet?"

"No," Genevieve replied, shaking her head. "My daughter married one, though."

So she did have a daughter. "And what happened to her? She didn't want to live forever?"

"No, my Angelica was more pragmatic," Genevieve explained. "She believed we were only supposed to live on this Earth for a short time and then move on to something better. That was a belief I couldn't get behind."

"She was religious?"

"She was a Christian," Genevieve said, her disdain evident. "I tried to explain the stupidity of that choice, but she wouldn't listen."

"Maybe she didn't think it was stupid," I said. "Maybe she wanted to believe in something bigger. Maybe she was right."

"She died when she was 32, in childbirth," Genevieve shot back. "How right could she be?"

"So she married into the Olivet family, had a child and cast off your beliefs," I mused, thinking of my father. "That must have driven you crazy."

"It didn't sit well," Genevieve agreed. "I went back to Salem before her death and tried to change her mind, but she was adamant she was right. Look how that turned out for her."

"Kids," I shrugged. "They're going to follow their own path, no matter what you want them to do."

"This is true," Genevieve said.

"How come none of the history texts mention her?" I was stalling for time. The longer I kept Genevieve talking, the longer Aidan had to realize I was in trouble.

"Angelica went to great lengths to disavow any ties to me," she replied. "She changed her last name before the problems in Salem arose. She knew what I was doing. She wanted to leave. She just couldn't come up with a plausible reason for her husband to uproot his entire existence, though, so she stayed."

"It must have been hard for her," I said. "And you, actually. Did she make you pretend you didn't know her?"

"We made an ... exchange," Genevieve said. "I agreed to keep her secret, if she agreed to keep mine."

"And did she? Keep yours, I mean. It must have been hard for her when she found out you were sacrificing innocent women to protect your secret."

"You understand this better than I could have hoped," she said. "Yes, when it became apparent what I was doing, Angelica had some ... issues."

That didn't sound good. "And how did you handle those issues?"

"Do you think I killed her?"

"No," I replied honestly. "You said she died in childbirth. That would have been long after you fled Salem."

"You are correct," Genevieve's smile was genuine, if no less creepy. "I considered killing her. I know, coming from a mother that sounds horrible. I was at a crossroads, though. I didn't want to leave my home, but I didn't want to kill my daughter."

"She told the truth, didn't she?"

"She did."

"That's why you ran."

"Yes."

Griffin was silent next to me. The only reason I knew he was still listening was the occasional tightening of his hand on my shoulder.

"So you ran, ending up in London," I said. "Where did you go after New Orleans? The texts lose track of you."

"I think the proper question is, where haven't I been," Genevieve said. "I have lived many places. I have been many people. I have loved many times. I have lost many times. And yet, I remain."

"Is that really living, though?"

"Is what living?"

"Going through life without family?"

"You have to make certain adjustments when you choose to live as I have," Genevieve said. "For a long time I convinced myself that family wasn't important."

"Did something change your mind?"

"Time," Genevieve said. "Living forever has its benefits. It also has certain drawbacks."

"Like?"

"Like losing your anchor, your focus," she said. "When you find yourself drifting with no purpose other than extending your own life things start to shift into perspective."

"And what things shifted for you?"

"The things you might expect," Genevieve admitted. "I found that I wanted more. I wanted a family. I wanted to be with my blood, however far removed."

She wasn't making a lot of sense. "Exactly how did you extend your life and not become a wraith?"

Genevieve smiled. "I cast a spell," she said. "I agreed to provide them with ... nourishment. As part of the spell, though, part of the life essence they were absorbing was passed on to me."

Huh. "Then why aren't you a wraith?"

"Because I'm not the one procuring the souls," she replied.

"I still don't get how that works," I admitted.

"It's a long process, a hard spell," Genevieve said. "Each time I cast the spell, it gets harder in some respects. It has been worth it, though. I've seen more marvels than a woman of my time could imagine.

"Of course, while my wraiths are stronger than normal wraiths, they also burn out quicker because they're not getting the same amount of nourishment they normally would," she continued.

"I bet you didn't tell them that when you partnered with them," I grumbled.

"No," Genevieve chuckled. "No, that wouldn't go over well."

We lapsed into silence for a second.

"How did you lose the grimoire?" I asked finally.

Griffin stirred next to me, clearly approving of my question.

"That isn't the exciting story you likely think it is," she replied. "I moved to Detroit to find some of my descendants. Unfortunately, the woman who lived next door realized what I was; I'm still not sure how. I thought I had the situation taken care of, but I was wrong.

"I didn't realize until it was too late," she continued. "There were fifty people on my front lawn, torches in hand – some things never go out of style

– and I didn't have a lot of time to think. I thought I could come back for the grimoire, but it didn't happen. I got distracted. The computer age has been a godsend, though. Finding it in Brian Harper's clutches was a stroke of luck."

"If you've lived this long, why did you need it?"

"Because it's mine."

That sounds reasonable – if you're crazy.

"So, you tracked your family lineage to the Detroit area and settled here before being forced out," I said. "Then what?"

"Then I wandered for a while, never taking my eye off my family but not getting close enough to actually contact them until a certain opportunity arose," she said, clearly relishing her story.

I was almost afraid to ask. "What opportunity?"

Genevieve clapped her hands together excitedly. "I was hoping you would ask that." She moved toward us, reaching into the pocket of her dress and pulling a small trinket out as she approached. "Open your hand."

I wasn't sure it was a good idea, but I followed her order. She dropped the trinket into my palm and then moved a few paces away, waiting for my reaction.

I exchanged a wary glance with Griffin and then focused on the piece of jewelry in my hand. It was a ring – a wedding ring, to be exact. There were no discernible markings and, while it was gold, it didn't look particularly valuable. My eyes caught sight of some markings on the inside of the band, so I peered closer.

My love, my heart, forever. Cormack.

My heart clenched in my chest. "This is my mother's wedding ring," I rasped, confusion washing over me.

Griffin's face was unreadable, but his body stiffened at my words.

"How did you get this?" I pressed.

Genevieve smiled even wider. Seriously, she's lived for more than 300 years and she can't get some porcelain veneers or something? Heck, dentures would be better. "Think about it."

My mind was blank. "I don't ... ."

"Think about it," she pressed.

There was only one possibility. "We're related to the Olivets, aren't we?"

"Don't you know?"

Unfortunately, paying attention to the family tree had never been a high priority during my formative years. Still, the proximity of the vaults was a big hint. "I don't know," I admitted.

"So, you claim you're all about your family and yet you know nothing about your family?"

"I know that my family is my father and brothers," I replied. "I don't know about my ancestors. I've never really cared."

"Well, your ancestors are the same as mine," Genevieve said. "You are my family."

Great. I was descended from crazy. In hindsight, that shouldn't have come as a surprise. "You still haven't answered my question," I said, choosing my words carefully. "How did you get this?"

"From your mother, of course."

"But she had this with her ... she had this with her when she died," I said, a host of possibilities rushing through my mind. "The coroner identified her body, but the fire inspector said that the fire was too hot and the ring was lost."

"Aisling," Griffin started, but I ignored him.

"She died in the fire, right?"

"She did not die in the fire," Genevieve replied. "She was badly injured, very badly. I managed to get her out, though."

"How?"

"She was the last adult female of my line," she said. "I was watching her for a long time, watching all of you really. She took such joy in being a mother. She always had a ragtag group of you at her side.

"I wasn't sure at first – sure that I wanted to approach her," she continued. "She didn't seem special, and the probability of her being interested in what I had to offer was minor. It wasn't until the fire that I made my decision."

My heart was hammering in my chest. "You took her from the fire?"

"I did."

Hope sprang. "Is she alive?"

Genevieve smiled. "If she was alive, why would I need you?"

Hope died. "She's dead? She's dead?"

"She's gone," Genevieve confirmed. "That's why I came for you."

She was dead. She had lived longer than we thought, but she was still dead. It was like losing her all over again. I had so many questions. How long did she live? When did she die? Was she a captive? How did she die?

Griffin filled the overwhelming silence for me. "Why Aisling? Why not one of her brothers?"

"Men are such wastes," Genevieve replied. "They have no potential, no strength. They're considered the stronger sex, but they're not. They're weak. Their strength always fails. Always. That's not the case with women. Women are really the stronger sex, even though we're never treated as such."

Griffin glanced at me, trying to gauge my mental state. "I'm not disagreeing with you," he said. "If you're only interested in Aisling, why did you keep me alive?"

"As a gift for her, of course," Genevieve replied. "She would hardly trust me if I killed you. Although, to be fair, I have no idea what she sees in you."

"She's never going to trust you," Griffin countered, ignoring the jab. "You took her mother, kept her locked up, let her die away from her family. How does that equal trust?"

"Lily would have died in that fire," Genevieve countered. "I prolonged her life, gave her something she would never have had without me."

"What's that? Loneliness? Sadness?"

"You can never understand," Genevieve waved off Griffin. "Your mind isn't big enough to grasp what I'm offering here."

"And what are you offering?" I asked, my voice shaky.

"Eternity, of course," Genevieve said. "There are so many things I can teach you."

"How to kill people? How to lose my soul? How to watch my family die? Thanks, I'll pass."

Genevieve pursed her unnaturally red lips. "I don't think you understand."

"I understand," I argued. "I understand what you are, and I'm not interested in becoming like you. I'm fine being me."

"Being you? And what are you? A failed secretary? A college dropout? A pawn for your brothers to move around the chessboard? I can give you so much more. I can give you everything." She'd obviously been watching me for a long time.

I shook my head, rage coursing through me. "Can you give me my mother back? Can you give me the option of choosing my own life? Can you undo all the evil you've perpetrated?"

Genevieve didn't look happy. "I can give you forever."

"I don't want forever," I spat. "I want my life to be what it is. I don't want to live forever. I want to live what I was meant to live and then move on, like I'm supposed to move on."

"You're so much like Angelica." Genevieve meant it as an insult, but that's not how I took it.

"Good," I said. "Because I'm never going to be like you. Angelica is the hero in this story, not you."

"That's your final answer?"

"That's my only answer."

"So disappointing," Genevieve mused.

The room was silent now, my proclamation sucking the air out of the small enclosure. Griffin was tense, waiting. Had I just given Genevieve a reason to kill us both? She wasn't armed, and the wraiths were still outside, but something told me she had ways to protect herself.

The silence was interrupted by a loud bang on the other side of the door. I jumped. Griffin did, too. I could hear loud voices outside of the mausoleum.

"Aidan," I breathed.

"I think he has backup," Griffin agreed, craning his neck to hear more. The voices weren't clear, but there was definitely more than one person yelling on the other side of the door.

I glanced at Genevieve; she looked alarmed by the sudden disruption in our conversation. "Who is that?"

Hope swelled again. "My family."

"I am your family."

"No, you're not."

The mausoleum door flew open; only it wasn't Aidan standing there. Cormack Grimlock is a terrifying man under normal circumstances. Threaten one of his children, though, and there is no measure for his rage.

Dad's eyes flitted over to me, checking to make sure I was okay, before focusing on Genevieve. "I think you'll find that your first mistake was touching my daughter," he growled, brandishing a sword and repeating the words I had heard Aidan say only a night before. This is why he has so many "heirlooms" in the house, I thought, fighting the smile that was taking over my face. Boys like their toys. "I think you'll find your second mistake was underestimating exactly what I would do to get her back."

"You're no threat to me," Genevieve said, although she didn't look convinced. "I am the end of time."

Four other figures – all familiar – tumbled into the mausoleum behind my father. Each carried a sword and breathed heavily. Dad didn't move his eyes from Genevieve's face, though. He was focused.

"Then let's end your time," Dad said, his face grim. The sword flashed forward, slamming into Genevieve's chest.

For one breathless moment, I thought it was over. Unlike the wraiths, though, she didn't crumble into dust. The only change in her demeanor was a crazy laugh. "I am immortal."

Dad frowned, pulling the sword back. Instead of the red blood you would expect, the liquid coating the blade was black.

"Chop off her head," Redmond suggested. "Let's see her survive that."

Dad didn't need to be told twice. He reared back, this time taking a wide arc. Genevieve's eyes flashed in surprise, worry reflected there for a split second, before the sword hit its mark and separated her head from her shoulders.

Genevieve's head hit the ground with thump, her body tumbling beside it a second later. It wasn't long before both started oozing and melting into the floor.

Gross.

Now it was over.

THIRTY-NINE

Dad was sitting at his desk, flipping through the newspaper, when I finally mustered the courage to approach him.

It had been three days since the unfortunate events in the mausoleum, and the good news was that my brothers and father had finally started to calm down. Let me tell you, seventy-two hours of recriminations and intelligence jabs are not fun.

Since he hadn't noticed me I knocked on the door to get his attention. Dad glanced up, dropping the paper and motioning for me to enter. "Is something wrong?"

"No," I shook my head. "I just thought you should have this."

I had told Genevieve's story multiple times since my rescue, but for some reason I had left out the part about the ring each time. Now, though, I knew it was time. I placed the ring on his desk and took a step back.

I expected yelling. I expected anger. I expected accusations. Quite frankly, I expected him to try to ground me. What I got was tears.

"Where did you get this?"

"Genevieve had it," I said.

"Why didn't you tell me?"

I searched his face, but there was no anger there. "I don't know."

Dad fingered the ring, reading the words inside the band, and then clasped it in his hand. "It's hard to fathom," he said after a moment. "Your mother was alive, and I didn't know it."

"How could you?" I asked, slipping into one of the chairs across from his desk.

"When two souls collide and latch on to each other, you should know."

That seemed like a heavy burden. "If you should have known, then I should have known, too. She was my mother."

Dad smiled, the expression surprising me. "You may have been her daughter, but the connection we shared was different."

"Different how?"

"Not greater. Not better. Just different. You'll understand. Someday soon, if I read Detective Taylor's intentions correctly."

I blushed. "I haven't spoken to him since it happened. I think we freaked him out. He's done. I think you're reading the situation wrong."

Dad sighed. "That man sat outside your condominium to make sure you were safe," he said. "He kept our secret. He sat through two meals with your brothers – even though they were nothing but obnoxious to him. This whole situation may have confused the lad, but it hasn't deterred him."

"How can you be sure?" I tried to keep the hope from overtaking me.

"Because you're not that easy to forget," he replied.

"How do you know that?" I asked curiously.

"Because you are your mother's daughter."

I smiled, despite myself. "Not just hers, Dad."

LATER THAT NIGHT I WAS ENJOYING HAVING THE CONDO TO MYSELF – the fourth season of *The Walking Dead* in the Blu-Ray player -- when there was a knock at the door. I hit the pause button, biting my lower lip as I considered who could be on the other side.

No wraiths had been sighted since Genevieve's demise – and my brothers had managed to sweep out the goo so none of the Olivets would notice the mess – but I was still momentarily scared.

I tamped down the fear and moved toward the door, peering through the peephole before unlocking it. The figure standing on the other side was a welcome – if terrifying – one.

I took a deep breath, glanced down at my furry Hello Kitty pajama bottoms, and ran a hand through my hair. What the hell? I opened the door and came face to face with Griffin.

"Hey," I greeted him, hating how timid I sounded.

"Hey." He seemed just as nervous.

We both stood there awkwardly for a minute.

"Um, do you want to come in?"

"Sure."

I opened the door wider, letting Griffin in – my body tensing as we brushed together – and then closed the door behind him. When I finally gathered my courage and looked up, he wasn't there.

I wandered into the living room. He was standing in front of the television, his eyes trained on the screen. "This is a great show."

"It's one of my favorites," I agreed.

"Who is your favorite character?"

"Daryl."

"I like Rick."

I laughed. "Of course you do; he's a cop."

Griffin lifted his eyes to meet mine. "Right, because only a cop could like another cop."

I couldn't believe how nervous I was. "So, um, how are you?"

"How are you?"

"I asked first."

Griffin smirked. "I'm okay."

"Good."

"How are you?" He repeated.

"I'm better."

"Better than what?"

"Better than I was," I admitted. I considered sitting on the couch, but that seemed the wrong move. Instead, I stood there like an idiot, my hands clenched at my sides.

"You're okay, right?" Griffin seemed stuck on repeat.

"I'm better than okay," I said, and it was the truth.

Griffin looked confused.

"I gave my dad the ring tonight," I said. "I hadn't told him about it for some reason. I don't know why."

"Do you know why now?" Griffin looked curious.

"Fear? Is that a lame answer?"

"No," Griffin shook his head. "I think that's understandable. How did he take it?"

"I thought he would be angry."

Griffin waited.

"He cried."

Griffin swished his lips to the side. "That sounds about right."

"How?"

"He's got a piece of her back, another piece anyway."

I realized what he was saying. "Another piece besides me, you mean."

"Yes."

"I never understood before," I said, my emotions running deep.

"Understood what?"

"I always thought he hated having a daughter," I said. "I thought he would have been happier if I was a boy."

"And now?"

"Now I still think it would have been easier if I was a boy," I replied, the realization not filling me with anger for a change. "I just don't think he wishes I was a boy."

"That's progress, right?"

"It is," I agreed.

"If it's any conciliation, I'm pretty happy you're not a boy."

My heart started thumping harder. "And why is that?"

"Because, if you were a boy, I would feel pretty stupid doing this." Griffin was across the room, his mouth on mine, before I had a chance to think about what was going to happen. The kiss was deep, full of yearning and more combustible heat than I ever thought possible. I sank into it, despite the misgivings tickling the back of my mind. Exactly how was this going to work?

Griffin's hands were at my waist, tugging at the hem of my shirt. I pulled back, despite the hormones coursing through my body. "Are you going to run away tomorrow morning?"

Griffin's lips pressed back against mine, not bothering to answer. I couldn't go through that again, though, so I pulled back.

"I'm serious."

Griffin smiled, clearly enjoying my consternation. "Aisling?"

"Yeah?" I was having trouble catching my breath.

"Shut up."

This time I didn't fight Griffin's intentions – or his mouth. I just let myself fall. Again.

Printed in Great Britain
by Amazon